MW00638465

Paperback ISBN 978-1-78705-847-7
ePub ISBN 978-1-78705-848-4
PDF ISBN 978-1-78705-849-1

Published by MX Publishing
335 Princess Park Manor, Royal Drive,
London, N11 3GX
www.mxpublishing.co.uk

Cover design by Brian Belanger

The Magnificent Mac
Of Tessa Wiggin

By

Kim Krisco

To

Sararose the Druidess of Willowrun.
Thank you for your unflagging support,
editorial advice, ideas, and eagle eye.

ONE

THE FRAGILE VEIL of life's daily routine was unraveling under the weight of Tessa Wiggin's wonder and apprehension. As her dust rag traced the window moldings, raindrops began tapping on the glass. *Sacred water* Tessa thought, longing to feel their cool caress on her face. When she was born, a parish priest poured holy water over her and gave her to God. Thirty-six years later, she was preparing to be baptized again—this time in the waters of rain and river.

As raindrops speckled the glass, Tessa noticed that each windowpane framed a watercolor miniature of the verdant Welsh landscape she loved. St. Matthew's feast day was less than a week away, and the heather-clad hills and moorland were bathed in sunlit reds and golds. It was seed-fall, the time Tessa loved the most. When she walked on the moors and meadows, seeds covered her shoes and found their way into her pockets and hair. When they fell to the ground, the seeds held fast to their own distinctive promise.

The elfin lines of Tessa's mouth suddenly turned up as she saw a lumbering figure walk through the main gate. Nell had not called since the night of her anointing eight months ago. She carefully slid the side table in place and centered the hand-painted kerosene lamp on the doily. She was new to housekeeping, and this ancient manor demanded more skills than she had to give. Tessa removed a head covering and shook out her long black hair as a booming knock echoed from the front door. She winced when she saw her workmate Clark hurrying down the hallway toward the entry.

"Crazy Nell is here," he said from the parlor door. His jaw tightened, and his chin dimpled as he measured his next words. "If she must come, have her go to the back."

Tessa tossed her dust rag aside, swept a strand of hair from her sweaty forehead, and strode toward him. "Nell has the best herbs in Gwynedd." There was a metallic edge to her voice, and her emerald eyes narrowed. Poking a finger gently into Clark's chest, she added, "Nell is my friend and can enter where she may."

"You think herbs are the answer? The sisters arrive in four days, and we do not have time for wasting." He gingerly placed his hand on her shoulder. "Don't get caught up in all that nonsense again."

Tessa brushed Clark's hand aside and set him back on his heels as she strode wordlessly into the hallway. He huffed and tucked a lock of auburn hair behind his ear.

The hinges of the manor's massive hobnail door groaned as Tessa opened it just far enough to allow entry. Nell Rees had an enigmatic closed-lipped grin and bright blue eyes that popped from her sun-dyed face. Standing about five feet, Nell was heavily bundled in layers of clothing: men's britches beneath a mouse-brown skirt, bulky grey-green sweater pulled snug around her neck, and a worn black Brixton tiller hat over her ears. A covered basket was looped on one arm.

"Morin', Nell."

"Bore da, Miss Wiggins," Nell echoed in her thick Welsh brogue.

"*Croeso, dewch i mewn.*" Tessa stepped back and motioned for the old woman to enter. "What do you have for me today?"

As Nell passed, the acrid smell of a wood fire permeated the air. Her eyes flitted about the hall, finally resting on Clark, who looked on warily. Nell smiled at him and offered a nod. Clark returned the nod.

Tessa put a hand on Nell's elbow. "There is a chill in the air," she remarked, eyeing Clark. "It looks as though you could do with a cup of tea. *Dewch ymlaen*—come along to the kitchen." Tessa led the way toward the back of the manor house. Water trickled from the brim of Nell's hat and the hem of her skirt as she waddled behind Tessa, clip-clopping on the oak floor in boots that were too large for her. Tessa restrained a grin when she heard Clark groan.

Fetching a tin of tea from the pantry, Tessa returned to find Nell lingering in the doorway. She pulled a chair away from the slab-oak table that sat in the center of the kitchen and motioned for Nell to come in. After kindling a flame under the kettle, Tessa sat next to Nell, who had arranged a neat row of emerald bundles along one edge of the table.

"Crazy Nell" she is called by some, but not the locals—the *Cymry*. They know Nell as a *dryw*—a seer and a bard. The olde way and olde gods still remain in Wales. You can still see people drop a pin in a well or leave a tiny rag on a bush in the woods, bowing their head for a moment before moving on. Ganna had told Tessa *she* was a bard—a verse maker, adding that bards were mightier than kings or warriors and that a poet's word-songs can shudder people's bones and transform their hearts. Nell's words had that kind of power, though she seemed oblivious to it.

As Tessa made two cups of tea, she surveyed the packets of plants, fully expecting she might hear Ganna's voice in her head—herbs being the old Druid's specialty. But she wasn't aware of Ganna's ethereal presence. This fact offered only modest relief, for Tessa knew that she could not escape Ganna's spirit.

"You've been busy, Nell."

"I have reaped the forest's bounty for you." The crone patted the contents of the herb hamper in her lap. "I heard you was ailin', missy."

Tessa's lips tightened. "How do you know these things? Never mind, I suppose the whole district knows."

"Pay them no heed, missy," Nell said. Noticing the vacant look on Tessa's face, she added, "She is with you now, isn't she?"

With those words, Tessa found herself again surrounded by the elders of the Iceni tribe in a candlelit sea cavern. Ganna had drunk from the bowl of poison and pulled her closer: "My spirit passes now to you." As her final breath escaped, Tessa wondered then if Ganna's spirit would come to her. Eight months later, she had her answer. She's afraid, and rightfully so. I know her fear, for her story is mine as well.

As the wooden hamper lid banged shut, Tessa startled and put on a smile. Pointing to the emerald parcels, Nell continued, "Here we have mugwort, madder, and tutsan." Her finger rose in front of her

3

protuberant nose. "Anyone who partakes of these will not languish long from melancholia or need to fear for his life." Nell grinned slyly. "I do have a wee bunch of red clover."

"Red clover? For . . ."

"For those hoping to be in the family way," Nell said, holding out a bouquet of roundish red buds.

Tessa chuckled. "You should be ashamed, Nell. You know I'm unmarried."

"I was just thinkin' on that gentleman in the hall—wonderin' if ye might break the lucky groat together."

"Marriage is the last thing on his mind."

"Maybe so, but if he's like most menfolk, he'd be keen to have ye in bed." Nell tittered.

Tessa pushed the crimson flowers away. "I'll have none of that—the man or the clover. Anyway, he thinks me a shrew."

Nell shrugged. "There is a hint of the shrew in every good woman." Nell retrieved a long stem bearing large, broad leaves and held up the leafy spray for Tessa's inspection. "Maybe some comfrey for broken bones, hearts, and spirits."

"Do you have anything for a sore throat? Eva is ailing."

"*Annwyd*, aye. Sage. Sage and honey in hot tea." Nell probed her basket and held up a grey-brown bundle of desiccated leaves.

"Truth is, Nell, I don't know what ails me." Tessa paused to search for Ganna's spirit but could not find it. "I cannot stop wondering how I got to this place."

"Choices."

"Aye, but choices my mother would never have made, or my sainted brother Rory, or—"

Nell pointed a finger at Tessa, and her eyes narrowed. "If you make your dead into saints, you'll be cursed to live in their shadow."

Nell's words touched Tessa's heart. "Thank you."

"For what?" Nell grinned. "You haven't bought anything."

"I'll take some sage and comfrey."

"And what of this?" Nell asked, drawing a colorful mushroom from her hamper.

"That's it then?" Tessa asked.

"The last of the season."

"The little saint?

"That's what our people call it. Fruit from an earth that is wiser than all of us." Nell's eye's widened as she admired the red-capped mushroom cradled in her palm. "Now you know what to seek. It often shelters at the foot of trees."

Tessa warily touched the crimson fungus with the tip of her finger and rubbed the white dapples dotting the crown. "How does one take it?"

Nell shrugged. "You can eat it like this or dried." Holding up her steaming cup, she added, "or you may drink it in a brew."

"It is poisonous for me?"

"Not just one," Nell said. "And why do you fear death? Maybe the desire not to be you is what you've sought all along."

Tessa's breath caught. She nodded and pulled a small purse from her apron. "What do I owe you?"

The old woman's eyes rolled about, and her lips puckered. Finally, Tessa placed two shillings on the table and took the bundles of comfrey and sage.

Nell picked up one coin and rubbed it between her fingers. "Thank ye, Miss Tessa, this will do." Leaning forward, Nell pursed her lips. "If you will excuse me for saying so, there may be no herbs for what ails you." She placed her right hand on Tessa's chest. "The past is in the past. But things ye've done and seen—or things ye've not done and dreamed—canna be denied."

The bundle of comfrey quivered in Tessa's hand. "But they can drive you mad."

The old woman took her hand away and began gathering up the herbs. "Sometimes, the proper way to deal with what happens is to lose your mind," she said, pushing the mushroom toward Tessa.

"That's what Ganna tells me . . . told me."

"She is a wise woman."

"Was. Was a wise woman," Tessa mumbled.

"Lose your mind and find your heart."

"Nell, you are a salve for my soul." Tessa chuckled as she put the mushroom and herbs into the tea tin. "*Diolch I chi*. Please finish your tea and let yourself out."

Nell watched as Tessa rose from her chair, walked to the kitchen door, opened it, and stood for a while silhouetted in the doorway. Gazing out beyond the garden to the forest, she kicked off her shoes and pranced into the waiting rain.

In the dining room, Clark pressed his hands against the window as he watched Tessa lifting her arms overhead and swaying side to side as if buffeted by the wind. A rolling rumble of thunder and brilliant flashes in the clouds halted Tessa's whirling, and she called out in a strange tongue. Clark shook his head and dashed to the closet to get Tessa's mac, but she was gone when he got to the open kitchen door.

He turned as Nell was rising from the table, having gathered up her things. She smiled as she shuffled toward him, chuckling and stopping only for a moment to pat his arm. "Yes, my boy, we're all a little mad," she said, stepping into the rain.

TWO

FEET SPLASHING through moor grass and rush pasture, Tessa hurried toward the forest encircling Ceridwen manor. She never took her eyes from the tree line even as the rain, mud, and mire spattered her face.

Tessa halted as she felt it—the veil that enfolds the woods. She stopped and bowed her head. The shroud parted, and Tessa stepped through. Upon entering, she turned back and watched her footprints filling with rainwater. *In the end, it washes us all away*, she thought.

Tessa gently walked among the tree shadows. She told herself that her body should be cold, but the coolness remained outside her skin. In the dimming light, she watched the treetops gathering rain on branches, needles, and dry leaves to fashion them into crystalline pearls that fall and bless the earth. The air was filled with soothing scents: petrichor rising from the russet grass, the sweet smell of lavender and thyme, and fungi waking up and releasing their musty bouquet. As Tessa walked on, the wood-like layers of dried leaves crumbled beneath her bare feet and gave off the smell of an old tea shop. Then came the woody-sweet ether of cedar.

There before her was the majestic evergreen conifer—the symbol of endurance, eternal life, and immortality. Tessa ran her fingers over the ridged brown and black bark and went to her knees. Placing both hands against the trunk, she rocked back on her legs, closed her eyes, and prostrated herself before the tree.

When her eyes opened, she saw redheaded mushrooms peeking out beneath brown needles and tiny cones. Plucking one, she put it into her mouth, chewed, and waited.

Eventually, a mild euphoria began to overtake her—a feeling of buoyancy. Then as if each of her senses popped in her brain, she heard individual raindrops splatting around her, inhaled the woodsy balsamic scent emanating from the bark, and in the same moment saw countless woodland creatures skittering among the limbs and along the forest floor. Then came a flutter of wings that brought her back into her body. A brownish bird streaked overhead. Tessa felt compelled to follow. Rising, she searched among the trees until she found the bird again working on the ground. It had made a scrape in the dirt and was laying down yellow leaves of grass to make a nest— a home. *Why now?* she wondered as the enigmatic construction continued. Plucking stems one at a time; the skylark wove a natal cradle a strand at a time. Tessa watched for a long while before her gaze went to another beautiful bronze-colored skylark in the branches above. It was watching the nest-making—and she was watching it. As the observer bird turned its beady black eye on Tessa, she heard a voice—neither outside nor in: "Doubt keeps you earthbound. Faith gives flight." The watching bird flew upward, and Tessa followed.

She was rising high above the forest at great speed. Ceridwen became a speck of sandstone, roads and rivers were shriveling into lines and scribbles, and all the earth's colors were melting into grey-brown smudges pushing against the edges of an azure ocean.

The sun blinded her for a moment, and when her eyes opened again, crystalline threads shot out in all directions like fireworks crisscrossing the surface of the earth and arching over the horizon. The gem-like filaments bourgeoned into glass cobwebs coming closer. Suddenly she was entangled in the crystal threads and began to tumble down faster and faster. Through the clouds, over the forest—down and down. She was plummeting to her death, but there was no fear or panic but only serene acquiescence as she vanished into the blackness of the forest.

When Tessa's awareness shifted again, she found herself on her back gazing up through a pale bluish light shining through a black netting of tree needles. It was dusky and quiet. Wet and cold now, she got to her knees and hurriedly picked the mushrooms spread around the base of the cedar tree. Putting them in the pocket of her apron, Tessa pushed herself to her feet and began walking.

When she found her way out of the forest, she looked for something familiar, but it was all strange—different. Then a speck of light appeared in the distance and she instinctively moved toward it.

The amber light grew larger and bobbed in the air. Then a voice called her name. Her feet moved faster now as she stumbled through the thick wet grass.

"Tessa, is that you? Tess?" Clark wrapped his arms around her just as she lost her feet.

Then she was moving again. Clark had her in his arms. The lantern in his hand hung beneath her and cast shadows on his face, but she could see his wide-eyed look of concern. She felt the power of his legs driving into the mud and huddled closer to his chest for warmth. "We're going home, Tess. We're going home," he repeated again and again. He was talking about Ceridwen, but Tessa knew that home was someplace she has not yet been.

Eva, Tessa's ward, was waiting at the door. She helped Tessa upstairs and drew a warm bath, and afterward settled her into bed. Clark was waiting in the kitchen when Eva came down to make her report. "She's fine for now," Eva began. "No cuts or bruises."

"Did she say anything?" Clark asked.

"Not really, some gibberish about 'who's watching the watching-bird', whatever that means. I found these in her apron." Eva laid the redheaded mushrooms on the table. "I guess she was picking 'em."

Clark's head cocked. "Like the one I found in the tea tin," he said. "It's crazy Nell. She's got Tessa mixed up in some nonsense. Throw'em in the dustbin."

"She may be asleep now, but when I tucked her in, she asked after you—wanted to see you. Anyway, I left the lamp burning."

9

Like a sunflower seed in his gardens, Clark's relationship with Tessa was slow to sprout as it grew from co-worker to friend, but then it abruptly bolted and flowered.

Clark listened for a moment at Tessa's door before opening it. She was sitting up with blankets pulled up tight around her neck. He stopped just inside the door. "I came to turn down the lamp."

"Come here, Clark."

As he approached, she patted the bedside. "Stay a moment."

He nodded and sat.

She put her hand on his. "Thank you for coming for me. I can't explain it. Everything looked different in the dusk. I'm not sure I could have found my way back."

"I was lucky. I thought for sure you were lost in the woods."

She shivered and pulled the quilt up tighter about her. "I wonder if I will ever get warm again." She lowered her head. "Clark, this isn't proper, but could you warm me?" She moved over to one side of the bed as he took off his boots and prepared to lay down.

"No, under the blanket. Take off your clothes."

He stood motionless.

"If you wait much longer, I'm going to feel unwanted," Tessa said.

Clark's britches, shirt, and underclothing came off in a few swift movements, and in a moment, he was in bed with her. He ran his fingers over her cheek and down her neck. "Your hair is still wet."

Tessa laughed. "But you're going to keep me warm, aren't you?" She took his hand from her cheek and slid it under the quilt. He turned back toward the bedside lamp. "No. Leave it on. I want to see you."

He rolled over on his side and slid his hand under her breast and down her belly. Tessa closed her eyes as his rough hand traced the curves of her body. She knew if she were to reach for him, he would stop, but she didn't want him to.

She smelled the tobacco on his breath as he slid closer and kissed her. His lips were soft and dry. She put a hand behind his head and kissed him deep and long. She felt his body tense as his mouth opened wider. His fingers slid down her back and pushed at her hip, but she didn't move.

His kisses came harder, and his breath quickened. She had the scent of him now, and he had hers. She closed her eyes and shifted her weight slightly, opening her legs, and he was on her . . . over her . . . in her.

She opened her eyes. "I see you."

THREE

THE FULL MOON spilled through the curtain and stretched like a silver blanket across the foot of Tessa's bed. She hadn't slept since Clark left. It was the mushroom, she reckoned as her mind spun in a cycle of battered memories and mounting fears.

The moonlight summoned recollections of her grandmother and her timeworn Irish stories about the phases of the moon and what each conjured for the people of the earth. Her last evening with Benjie was a full moon. The night before he went off to the war, the little money they had bought one glorious night at Claridge's. The room was elegant beyond belief, with a huge poster canopy bed. They drank wine and stayed up all night planning the home they would build, the garden she would tend, and the two girls and one boy they would have. Those children and dreams died with him.

Growing up in Spitalfields and sleeping on a rickety cot, Tessa had imagined that a soft, warm bed would mean a happy life and home. And eight months ago, when she first laid eyes on Ceridwen Manor, she thought that impossible dream had come true, for here she was in an elegant bed.

Ceridwen had been named for an enchantress from medieval Welsh legends. It perched on the weather-beaten horizon like a gilded eagle, its chiseled sandstone façade an odd amalgamation of Tudor and Jacobean styles. Almost as an afterthought, two Victorian-style wings spread out from each side, tenuously attached by leaded glass galleries.

The antiquity of Ceridwen manor suited Tessa. She had always believed she was born for another age. The present one, with its raucous machines and cataleptic people, offended her senses and sensibilities. In Wales, you cannot live in the present, surrounded as you are by rotting relics, ancient laments snagged on craggy cliffs, and wind-ravaged castles with weary ghosts.

The walnut-paneled bed chambers of Ceridwen were gloomy affairs. And looking up at the red velvet canopy above her, Tessa imagined she was lying in a coffin. Such a thought was not unusual, for death had been a frequent visitor throughout her life. Tonight, as the misty wind rattled the brass curtain pulls, Tessa could hear the reaper's boney knuckles knocking.

A new day draws near, Ganna announced.

Tessa startled. "There you are, Ganna. I thought you had deserted me."

You hoped I had.

"I say what I mean. You have been silent of late."

My presence is causing you distress.

"Distress?" Tessa feigned laughter. "People say I'm not myself, and your presence gives new meaning to that well-worn notion. I would have hoped that the promise of becoming 'Nature's handmaiden' would allow me to accept your presence, but . . ."

So, you've come to regret your decision to shelter my spirit.

"If so, it's one of many regrets I am drowning in—regrets about what I've done . . . not done . . . and all the nameless regrets awaiting me."

Don't summon regret. It nurtures self-loathing.

"The truth hides in our regrets, Ganna. When I see mine, I realize my life has been but a feeble attempt to survive."

Then our union should offer solace, for you are destined to be the peoples' connection with The Mother.

"Not me, you. I am living your life . . . having your thoughts and lately even your memories."

I will travel more . . . be a teithiwr when I am not with you or teaching you. I will come and go. But you must understand that I may not be at hand if you need me because I will be resting in another realm. And you must know that we can only be apart for a short while before my spirit becomes wholly untethered.

"Yes, and as you leave, my spirit wants to follow, and for a time, I become a hollow plaster figurine forlorn in this world."

Loneliness has been my constant companion since I fled Suetonius Paulinus. I crave companionship and am blessed by yours. Trust me for a while longer.

"Companions walk side-by-side. My spirit chases after you and doesn't even glance back on the body it's leaving behind."

I'm sorry. It's not what I intend. You must trust me.

"I want to but . . ."

The world has taught you not to trust others, and you are overcoming that conviction. But the world has also taught you not to trust yourself, and you must heal that part also.

Tears formed in her eyes. "I'm sorry, Ganna. It's the mushroom . . . the fantastic visions."

Ah, so you found them.

Tessa nodded.

As I had hoped. What you experienced is the truth of things. Understanding and acceptance come later. I will go now and leave you to greet another day, but please, I beg you, continue to do as I bid and await my return.

And Ganna was gone as quickly as she had come.

With a steaming cup of tea in hand, Tessa shook off her early morning angst and sang as she made her way in her nightdress and stocking feet to the windowed gallery adjoining the great hall. Her lilting voice echoed in the corridor:

> *And we'll all go together*
> *To pull wild mountain thyme*
> *All around the bloomin' heather*
> *Will ye go lassie go?*

It was Clark's song, as he often sang or hummed it. She wondered if it was just another way he was trying to woo her. Their penny dreadful courtship, the housekeeper and the chauffeur, ensued almost from the moment they met last year at the Davis sister's home in London. "Love is not enough," she told him when he declared himself. A smile came to her lips as she recalled how sweet he was in his struggle to make a case for himself. Amid his awkward speech and stuttering words, he mentioned her loneliness, which surprised her, for Tessa believed she had vanquished that feeling.

The steam from her cup fogged the gallery window as she awaited the sun's first kiss on the garden behind the manor. Clark was an enigma to her. Belying his rough ways and ungainly manner, he had crafted the most resplendent gardens at Ceridwen. It seemed to come naturally to him. Against a backdrop of towering rhododendron and azalea bushes, he created a patchwork of evergreens that sported every shade of green on earth. Among them, he put small patches of flowers. All but the hardiest blooms had faded in the chilly winds that announce the fall season on the Welsh coast.

Clark's special gift was a bed of mahonia planted just outside the back door. One of nature's paradoxes, the mahonia bloom in the dead of winter—a spray of luminous yellow spikes flaunting golden blossoms that burst forth above an undergrowth of emerald holly. Clark had said that they reminded him of her—the prickly holly warning all to stay away, but if you can get close enough, you can inhale delight.

As a rosy glow chased the shadows into the corners of the garden, a movement caught Tessa's eye. A small animal—a bird. *The skylark.* It must have sensed her presence because it stopped pecking in the dirt and turned toward her. She half expected to hear the voice again, but it soon went about its business. Then another shadow—something in the morning mist, a waif-like silhouette reminiscent of the one Tessa had spied when Maeve waited in the phantom fog last January. This morning the figure was Eva. Her back was to Tessa—her shoulders shaking.

"Good morning, Tess." Clark had approached unnoticed. Following her gaze to Eva, he added: "The whole house is up early today." He pressed himself against her back, folded his arms around her waist and placed a light kiss on the back of her neck. It felt good to have him at her back. They were lovers now—something she was afraid she would come to regret. The first time was just three weeks ago. She could still recall the wonderful revelation that evening.

Tessa had expected that Clark's pent-up passion would burst upon her in a frenzy, but the tables turned. It was she that wanted him—wanted his lips on hers, wanted to feel his weight. When she reached into his bedclothes, he stopped her hand. Instead of stroking and kissing, he held her. Then gently, cautiously, he ran his hands over the small of her back and hips. When their bodies finally joined, she felt something beyond sexual pleasure. Her eyes were closed when she climaxed, and when they opened, he held her gaze. He did not spoil her feeling of delight with words. But lovely moments like this were rare because everywhere other than the bedroom, Clark questioned what she was doing or why she was doing it. It bothered her because it was redundant, for she continually asked the same questions of herself.

"It's good we're up early," he said. "There is much to do if we're to be ready when the ladies arrive the day after tomorrow."

"*Ni allaf ei gredu*. Is that all you think about, Clark?"

"We have responsibilities. The sisters put their trust in our caretaking, and we cannot afford to lose our positions."

Tessa wheeled about and pushed him back with a hand. "What about Eva out there crying?"

"She's eighteen but acts like a child—only thinks of herself."

"Would that your heart might be as astute as your head. She was abandoned, abused by stepparents, sold into slavery and—"

"I know the story, Tess. I feel for her. But now she has a good life, a warm bed, plenty of food, and an opportunity to make something of herself. She is a fortunate woman. You've made a good home for her."

Tessa sighed. "I can barely make a home for myself, but I try to take care of her." Tessa's eyes glistened as the memory of her little sister Evangeline assailed her mind.

Clark's concern for Tessa had been growing for weeks. Her disappearance into the woods yesterday confirmed his worst fears. He squeezed her shoulders. "Tess, we need help. Maybe Mr. Holmes or Dr. Watson—"

"No, Clark, just some time! It's been only eight months since Imbolc. Promise me you'll keep all this between us."

He awkwardly withdrew his hands and nodded.

Tessa took a breath. "I can take care of myself. As you say, there is much for me to do, but I will first tend to Eva."

"Go to her then but let me get your sweater and slippers."

Eva, who shunned the sun, was comfortable in the morning mist. Her auburn hair fell in long tresses down her back and curled in the moist air. Her lips were thin, and her mouth was set in a manner that made her appear strong and resolute. It was a practiced look that had become her first line of defense on the streets of London. Desperate to escape a dreary life in the basement laundries of the city's East End, Eva had fallen prey to the storybook promises of white slavers. Tessa rescued her before she was shipped out to Port Said. Now, a year later, Tessa's promises rang hollow—not because Eva couldn't trust Tessa, but because Eva could no longer trust her instincts.

The young lass started when Tessa approached and surreptitiously wiped her eyes with the sleeve of her flannel nightdress before turning. Tessa put a cup of steaming tea in Eva's hands. "What is it?"

"It is deadly dull. I don't belong here. There's nothing for me in this wilderness. I want to go home to the city . . . to London."

"The city is not a home; it's a place. Home is where both purpose and peace come together."

"I have neither of those here. I miss my sisters."

Tessa's scowled. "The Sisters of Scáthach live in a dream world."

"A dream you turned into a nightmare when your friends raided our family and murdered Mistress Maeve. You think because you saved me, that you own me."

"Go to town, Eva. Make friends."

"I don't speak the language. I'm an outlander. And Blaenau Ffestiniog can hardly be called a town—a bunch of crumbling stone buildings surrounded by heaps of slate tailings." Eva turned a defiant face on Tessa. "You don't understand."

Tessa smiled. "I felt the same when I was your age . . . that I didn't fit in, that I was in the wrong place, doing the wrong things. You'll find that happiness has little to do with where you are and everything to do with who you are.

"I don't know who I am, but I won't find out here."

"Give it time. You might see how wonderful this place is."

"This wonderful place doesn't seem to be doing *you* much good. Bickering with Clark. Babbling all hours of the night to some old ghost . . . your blank spells. Maybe you'd best leave here too before they put you away!"

FOUR

IT WAS THEIR PRACTICE to take turns, and it was Sherlock Holmes's turn to visit his friend Dr. John Watson. However, Holmes remained resolute in his vow to stay in the Sussex Downs until he completed his masterwork on crime and criminals. It had become an obsession of late.

Having secured a publisher, Holmes was eager to have his manuscript in print. His magnum opus was the culmination of three decades of work, experience, and experimentation. It featured his most famous cases, as well as those Watson never penned. As such, the contents of Holmes's manuscript were becoming a source of intense curiosity for the good doctor. And now, a recent letter from Clark Button and a minor mystery vanquished what remained of Watson resolve not to visit.

He made the two-hour journey from London's Victoria to Berwick Station in East Sussex, then proceeded by rickety dogcart to a traditional thatched roof stone cottage on the Eastbourne to Brighton Road. The doctor would never admit it to Holmes, but he looked forward to shaking off the soot of the city and feeling the touch of the sun and sea breeze on his face.

Arriving at Holmes's cottage, Watson stared at the bramble obscuring Holmes's front door. He was momentarily engulfed in bittersweet memories of his twenty-five-year partnership with the illustrious detective. He had assumed that they would share their later years, so it was a shock, six years ago, when Holmes showed him the deed for the cottage he had purchased for his retirement. For a time, Watson consoled himself with the belief that Holmes would tire of the provincial life and return to the city. But he was wrong—proving again that even those closest to Sherlock Holmes could not plumb the full depth of the man.

The doctor knocked several times before Mrs. Thornton answered. "Good day to ya, Dr. Watson. We were not expecting ya. Will ya be stayin' for lunch?"

Catching a whiff of something delicious bubbling on the stove, Watson answered, "If I may."

The housekeeper put on a smile and took the doctor's hat and coat. "It's good you've come, sir."

"Why is that Mrs. Thornton?"

"You will see for yourself, sir," she replied, pointing toward the office. "The old dragon is in his lair."

Watson straightened his coat and tie, took a long breath, and knocked on the study door.

A voice called out: "Enter, Watson."

Holmes was hunched over a typewriter. His hair was disheveled, and when he looked up, Watson saw Holmes's puffy face and red-ringed eyes.

"I expected to find you at your desk, Holmes. But it appears you've been at it too long. You look dreadful, old man."

"If you've come to poke at my foibles, you best stay in your London burrow," Holmes grumbled.

"Nonsense, Holmes. It's a tolerable journey, and I wanted to see you on a couple of matters. Your tenacity with regard to completing your manuscript is admirable, but you must get some rest."

"Yes, sleep that knits up the ravell'd sleeve of care. Would that it was so."

"It seems this manuscript has cast a large shadow over you, Holmes."

"It was not only the manuscript that kept me up last night but strange dreams."

Watson's brow rose in surprise, for his friend rarely mentioned such things. Holmes had long since explained dreaming as nothing more than the brain sorting and filing the previous day's activities. "I recall that you do not put much store in dreams."

"True, Watson, but this dream was remarkably vivid."

"So, the work on your manuscript has stimulated some graphic imaginings?"

"That may explain it, Watson, but last night it was if I were actually visited by that old woman who died in the cavern last February."

"Ganna?

"Yes. She was lying on the slab where she died, and then she rose and beckoned to me," Holmes exclaimed with a hollow chuckle.

"What do you make of it?"

"Nothing, never mind. I apologize," Holmes said.

Like some men, Holmes was crippled by antipathy toward emotion. For him, the world was a safer place when one used reason and a more precarious one if put at the mercy of one's feelings. With a casual wave of his hand, Holmes dismissed the troubling digression: "Let's not get caught up in nonsense."

Sensing the door close on Holmes's interior life, Watson changed the subject. "Rumors are swirling about London regarding your forthcoming book. It's even reported in the papers. What's it called?"

"*Theories and Practices of Crime and Criminology.* And I would add that I am disappointed that John Wiley & Sons has fallen prey to asinine commercialism. It appears they think my book is to be promoted like a sideshow in a grotesque bourgeois circus!" Holmes's jaw tightened as he pointed at Watson. "They had the gall to request a tantalizing title." He smiled and settled back into his chair. "When I suggested: 'Blood, Guts, and Vampires,' they demurred."

Watson laughed. "Well, judging from your sleepless nights, I would guess *Blood, Guts, and Vampires* is past due at the publishers."

Holmes harrumphed and placed his hand on the document cover. "This manuscript is my legacy. It is not a simple saga in *The Strand* for the jaded masses. It is a definitive work on the criminal mind and the modern means and methods for bringing the lawless to justice."

Though miffed by Holmes's gibe, Watson soldiered on. "But it undoubtedly contains tantalizing cases and singular criminals."

"I suppose it does—cases you know well and some you do not. Indeed, thanks to Wiley's circus barkers, I have been accosted by former clients begging me *not* to include their cases—some appeals bordered on threatening. Of course, I intend to change names, dates, and places, but that may not be enough for some."

"Come, come, Holmes. You've done much good in the world. You are respected, admired, and have many friends."

"And enemies as well."

"Indeed, but the worst of them are dead and gone."

"I wonder . . ."

Watson chuckled. "Moriarty, you mean. Must we go there again?"

"His body was never found."

"You're speaking gibberish, Holmes. It's been over twenty-five years. Really now, you must get some rest."

"You're right, of course." Rocking back in his chair, he put on a smile. "So, what brings you here other than a meal?"

"Mrs. Thornton's cooking smells delightful, but I did not come to dine." Watson retrieved a letter from his jacket pocket. "This letter came from Clark Button."

Holmes resumed pecking at the typewriter with two fingers. "Tessa's friend?"

"Yes." The doctor opened the letter and held it out, but Holmes did not look up. "Mr. Button is concerned about Tessa's health and well-being."

Holmes stopped typing and snatched the letter. Watson took a seat as his friend bent over the missive, mumbling as he read: "Anxious . . . sleeplessness . . . babbles . . . blank spells. What's wrong with her, Watson?"

"If this report is accurate, Tessa may be suffering from mental strain."

Holmes fell back in his chair. "I might have seen this coming."

Watson leaned in. "You think this has to do with the killing of Maeve Murtagh and the death of that old woman you dreamed about?"

"I need to tell you something. I did not kill Maeve." Watson's eyes swelled saucer-like, and his mouth went agape. Holmes had told Inspector Walls, indeed everyone, that *he* had killed Maeve Murtagh in self-defense when they raided the lair of the Sisters of Scáthach.

"Maeve ran herself onto a saber that Tessa held. Poor Tessa pitied Maeve and didn't want her to go to the gallows . . . and that old woman on the altar took poison from Tessa's hand. It was some arcane ceremony where Tessa and that band of Celtic zealots helped Ganna put an untimely end to her life."

Watson leaned back in his chair, shaking his head. "Such events would rain down enormous guilt upon Tessa."

"So, we may know the cause of Tessa's distress, Watson. What of the cure?"

The doctor's voice took on a pedagogical tone as he described possible therapies for Tessa. However, Holmes was unable to bring his attention to the conversation as his mind was clouded with memories.

Tessa was six when Holmes met her thirty years before. She had tagged along with her older brother Rory, who led the gang of street Arabs that Holmes called his irregulars. He remembered the first time he laid eyes upon her grimy little face . . . her black hair sprouting in all directions . . . the hem of her dress lying unraveled on the ground. There was a patch pocket sewn onto Tessa's dress. Holmes asked her what was in it. The wide-eyed waif peered into her empty pocket and shrugged. He recalled how her bright green eyes dilated and tracked the penny he placed in her pocket. In that moment, Sherlock Holmes became the "penny man." To this day, he often gives Tessa a penny when they meet.

"I'm sorry, Watson, I lost your train of thought."

"I said, we need to assess Tessa's situation for ourselves."

"You're the doctor. My presence will only complicate matters."

"But she trusts you—loves you."

Holmes winced. "Tessa needs a doctor. That's why Clark sent the letter to you. If you believe my presence is required, I will come." Holmes nervously patted his pockets for his pipe.

"You're troubled, Holmes."

The detective's eyes grew dim. "Something happened to Tessa in that cavern—something we may never understand."

"Strange things happened to everyone who pursued mad Maeve and her Sisters of Scáthach. Clark nearly lost his arm, Eva was traumatized, and poor Professor Stone has not been the same since. In the middle of it all was Tessa. I have a colleague with whom I will consult, Holmes. We'll soon have her on the mend."

"Spare no expense, Watson. I will stand for any fees."

"Yes then, very well," the doctor muttered, seemingly in agreement.

"Something more, Watson?"

"Another curious matter. Possibly nothing."

Holmes chuckled. "If it were nothing, you would not bring it to my attention. What is it?"

"A strange visitor called on Augustus."

Holmes had enlisted Professor Augustus Stone's help in tracking Maeve Murtagh and her murderess band of Celtic women. Afterward, the professor invited Dr. Watson to share his palatial three-story residence in Belgravia.

"A strange visitor, you say, Watson?"

"A woman who claimed she was Amelia Bauer, an archeologist from Austria."

"From your depiction, Watson, may I assume that there is no such person as Amelia Bauer?"

"On the contrary, Stone knew an Amelia Bauer by reputation. She is indeed a noted archeologist, but he has since learned that Frau Bauer died of the Spanish flu a year ago."

Holmes lit his pipe and leaned back in his chair. A good portent, as Watson knew Holmes was intrigued. "What did the woman want?"

"I was not present. She came to Augustus on the hunt for Celtic treasure. Stone called it . . . well in English, it is called the "blood of the slaughtered." Mythology has it that there is an undiscovered two-thousand-year-old horde of gold and silver on or near the Island of Anglesey."

"Ah-h-h, the lure of buried treasure," Holmes remarked.

"Stone insists that if it were to be found, it would be the find of a lifetime."

"But the professor fears the treasure will be looted."

"There you have the gist of it, Holmes."

"What brought her to Stone?"

"You recall how the papers treated the whole business with the Sisters of Scáthach and Maeve Murtagh—a witch's coven and all. Stone was quoted in some of the stories as an expert on Celtic culture."

"He deserves that appellation—although, I fear he lets his imagination get the best of him, especially with regard to the old woman who died last February."

"Aye, Stone believes Ganna was a druid."

"*That* is not beyond belief, but Stone believes she was a two-thousand years old druid!" Holmes smacked his hand on the desktop, "It is that kind of nonsense that may be driving poor Tessa mad."

Holmes rose and began pacing before the hearth. After a few draws on his pipe, he returned to his chair. "So, this imposter wanted to pick the Professor's fertile brain. Was she successful?"

"No. Stone was suspicious from the start. He said there was something about her accent or lack of it. I believe it was her manner as well. It made him want to check her credentials so, he asked her to come back at a later time."

Holmes smirked. "And the old boy wants me there when she returns?"

"I believe you owe him the courtesy of a visit. We may never have caught Maeve and saved Tessa without his help."

"Watson, you do not need to remind me that we are indebted to the man. If you detect any reticence on my part, it is solely due to my concern for Tessa. I believe our attention is best focused upon her. However, I will go to Stone if you will pay Tessa a visit. I'm certain we can make quick work of this little mystery."

FIVE

HOLMES ENJOYED A SINGULAR CAMARADERIE with Augustus Stone. He believed it was due to the Professor's profound grasp of arcane knowledge and dedication to his profession, but indeed they shared much more. They were misfits. Sherlock Holmes and Professor Stone, each in their way, were obsessive seekers of truth. This set them apart from a large part of humanity. Like many misfits, they immersed themselves in their work. But even when their singular quests were rewarded, they experienced only momentary solace, for both ancient history and criminology imbued their pursuers with a cynical attitude concerning the plight of humankind.

Holmes's knock brought Professor Stone to his door. "Sherlock, you are a rare and welcome spectacle. John said you would come, but it was too much to hope for."

"Nonsense, you know I enjoy a little mystery."

Stone was a balding, pear-bellied man who, despite weighing more than eighteen stone, moved in a confident British style as he ushered Holmes into his library. His eyes sparkled with blissful expectancy as they settled into their chairs.

"John is not here. I assume you know he's on his way to see Miss Wiggins?"

"Yes. When does Frau Bauer—if I can call her that—arrive?"

"I expect her in an hour's time."

Holmes yanked on the gold sovereign fastened to the chain on his vest and opened his watch. "Two o'clock then. Was this the time she called upon you two days ago?"

"Yes. It was clear she traveled some hours by train. I recall that she had to cut short her interview because she wished to catch a return train. She remarked it was the last of the day."

Holmes retrieved a small diary from his coat pocket and made a note. "What time did she depart?"

"Just after three."

"So, we now know two things about this mystery woman: she is likely *not* an archeologist, and she resides some distance from London. Let us use the remaining time we have before her arrival to gather some additional facts."

As the two o'clock hour approached, Holmes had filled five pages in his diary. He knew the approximate time of the mystery woman's train departure and, through other small details, deducted the station from which she had departed—Euston. He also knew it had been raining at the place from which she had come by the damp umbrella that Stone noted—an umbrella with a gold knob. Her accent made her British despite her Germanic surname, and she used medical terms in her conversation with Stone such as acute, delusional, and neurosis.

The most curious thing of all was that she mentioned Ganna's name, claiming that she learned it from newspaper stories reporting last February's events. Holmes had filed away all the newspaper clippings from that case and knew for a fact that none of them carried Ganna's name. References were only to an "unidentified older woman."

"Now, Professor," Holmes continued, "tell me about the treasure the woman was seeking."

"*Gwaed y Lladdedigion* is what it's called: the blood of the slaughtered. It is said to be buried somewhere on the Island of Anglesey. At the time the Celts inhabited Anglesey, it was called *Ynys Môn* by local tribes, and Mona by the Romans."

Stone's voice took on a professorial tenor as he explained that this treasure was likely a cache of sacrificial offerings. "In AD 50 the

Romans controlled most of Britain except the Welsh tribes. The date is not clear, but around AD 57 the Roman general Suetonius Paulinus decided that enough was enough and led his legions to a final reckoning on the island of Mona.

"This island was significant for the defending tribesmen because Anglesey was the sacred home of the druids, the spiritual leaders of the Welsh people, and most of the druids lived there. The island was also a handy bolt-hole for tribesmen fleeing from Roman persecution. The Romans—always a superstitious people—believed that the druids practiced all sorts of evil rituals, even human sacrifice they believed was carried out on this shadowy isle."

Stone retrieved a massive volume from a nearby shelf and paged through it. "Here we are, Holmes. The Roman historian Tacitus recorded the invasion of Mona." He read:

"In view of the shallow channel that separated the mainland from the island, Paulinus constructed a flotilla of boats with flat bottoms. By this method, the infantry crossed; the cavalry did so by fording or by swimming at the side of their horses. On the shore stood the forces of the enemy, a dense array of arms and men, with women dashing through the ranks like the furies. The druids poured forth dire imprecations with their hands uplifted towards the heavens, striking terror into the soldiers. Then, reassured by their general and inciting each other never to flinch before a band of females and fanatics, they bore down upon them, smote all to the earth, and wrapped them in the flames they had themselves kindled."

Stone slapped the book closed. "It was a massacre, Holmes. Men, women, and children—armed and unarmed, young and old— fell under the swords of the Romans'. The bodies of the dead and dying were unceremoniously hurled onto makeshift funeral pyres.

Suetonius and his soldiers then set out across the island, setting fire to the druid's sacred oak groves, smashing their altars and temples, killing anyone they found, and taking everything of value.

"It is believed that the druids, realizing that they could not stand against such a mass of well-equipped soldiers, gathered up the gold, silver, and weapons intended for offerings to their gods and hid the cache before the Romans attacked. It appears that Suetonius Paulinus did not get the treasure, but he crushed the heart of the Welsh resistance. The restoration of these offerings would mean a lot to historians like me, but it would mean far more to the Celtic people who lost their spiritual driving force to the Romans. I relish the thought of finding this prize."

"And where would you look, Professor?"

"Water. I would focus my search on watery places. Offerings were usually cast into the water because the Celts believed it spans the three realms of Otherworld, Surface World, and the Heavens. But there are so many rivers, streams, ponds, and bogs in Anglesey; I would not know where to begin."

"A dilemma obviously shared by our mystery lady." Holmes checked his watch. "It's half-past two. The lady has missed her appointment. She may have been as suspicious of you as you were of her. However, I believe I have all the details needed to find her, save a good description. If you have paper and a sharp pencil, you might help me sketch the mystery lady."

"Then you will aid me in preventing a greedy plundering of this Welsh treasure?"

"Professor, let us keep in mind that we are not certain there is a treasure."

"This imposter had knowledge and information that one does not find in books. She seemed to know details about arcane worship ceremonies and the lineage of the Iceni tribe that the old Druid Ganna claimed as her own. She is convinced that there is a treasure and seems well along on its trail. And I believe that her intentions are not honorable."

The professor provided a detailed description of the woman who called herself Bauer. Holmes made a sketch and tucked it into his notebook. "The fact that she knew Ganna's name would support your belief that she has deeper knowledge and knows more than she shared. She may have been one of those at the Imbolc ceremony where Ganna took her life, and Maeve was killed. If so, it would seem odd that she sought you out to garner information. I do not wish to speculate until I learn more, but maybe she imagines you are after the treasure also."

"I know little beyond what I just told you, Holmes."

"About a treasure, Professor, but what do you know about Ganna, about the mad Sisters of Scáthach, and the whole business around that terrible night? No Professor, this mystery lady may be up to something beyond simply seeking treasure."

"Where does that leave us?"

"If this woman contacts you again, call me. I must return to Sussex and put the finishing touches on my manuscript which is past due at John Wiley & Sons. Then I will look into this matter."

"Thank you, Holmes. I'm a poor host. Let me offer a cup of tea before you leave." The professor put his hands on his knees and pushed himself to his feet. "This business with Tessa and all . . . it's a difficult time for John and you, so I appreciate your help. Watson has been knocking on the doors of several doctors in the city, and I am certain Miss Wiggins will receive the help she requires."

"I appreciate that, but it would be premature to assume that Tessa is suffering any serious malady. As you say, your house-mate is paying her a visit as we speak, so we will soon know more."

"Holmes, I'm not certain how to say this . . ." Stone's eyes looked upwards in thought as he put a finger to his lips. "Have you considered that Tessa may be struggling in the aftermath of Mauve Murtagh's and Ganna's deaths?"

"I am certain she is. I too harbor regret and doubts about what happened that dreadful night."

"You are, of course, aware that we part ways regarding our interpretation of the events that surrounded that band of Celtic women we hunted. To put it bluntly, you think me a little mad."

The corners of Holmes's mouth turned up as the professor made his point. "You are *implying* that if Tessa shared her experiences regarding Maeve and Ganna with others, that *she* may appear to be mad as well. But you forget Professor, I was there the night Maeve was killed, and before that on all-hallows-eve when lightning felled that massive oak tree allowing the Sisters to eluded us."

"The night Ganna eluded us with a storm she summoned."

Holmes bolted from his chair. "You cannot believe a human being can conjure lightning and rain like some god on Mount Olympus." Holmes returned to his chair and took a breath.

"I am not a fanatic, Holmes! I know what I saw!" Stone shouted. Then his shoulders relaxed. "I apologize. It appears I am still chaffing from your ridicule."

The detective nodded. "When human beings are not able to fully explain an experience, they fall prey to superstition and fear. The rational mind is our only defense."

"I agree, but not everything that happens can be reasoned away. The druids of old possessed a command of the natural world and our relationship with it. It's not only reason and science that must be weighed. Our deeper instincts must be considered. It is there that the truth may rest. If we ignore what we instinctively know to be true, we *invite* madness."

SIX

POURING RAIN STALKED WATSON as he made his way from the station at Blaenau Ffestiniog to Ceridwen Manor. The driver of the cart laid a canvas over the doctor's knees. An umbrella covered his head and shoulders. These were futile gestures, as the ride to Ceridwen would take the better part of an hour, and the rain was already working its way through his stitching.

Watson observed the water pooling around his shoes on the floor of the dogcart. Dylan, the driver, failed to hide his amusement as Watson's grumbling grew louder with every mile. "I suppose, sir, you would not be surprised to learn that Gwynedd is one of the wettest places in Wales."

Watson harrumphed. "Wales! In the entire empire, I should say. How much further, Dylan?"

"Not far now, sir. If ya cen squint the rain from your eyes, ya may make out Ceridwen on the left."

The angular rooftops of Ceridwen Manor cut a jagged line across the horizon. Before Watson could express his relief, the cart lurched to a stop. "'Ello, what 'ave we here?" the driver exclaimed. Just ahead, a lone figure was trudging toward them with something in hand.

"Oh, good grief," Watson exclaimed as the figure came into view. Throwing the canvas off, he climbed down from the cart and hurried to a sopping wet woman. "Tessa, what are you doing in this maelstrom?"

She pulled her arm back as Dr. Watson reached out. "So, he did call you. I knew it." She shivered and dropped her suitcase. Watson wrapped his arm around her and led her to the cart. Dylan retrieved the suitcase and followed.

Watson draped the canvas around Tessa's shoulders. "Now, my dear," I'm here for you." Then turning to Dylan: "Come along, we must get her into dry clothes quickly."

Tessa had regained her composure by the time the dripping trio knocked on the nail-studded doors at Ceridwen. A grateful Eva answered the door, explaining that Clark was searching the grounds. The young woman took Tessa upstairs as Watson shuffled and dripped his way toward a cozy hearth in the parlor. As he waited, he removed his boots and placed his socks over the fender by the fireside.

Clark had seen the dogcart leaving and hurried inside. "Tess, Tess, are you here?"

Watson called out: "She's upstairs."

Clark followed the call to the parlor. "Dr. Watson, how is she?"

"Drenched, like me, but otherwise fine. Eva is tending to her."

"Let me hang your coat and get something for your feet—and maybe a wee dram of whisky."

"That would be most welcome."

As the two men settled in before the fire. Clark sipped from his glass and stared into the flames. He had come a long way from the Millwork Dock on the Isle of Dogs. Born into a family of 'wharfies,' he had scratched out a living on London's East Side—a genesis he shared with Tessa. Like many on the docks, he occasionally helped himself to "useful cargo." One night he was caught and spent six months in Newgate for the crime. Petty though it was, Clark was unable to regain his position on the wharf. As with Tessa, his only choice was to go into service. This is where his luck changed, for the Davis sisters were known for giving ex-convicts another chance. He started as a chauffeur, but he discovered a love for gardening during the six years he had been with the Davis Sisters. It was not music but rather nature that soothed Clark's savage breast.

"I'm worried," Clark said. "Tess is not one to run from problems. I drove her away by making too much of her difficulties."

"How has she faired since you wrote to Holmes and me?"

Clark downed the remainder of his whisky in a quaff. "Her spells continue."

"Spells?"

"That's what I call them. A couple of mornings ago, I saw her barefoot, standing in the rain, waving her arms about and shouting nonsense. There are times when she wanders off onto the moor or into the forest nearby without a word. Most recently, she vanished into the woods for the better part of the day. She was confused and senseless when I found her wandering in the muck and mire just before nightfall. She nearly caught her death." He went to the sideboard and poured another drink. "When I attempt to talk about these things, she says that she can't recall them. If I press her for an explanation, she gets angry and walks away or secretes in her room."

Watson opened his notebook and made an entry.

Clark held up his glass with a questioning look. "Another doctor?"

"No, thank you."

Clark swirled the glass of whiskey and dropped into his chair. "She's up at all hours. And out of nowhere, she's speaking Welsh. I don't know what to do. That's why I wrote to Mr. Holmes and you."

"I have contacted Dr. Kraepelin in the city. When I told him where Tessa resides, he was quick to tell me of a prominent psychiatrist—a Dr. Mayer, who recently arrived in this country to take the superintendent's position at Hellingford Asylum—"

"Asylum!" Clark's body stiffened. "You don't think—"

"No, no. I'm simply saying that a qualified psychiatrist is in practice nearby should he be needed."

Clark cocked his head. "I thought Hellingford was shut down."

"Yes, yes, Kraepelin made that point. However, it appears the hospital has a benefactor. I feel woefully unprepared to make a diagnosis, so we need Dr. Mayer or Kraepelin to see Tessa."

Clark downed his drink. "I don't mind saying that I'm worried. Eva says that she often hears Tess talking to herself in her room—as if in conversation. Eva thinks she's talking to that old woman who died in the cavern."

"Holmes and I feared as much," Watson said. "Tessa may be having hallucinations. Does she tend to her duties?"

"No. That's another thing. I'm concerned that we may lose our positions, and I told her as much."

"And?"

Clark turned frightened eyes toward Watson. "She says this is not her home—that she doesn't belong here. A few months ago, she told me Ceridwen was the place of her dreams. Now she's running away."

"It was an emotional response, Clark. An impulsive attempt to flee—not a plan."

"She guessed that I sent for you and pressed me about it. I never admitted that I wrote to you and Mr. Holmes, but she somehow knew. Lies do not escape that woman. I'm certain she will never agree to see a doctor, and if we press the point, she will leave for good. One thing more, Dr. Watson, the Davis sisters arrive tomorrow, and the cook Gwenda comes today. All of them are generous to a fault, but I fear they will find all of this too much. I want to introduce you as a friend of Tessa's here only for a visit."

"I understand. But the Davis's may have a need to know at some point."

A slamming door upstairs brought both men to their feet. Eva stomped down the stairs and posed at the parlor door with her hands on her hips. "She's impossible."

The nurturing physician in Watson came to the fore at that moment and he decided to check on Tessa.

Watson's gentle knock brought Tessa to her door.

"Are you alone?" she asked.

"Yes," he replied.

The door opened wider. "You're welcome only as a friend."

"Then I come as a friend," Watson answered.

Tessa and Watson shared a singular relationship, as they both loved Sherlock Holmes—not an easy thing to do. It takes time and tenacity to see past the man's subtly masked arrogance, dark moods, and obsessive rationality. Watson was always able to see the tenderness that lay beneath the detective's actions and activities, but until Tessa came along, Holmes seldom displayed love and kindheartedness. Like the daughter he never had, Tessa could see that Holmes concealed his feelings it to protect his heart, which was more tender than he would admit.

As he waited in the parlor, Clark watched the rain blasting the windows and ravaging gardens he had painstakingly tended all week. His heart sank as we watched the flora bowing in surrender to the storm. Gwendoline and Margaret Davis would understand about the garden, but maybe not about Tessa. She had never told him that, less than a year ago, it was on Ganna's recommendation that the sisters hire her. Indeed, there were many things Tessa had never told him or anyone.

Clark harkened to footsteps on the stairs and turned as Dr. Watson entered the room. "How is she?"

Watson held out the palms of his hands, cautioning Clark to lower his voice. "She is fine for the moment. I could do little more than comfort her. She feels betrayed."

"Because I called on you. Did I do the right thing, Doctor?"

"Yes. Tessa needs a doctor's help as surely as she needs good friends. She is frightened."

"Of what?"

"I'm uncertain. She knows her behavior is erratic, so it would be reasonable to think that she is worried about her mind. If I can persuade Dr. Kraepelin to come, he can give us a proper diagnosis. If he cannot, we will seek out Dr. Mayer."

"I tell you; she will not stand for it."

"I hear you. But she will listen to Holmes. I will get word to him as soon as I return to the city. If I may, I'd like to stay the night and leave for London on tomorrow morning's train."

"Certainly. That would be at 7:40."

"It may take a day or more for—" Watson's eyes widened as he gazed across the room. Clark turned to see Tessa glaring at them from the parlor door.

"Yes, gentlemen. I heard you plotting. Poor, poor Tessa, she's lost her mind." She pointed her finger defiantly. "Act like men. Say it to my face. Tessa, you're mad!"

Clark shook his head. "I don't know what to think. How do *you* explain what's been happening to you?"

What could Tessa say? How could anyone comprehend the spiritual aching that accompanies the unrequited yearning to meld with The Mother? Divine madness shreds the fragile fabric of daily life.

SEVEN

THE NEXT DAY, after months of preparation, Tessa told the Davis sisters that she was ready for the Water Ceremony—*Seremoni Dŵr Cysegredig*. It had taken time for Tessa to prepare her heart and mind as guided by Ganna. She wove countless hours of silence into the routines of her daily life to cultivate inner focus. The ritual's Celtic rites were rooted in antiquity, performed for thousands of years by women elders of the Iceni tribe. She had partaken of the fly-agaric mushroom—"the flesh of the gods," Ganna called it. In that transformative journey, she glimpsed the elegant web of connections that embrace the earth, humbly accepting her place within it. In that experience, human mortality lost its meaning which opened the door to the Otherworld. Now she was ready to offer her life to The Mother.

Tears of love and gratitude streaked down Margret Davis's cheeks as she held Tessa's shoulders in her hands. "Gwendoline and I are overjoyed knowing that our tribe and its traditions will live on. Thank you, Tessa. You must prepare yourself for the ceremony. I have sent Clark to the city to retrieve items for me, so he will be away most of the day. Come to the well-chamber when you are ready. Do you understand what is to be done and why?"

"Ganna has explained it."

"Aye, this is an important night for Ganna as well. Gwendoline and I will be the ritual casters for the *imbas forosnai*, which is for you alone this afternoon. Later you will preside over the *Seremoni Dŵr Cysegredig*" with the other elders.

When Tessa entered the ancient room that housed the sacred well, the Davis sisters were waiting in their green robes. A candle was burning under a small iron pot that sat on the edge of the well,

41

and a pile of animal skins had been heaped in one corner of the small chamber. Next to it was a basket of dried oak leaves.

Tessa approached. Without a word, they removed her clothing. When she was naked, Gwendoline placed one of the larger animal skins over her shoulders and wrapped it around her body. Margaret retrieved the steaming pot on the ledge of the well and held it before Tessa. "There is nothing to fear. This brew contains the "flesh of the gods," which you know, and other herbs. Drink all of it."

The tannic tea was bitter and gritty in her mouth, but as she swallowed, Tessa felt a soothing warmth fill her belly.

Gwendoline and Margaret each, in turn, kissed Tessa's cheeks, guided her to the bed of skins they had prepared, and instructed her to lay down. As she curled into her nest, Tessa thought she heard the flutter of wings and glanced about. There was but one high window in the well-chamber, and nothing was there.

Gwendoline made a sign telling Tessa to close her eyes as she began sprinkling the dried oak leaves over and around her. Then came the skins. One at a time, each was draped over Tessa until all light was shut out and she was encased in complete darkness. As the many layers of skins were laid, the weight on Tessa grew greater and greater. The earthy smells of the hides filled her nose and lungs and cut out sounds until she could hear nothing but her own heart beating in her ears.

Then the dreams came vivid and quick—figments of memories and faces long gone—a parade of the past. Then the images slowed and stopped. There was nothing. . . almost nothing . . . faint crying . . . a child's cries. Tessa's body trembled. "Evangeline, I'm coming. I'm sorry . . . so sorry . . . I'm coming." Tessa cried out to her dead little sister over and over. Then suddenly, her entreaties stopped when she heard the flutter of wings, this time accompanied by a voice: "I am well, sister. Shed no tears for me. I love you."

"Ah-h-h-augh!" Tessa cried as she burst out from under the layers of hides—her arms stretching up over her head. Her breath, deep and heavy, slowed as her eyes went to the small square window above. There sat a shimmering skylark and, for a moment, the only two creatures on the earth were Tessa and that precious little being.

A cold draft sent a shiver through Tessa's body, and she hastily covered her nakedness with a skin as the sisters hurried back into the chamber. Wordlessly they put a green robe over her shoulders and quietly ushered her to her bedroom. "Until tonight," they said as they closed the door.

There was water and food on a table next to her bed, but she could not eat or drink.

It was real, Ganna said. *That's what you are wondering isn't?*

Tessa sobbed. "Thank you, Ganna."

Thank The Mother and Evangeline. Guilt forges the heaviest of earthly chains. Now, like your sister, you are ready to take flight. Eat and rest before the Seremoni Dŵr Cysegredig.

The ceremony's rites were simple, but it demanded that Tessa put her full heart and intention into every word and act. Five women encircled a low stone wall surrounding Ceridwen's sacred well. Tessa, the declared channel of Ganna's ancient spiritual knowledge, was joined by the surviving women elders of the tribe: Gwendoline and Margaret Davis, Gwenda the cook, and Nell Rees. They were dressed in long hooded robes of nettle green. Calm and ready, they rocked gently as Tessa intoned the ancient mantra: *"Ceissio y tu hwnt"*—seek beyond.

The dark chamber where they gathered was located at the far end of Ceridwen's great hall. It was a place without time. Moss-covered stone walls had originally been built to protect the well long before the construction of the manor centuries later. A hallowed underground river, the largest of many subterranean rivers thereabouts, fed the well. The Iceni called it "the boundless water." It was perhaps the greatest of their long-held treasures. With its powerful energies, water is the surest pathway to The Mother, and so the druids' strongest connection with the divine forces of the Earth.

The ancient anointing ritual that the women gathered to perform marked a turning point in the survival of the primeval druid lineage. Tessa's own grandmother had been a "keeper of the secrets"—a ritual caster for the tribe. Now, before Tessa could take her place as the tribe's Druid priestess, she must seek the blessing of The Mother.

The only light in the room came from a flickering candle resting on the short stone wall surrounding the well. The moon had not yet risen, but through the high opening in the tower wall, a dazzling point of light could be seen—the planet Venus announcing that it was an auspicious time for this ceremony.

Tessa watched the face of her twin floating on the well's glassy surface.

Look deeply into the water, Ganna told her.

The water rippled, and tiny furrows marred Tessa's image. *This is how I will look when I am old,* she thought.

Concentrate, Ganna reminded her. *When you are ready, retrieve the water.*

Tessa pulled her cowl down, took a small wooden bucket, and lowered it into the water. When the bucket was full, she pulled it up and set it atop the low wall. Reaching into the bucket with cupped hands, she scooped up the water, held it for a moment over the well, and washed her face. Dipping into the bucket again, she bent low and poured water over her head.

Now the knife, Ganna reminded her.

Tessa retrieved a crudely forged length of steel from her robe. It was wrapped in leather on one end and honed to a sharp point on the other. She held it over the well for a moment before breaking the blade on the edge of the stone. Holding both pieces in one hand, she closed her eyes and sang: "*Gadewch imi ddod adref at fy mam, Gadewch imi ddod adref at fy mam.*" Tears cascaded down Tessa's face and dripped into the well as Ganna's voice joined Tessa's in the ageless lament: "Let me come home to my mother, Let me come home to my mother."

Over and over, they chanted the lovely song, their voices harmonizing and deepening, becoming more resonant with each verse. Tessa's tears seemed never-ending. Her hand opened with the offering as the broken knife fell away. Her arm remained outstretched as blood from a gash in her palm dripped into the water below as she spoke: "Take my blood and my body. I give it freely for your use."

EIGHT

DR. WATSON RETURNED TO THE CITY only to receive another urgent telegram from Clark Button begging him to return to Ceridwen immediately. Without success, he had been trying to reach Holmes.

"I'm pleased the weather is more hospitable on this trip, sir," the cart driver Dylan remarked as they made their way toward the manor. "If I may ask, sir, is the young lady feeling better?"

"Miss Wiggins?"

"Yes, sir."

His innocuous inquiry told Watson the local gossip-mill had been busy. "She is well. My visit today is as a friend, not a doctor."

"Pleased I am to hear it, sir."

Watson sent a telegram ahead letting Clark know he was not able to engage Dr. Kraepelin and was arriving alone on the afternoon train. To make matters worse, Holmes had disappeared. Watson had made several unsuccessful attempts to contact the detective—two telegrams and three telephone calls. One call to Holmes's housekeeper, Mrs. Thornton, seemed to yield a clue to his whereabouts when she reported that, while dusting, she noticed Holmes's manuscript was not on his desk. She thought it likely he had gone to the city to deliver his book to John Wiley & Sons. However, a call to that establishment told Watson that Mrs. Thornton's surmise was incorrect.

"He's a gadabout," Watson mumbled in frustration.

The dogcart lurched, bringing the doctor's musings to an abrupt halt. Dylan pulled back on the reins and guided his horse to the side of the road. Looking ahead, Watson saw the reason: a large automobile was speeding toward them. The doctor stood and looked over Dylan's shoulder.

"It's the Davis sisters," the driver told him. "They're in residence." *Sotto voce,* he added: "Blasted machine."

But Dylan was only partially correct. The burgundy Daimler limousine did belong to Gwendoline and Margaret Davis, but the only passenger was Clark Button, who was waving wildly. Dylan held the reins tighter as the auto slowed and rolled to a stop alongside.

Clark lowered the window and took a deep breath. "Thank heaven, Dr. Watson," he began. "I only received your telegram a short time ago. I was afraid you would blunder into an unfriendly situation." Dylan's eyes grew wide at this new grist for the district gossip-mill. "I'll take Dr. Watson from here," Clark said before backing up the Daimler.

Clark got out and grabbed the halter of Dylan's horse and turned the rig back toward town. Watson stepped out, paid Dylan, and joined Clark in the front seat of the limousine. When the dogcart was some way down the road, Clark took off his cap and swept a lock of hair from his sweaty brow. "I could have handled that better."

Clark's harried manner told Watson he had disturbing news. "We will talk," he said, "but I could use a wee dram or two."

Watson held his curiosity in check as they drove in the opposite direction from Ceridwen.

The limousine made its way to nearby Porthmadog. As they came onto the high street, heads in the village turned, some men tipping their caps, thinking one or both of the Davis sisters were within. Pulling up across from the Golden Fleece Inn, Clark turned the motor off and slumped in his seat. "Ah, now to business," he said.

They took a table, and as Clark went to the bar for their drinks, Watson noticed a striking Waterhouse print of Jason and Medea that hung behind the bar. The beautiful black-haired maiden in the print looked remarkably like Tessa. The resemblance made him shiver, for it depicted Medea pouring poison into a chalice as her paramour looked on. Clark set two glasses on the table and, following the doctor's gaze, said: "Yes, a remarkable likeness."

"Medea was the *real* warrior, wasn't she?" Watson noted.

"That's Tess," Clark said before he sat and downed his whiskey in one quaff.

"Now, what has happened?" Watson asked.

"I was gone most of yesterday—on a fool's errand, as it turned out. It was dark when I returned and, after wiping down the auto, I went to bed. Later, I was awakened by strange singing coming from outside—or so I thought. It was faint, but I could hear women's voices singing a Welsh song. As our nearest neighbor is miles away, I knew the voices were coming from somewhere near. I followed my ears, and they brought me to the small chamber that houses the manor's well. The room was mostly dark, but I was able to make out Gwendoline and Margaret Davis, along with Tessa and two other hooded women. Tess was singing." Staring into his empty glass, he added: "I know Tessa's singing. She sings all the time. It wasn't her voice."

"Then your employers are complicit in all of this?"

"Yes. I can hardly believe it, but it's true. Now you see why I had to head you off."

"Indeed." Watson took a drink. "This is beyond my depth, old man. I wish Holmes were here." He downed the remainder of his whisky. "Tessa needs a proper doctor now. What do you think about paying a visit to Hellingford?"

❋ ❋ ❋ ❋ ❋

Sherlock Holmes waited in the hallway as Elis, the Davis's butler, took his card to Tessa and the sisters. After a considerable time, Elis returned to show Holmes to the drawing-room. "Miss Wiggins is indisposed, sir. The ladies will be with you momentarily," he said, attaching a slight admonishment: "You understand, sir, they were not expecting you." Holmes held up his pipe with a questioning look. Elis nodded. "Of course, sir. Make yourself comfortable."

Holmes did just that until a knock at the front door sent the butler scuttling down the hallway again. A moment later, Watson stood framed in the archway of the drawing-room. He bristled with indignation as he spied Holmes comfortably puffing away before a cozy fire.

"I received your message, old boy, and came as quickly as I could," Holmes said.

Watson took a deep breath. "You disappear for days, and then you arrive without a word!"

Holmes shrugged. "Really, Watson, from your telegrams and calls, I would think you would be pleased to see me."

"Ah! So, you received them but did not think to reply. Where have you been, Holmes, and how the devil did you get here? You didn't come on the afternoon train."

"No. I was in the neighborhood . . . have been since yesterday. Now catch me up."

Watson did just that.

Holmes listened intently to Watson's rambling report, interrupting only once when he mentioned Dr. Mayer's name.

"Mayer? The Swiss psychiatrist?"

Watson looked surprised. "You know Dr. Mayer?"

The detective had a fixed grin. "By reputation."

"Do you know that Mayer is nearby at Hellingford Asylum?"

"Hellingford." He smiled. "This all begins to make sense."

"What does?"

"Later, Watson. Tessa first."

"Of course. The upshot is that we need to get her out of this house and into treatment. Hellingford offers the opportunity for both, so I've made an appointment for her."

"If Miss Wiggins agrees," a gruff voice boomed from the doorway. There stood Gwendoline Davis, impeccably dressed and bejeweled. She sauntered into the room with her older sister Margaret—another creature altogether. Margaret's long grey hair was plaited, splayed down the back of her neck, and tossed over the shoulder of a drab brown dress. Both ladies were subdued in their graciousness.

Gwendoline took a seat opposite Holmes—her watchful companion standing behind her. "So, we have two distinguished gentlemen appear at our door—uninvited, I would add."

Margaret harrumphed, "What my sister means to ask is: why the devil are you here?"

Holmes remained unruffled. "We are here to see Tessa."

"She does not wish to see you," Margaret said.

Dr. Watson straightened in his chair. "You must know that Miss Wiggins is struggling emotionally. We're here to help her seek treatment at Hellingford."

Gwendoline cocked her head and squinted at Watson. "Really? You had a brief chat with Miss Wiggins a day or two ago, and you have quickly concluded that she should be shuffled off to an asylum?"

Holmes held up a hand to halt a rejoinder from Watson. "We are her friends. You know this. We insist upon seeing her."

Margaret's eyes riveted on Holmes. "I would remind you that Tessa is in our employ and under our protection. If she does not wish to see you, your tedious journey will have been in vain, and we will expect you both to leave immediately."

Holmes retrieved a penny from his vest pocket and held it out to Gwendoline Davis. "Please, give this to Tessa and tell her I wish to speak with her . . . alone."

Gwendoline rose, and with a perplexed look, accepted the coin. Then taking her sister's hand, they departed. The room remained gripped in tension as the two ladies exited. Clark stepped back from the doorway where he had been lurking. "You should be about your duties, Mr. Button," Gwendoline scolded in passing.

Clark waited until they left, then approached Holmes. "I assume Dr. Watson told you about last evening?"

Holmes nodded. "I concur with Watson's plan. The Davis's are complicit in Tessa's condition, and they are hiding something. Hellingford may be best for her."

"She won't go," Clark declared. "And I don't know as I want her to go."

"She will," Holmes countered. "Leave it to me."

NINE

HELLINGFORD ASLYUM AROSE like a tentacled beast crawling across the bleak Welsh landscape. "Bloody hell," Tessa muttered. She reached back for Eva's hand, trying to stop herself from asking Clark to turn the auto around. "It's enormous."

Ganna's frequent reminder resonated in her mind: *Your strength is there if you look for it.*

Clark slowed to a stop. Turning to Tessa, he put his hand on hers. His cap barely contained his auburn hair. He had donned his grey chauffeur's uniform so that those at Hellingford would know that Tessa was a proper lady. Sweeping a strand of black hair from her face, he frowned. "Why are you doing this? What power does Holmes have over you?"

"It's my choice, Clark. You know that many years ago, my brother Rory and I served as eyes and ears for Mr. Holmes. He paid us, but it was more than a simple exchange of services. He kept Rory, me, and countless other irregulars from the poorhouse. I have an opportunity to repay Mr. Holmes for all he did for my family and me—and for Eva. He needs eyes in Hellingford, and I can help him."

Eva leaned forward and placed her hand on Tessa's shoulder. "You don't have to do this for me. If I owe Mr. Holmes a debt, I will pay it."

Tessa's fears were humbled. At eighteen, Eva had faced abandonment, unbelievable cruelty, and a close brush with an ignominious death. Yet you would never know it looking at her now. But it was not so easy for Tessa—a woman had died at her hands, and now Ganna's presence shadows her.

"I'm not sure I can do this, Tess," Clark said.

She squeezed his hand and smiled. "My sweet boyo, voluntary admission is not an option. I need you to play your part. You yourself said I was barmy."

"Stop it, Tess. You know I didn't mean it."

She handed him the letter Dr. Watson had prepared. "Put this in your pocket. Let's get on with it."

✻ ✻ ✻ ✻ ✻

Sherlock Holmes had delayed a necessary conversation with Watson because there had not been a moment when they were alone. Even as Clark waved them onto the train, an elderly woman greeted them as they entered their compartment. When Watson grimaced, Holmes popped open his watch: "Shall we chat at ten?"

Watson seemed mesmerized by the austere autumn landscape rushing by his window. Holmes sat motionless, eyes closed, but a steadily tapping toe on the carpet showed that his prodigious mind was whirling away.

The woman sitting adjacent to Dr. Watson seemed dressed for a party or possibly returning from one. *No, going to a party*, Watson decided when he saw the gaily wrapped package stuffed into her tote bag, along with a newspaper and a knitted something-or-other. The gift was big enough for two Waterford wine glasses, or maybe a nutcracker music box or a brass tobacco canister. Try as he might, Watson could not recall the last party he had attended. He and Holmes were solitary men who traded adventures for festivities. But like a party, each adventure held a mysterious gift begging to be unwrapped.

The conductor's call turned everyone's head: "Crewe, Crewe Station," came the announcement as the train brakes squealed. The old woman tucked her knitting away in the tote and ambled out of the compartment with a passing nod.

Holmes held up his open watch. "Ten."

"You saw the *Crewe Chronicle* in the tote," Watson remarked.

"It appears you also did."

"Now Holmes, what in the blazes—"

The detective held up a restraining hand, retrieved a folded letter from his coat, and handed it to the doctor.

October 14, 1920

Dear Mr. Holmes,

To say that I look forward to reading Theories of Crime would be an understatement. I have followed your career almost from its genesis and was delighted to find that the insipid melodramas published by John Watson did not represent the full scope of your work. Apparently, there are many cats in the sack, since you seem to have saved your most tantalizing cases for last.

No doubt you intended to change the names, places, and dates of these unpublished cases to protect the innocent, and to ensure that you would not find yourself in a docket, sued for liable by Robert Ferguson, Neville St. Clair, or others. Or possibly you thought Theories of Crime might be published posthumously. But as the plowman poet noted:

> *The best-laid schemes o' mice an' men*
> *Gang aft agley,*
> *An' lea'e us nought but grief an' pain,*
> *For promis'd joy!*

I fear this will be the outcome, although I may be amenable to returning your masterwork for a price. However, I presently feel compelled to share at least some of it with the world. I believe you are a loyal reader of The

Daily Mail; however, I suggest you broaden your reading habits to include other publications in the coming month.

I know you will seek to find me. So realize that it will be a treacherous pursuit. Even if successful, some of the 'cats' will have already escaped the proverbial bag. Also, know that I am holding a rather scruffy feline by his neck—a secret that I doubt you have shared with anyone. I cannot say how much longer I will be able to maintain my grip on this rambunctious tomcat who has not reared his head in near thirty years.

Most sincerely,

Ahriman

P.S. You really should lock your cottage when you are away.

Watson dropped the letter in his lap. "Ahriman?"

"It's Persian," Holmes said as he retrieved the letter. "Ahriman is a destructive spirit—something akin to the devil."

* * * * *

Hellingford's immensity inspired awe. The epitome of Victorian design, the façade of the central three-story brick building with its many peaked roofs and chimneys cut a jagged line across the horizon. Several two-story wings sprouted in various directions, connecting to the central building via corridors reminiscent of the great houses' galleries. All the construction stood well behind a towering iron fence topped with barbed hooks turned inward. An ornate wrought-iron gate sat immediately adjacent to the road.

Clark squeezed Tessa's hand. "Here we go, Tess," he said, pulling to a stop before the gate. A large squat man wearing a cracked black leather coat stepped out of a gatehouse and lumbered toward the auto, his broad shoulders swinging. His face was all eyebrows and mustache. Bending lower to peer into the automobile, he revealed a brutish face. Smiling or frowning, no one could tell because his frothy ebony whiskers hid the man's mouth. He carried a strange pithy scent.

His dark eyes flitted to all three passengers before he spoke. "Alright and wha? Who be ye?"

Clark touched the brim of his cap with two fingers. "Miss Tessa Wiggins. We have an appointment."

The sentry cocked his head. "Aye, Miss Tessa. Under the doctor, ay?" His eyes widened and a smile blossomed on his face. "Like, wilcom' to Hellingford, Miss Tessa." He pointed to himself: "Cian."

"Thank you, Cian," Tessa replied.

As the gatekeeper's eyes softened, a sense of familiarity came over Tessa. *Surely, I would remember such a fellow*, she thought. Cian stepped back and went about swinging open the huge gates. Tessa caught him studying her intently as the glistening limousine passed through. She expected Ganna might comment, as she often did when she entered a new place, but Tessa was only aware of a peculiar foreboding that she ascribed to her own trepidation.

As they arrived at the front steps, three people emerged from the entrance: two dressed head-to-toe in white and another in a dark grey tailored dress sporting a black collar and bow tie. The dusky woman and her two acolytes waited passively on the top step, oblivious to the chilly air. The man had the body of a wrestler; his counterpart was a skeleton-thin female nurse.

As Clark came to a stop, Tessa turned to Eva, took her face in both hands, and gave her a brief kiss. "Wait here." Then to Clark: "Come on, Button, let's get on with it. Remember, take me in hand."

* * * * *

Watson pointed to the letter in Holmes's hand. "So, the visit by the would-be Amelia Bauer was a ruse? There is no treasure."

"It would appear so. Frau Bauer undoubtedly knew that you shared accommodations with Stone, and you would bring her contrived story to me in the hope that it would lure me away from my cottage."

"Clever and calculating."

"And well informed. It would be a mistake to underestimate this woman though she may have underestimated me. I was able to piece together small details of her visit to Stone and track her to Hellingford. But I thought it wise not to attempt entry."

"Aha! So, Tessa, once again, wears the cap of an irregular. I must say, Holmes, I *am* relieved. When you asked me to write a letter to commit Tessa, I had grave misgivings. How were you able to find this mystery woman?"

"She dropped too many breadcrumbs on her way to visit Stone. Her damp umbrella led me to trains serving the west, and a short list of routes where the last train of the day left Euston after three o'clock narrowed my search further. I rode both lines, showing my sketch of the woman to conductors and others. Finally, her umbrella—specifically the gold knob on the handle, caught the eye of an observant porter, and I was able to track her to Blaenau Ffestiniog. Knowing she would need transport—"

"Dylan!"

"Yes, Dylan provided the final link to Hellingford."

"But you did not go in?"

"My arrival would have alarmed the mystery woman and allowed her to escape or bury the manuscript even deeper in the bowels of that colossal building."

"Let us hope Tessa can find your manuscript before the bloody blackmailer can strike."

Holmes clenched his jaw. Of all the dastardly criminals and crimes he had dealt with over the years, he held that blackmailers and blackmail were the most cowardly criminals and the most heinous crime. It prayed on peoples' weaknesses and threatened to take away the thing human beings crave most in the world—love and belonging.

Holmes folded the letter and placed it back into his pocket. "Watson, there is considerable urgency here as I had not finished changing all the names and places in my manuscript. Whoever holds it has the means to blackmail our former clients and me as well."

"And what was that bit about a scruffy tomcat? What clandestine incident occurred thirty years ago?" Then, Watson blanched. "Reichenbach!"

Holmes nodded. "Indeed, a dark chapter in our lives."

"So that's what has resurrected your memories of Moriarty. My dear friend, you must know that it is more reasonable and likely that a former client or thief stole your manuscript."

"You're right, Watson, but I cannot seem to shed this lingering dread I have about Moriarty."

Watson was struck dumb. "Lingering dread? I did not imagine that such words could be found in your vocabulary. I should exalt in this moment, but instead, it worries me. Professor Moriarty is dead."

TEN

MRS. MAYER WAS ADORNED IN GREY, and there was grayness about her that went beyond her attire. Standing like a portrait by Sargent, she held herself apart from the nurse and attendant flanking her. *She appears genial,* Tessa thought, *but there is a remote unpleasantness behind her smile.* Ganna would later describe Mayer as one of those who sees only wood when they look at a tree.

Tessa waited in the auto as Clark retrieved her portmanteau and writing case from the boot. The nurse was waiting to take the cases. Clark tipped his cap and went around to open the door. Reaching inside, he took Tessa by the arm and guided her out and up the stairs. When she hesitated, he yanked her closer. Mayer's eyes grew wider as they approached. "I presume this is Miss Tessa Wiggins."

Clark nodded. "Yes, and you must be Mrs. Mayer."

"Beatrice Mayer. I'm the Director. My husband Doctor Mayer is occupied and regrets that he cannot be here to greet you." She extended a hand. "Pleased to meet you, Miss Wiggins," she said, as a politician might. Tessa did not take the Director's hand.

Clark deferentially removed his cap. "Miss Wiggins is understandably anxious."

"Of course," Mayer replied, maintaining her smile. "And you, sir?" she said to Clark.

"Clark Button. I am a co-worker of Tessa's."

"I see." Turning to Tessa, she observed: "No family then? The reservation was made by—"

"Dr. John Watson," Clark said.

Mrs. Mayer nodded and motioned toward the entrance.

The male attendant took his place behind the entourage following Clark and Tessa as they entered the asylum. A pungent iodoform smell permeated the air and beneath it the scent of the human-animal: urine, feces, and fear.

The Director turned to the attendant. "It doesn't appear we will need you, Angus. You may go." Then she instructed the nurse to wait outside before showing Tessa and Clark into her office.

Mayer took her place behind a massive oak desk. "Quite fortunate you are to find a place here. Hellingford is at capacity," Director Mayer began. "The Kaiser caused many casualties at Somme and other battlefields, but mark me, the war has left as many mentally afflicted here at home."

There was nothing to be said. The heartbreak of the Great War was still present two years after the armistice in *Compiègne*.

A masterful drypoint etching of a woman sat behind Mayer's desk. It bore an uncanny resemblance to her, and for some reason, looked familiar to Tessa. Like the woman in the portrait, the Director's chestnut hair was coiled like a rope behind her head. Catching Tessa's eyes, Beatrice Mayer turned to the portrait. "My mother. It barely does her justice."

"She was a beautiful woman," Tessa conceded.

"From this portrait, you would never know that she was horribly ill-treated in life." As the Director turned back to the desk, her eyes revealed that ghosts and troubled memories had momentarily possessed her.

Clark took a letter from his jacket and handed it to the Director. She opened it and read silently before looking up. "Everything seems to be in order," she said, holding the letter before her. "We have a certification from Dr. Watson, but it lacks clarity. He uses the term 'mental confusion,' and offers the opinion that restraint or confinement will not be necessary." She laid the letter down. "How would you describe your condition, Miss Wiggins?"

Tessa folded her hands in her lap and looked down sheepishly. "I have been through a difficult time," she mumbled. "I've been struggling to sort things out."

"Well then, let me add 'mental overexertion' until my husband can offer a more definitive diagnosis. She made a note on the letter, blotted it, and placed it in a folder. Tessa noticed that Mayer was not wearing a wedding band, although that is not unusual in hospitals. "The doctor's letter also indicates that he will stand for the expenses while you are in our care, so you will have a room on one of our fine rate-paid wards. You need not concern yourself about that."

"As I intend to repay him, I would like to know the costs involved," Tessa remarked.

A look of mild amusement came over the Director's face. "Now, now, we can work out the details later. You must focus all your energies on getting well, Miss Wiggins."

"You should know, Mrs. Mayer, that I do not intend for this to be a long stay."

Pulling back from the desk, her lips pouted in a manner intended to show sympathy. "Miss Wiggins trust me when I tell you that you are not in a position to evaluate your condition, nor appreciate how long you may need to be in residence. Be comforted by the fact that you are in excellent hands," she stated. "Accommodations have been prepared, and nurse Halper will show you to your room. Your things will be brought later. I would like a private word with Mr. Button."

Tessa wanted to spit in Mayer's condescending eye, but she knew that silence was the best way to protect oneself from the petty judgment of others. From the start, as a child walking the dangerous alleys of Spitalfields, Tessa had her own way of navigating the world—another way of knowing. She called it 'the small voice.' It wasn't her thoughts or feelings—it didn't seem to come from her. Ganna was the only one who knew and understood the 'small voice.' Others would think her mad.

Nurse Halper took hold of Tessa's elbow the moment she left the office, but Tessa yanked her arm back. "I will say goodbye to Mr. Button."

The nurse nodded.

The entry was chilly and damp. Tessa shivered. Halper took her hand—more gently this time. The corners of the nurse's mouth turned up. She was trying to reassure Tessa, just as Ganna had done on that dreadful night eight months before. Tessa trembled again as she recalled watching the ever-slowing rise and fall of old Druid's chest as the venom worked its way into her body. When Ganna took her last breath, Tessa clutched her hand tightly to welcome her spirit.

The moment Clark opened the door, Tessa pulled him to one side. The bitter tang of his tobacco was on his uniform and breath. "What did she say?" she whispered.

"Later, I don't feel good about this," he murmured.

"Keep Eva close. She wants to bolt and go to London." He squeezed her hand and nodded to reassure her.

As Director Mayer exited her office, she cast a disapproving eye on Nurse Halper, who quickly resumed her place at Tessa's side.

"Visit often, Clark."

"I will. We will. Mrs. Mayer feels it best that we give you a week to settle in before we return, but Eva and I will come regular after that." Tessa knew Clark had a kiss on his mind when he took her shoulders in his hands. She laid a hand against his broad chest and lowered her head. As he pulled back, she saw the unease in his eyes. "Goodbye, Tess."

Halper's hand tugged her along and even before Clark was gone. As the nurse marched Tessa down the hall, they passed a woman locked in a monotonous scuffle. Her eyes pleaded with Tessa as she passed.

"You are in Ward B," the nurse said as they came to a large oak door at the end of the gallery. Halper knocked twice. A lock clinked, and a large woman in a grey, black-belted dress opened the door. "This is Mrs. Mitchell. She is the matron and day-nurse in this ward. She will see to your needs. Mitchell, this is Miss Tessa Wiggins."

"Lovely," the Matron grumbled in a husky voice. "You're in B-16," she said, eyeing Tessa as if she were a sack of wheat wanting to be put away in the barn. Her hard eyes squinted and almost disappeared into her loose-skinned face. Tessa had encountered Mitchell's kind in the backstreets of London's East End. Her cold and measured manner told her that this was a formidable woman.

Matron Mitchell walked ahead and stopped at a door reinforced with black steel straps. A small square window was centered at eye level. In one smooth movement, the matron pointed to the room number, unlocked the door, and swung it wide. "Welcome to your new home, Miss Wiggins."

Tessa stepped across the threshold.

The room was generous in proportion but plain, austere, and stripped of color. The air was dank, stale, and smelled of mold. The utilitarian furnishings included a full bed, wardrobe, dresser, a Morris chair, and a small table with a lamp. In the corner sat a washstand with a chamber pot below. The windows were barred and covered with faded floral-print curtains.

As Tessa went to open the window, she caught sight of Clark and Eva driving out through the gate. Suddenly all the sadness and fear she had been holding back seized her. Doubts about this undertaking arose like some great creature writhing up from a sea of tears. These grim thoughts were interrupted by a metallic clank behind her. Mitchell was gone. Tessa rushed to the door and turned the knob.

Locked.

She pounded on the door. "What's going on?"

The noise brought muted shouts and moans from nearby rooms as Matron Mitchell's crimson-cheeked face popped up in the small viewing window. "Wiggins, you have just learned your first lesson: It's easier to get into Hellingford than to get out."

ELEVEN

IN A FRAIL EFFORT TO ESCAPE the sly demon self-doubt, Tessa paced about in her room. If there could be any solace for her, she knew it rested in nature. She went to the window and opened it.

It was the eye of the fall season, and Samhain was less than two weeks away. Pressing her face against the cold steel bars, she looked out onto fading grasses and browning bracken. She breathed deeply, welcoming the tannic perfume, recalling what Ganna taught her about the sense of smell—that it is rooted in the oldest part of our brains as undiluted knowledge. She closed her eyes and breathed in a rolling rhythmic pattern, savoring the sweet musky scents. Her body unwound. Calm and confidence replaced feelings of unease.

Looking out at the gatehouse, she recalled the strange earthy scent of the gatekeeper Cian. His size and appearance made him seem dangerous, but Tessa felt a strange kinship with the fellow. He likely benefited from the neglect of the modern world to become a simple man with simple ways, but Tessa sensed a rare primordial intelligence within the keeper at the gate.

"Where are you, old woman?" Tessa muttered. True to her word, Ganna had become a *teithiwr*—a wandering spirit, but Tessa knew Ganna had to return. She needed her reassuring presence and teachings now more than ever. The old Druidess had prodigious powers she shared with Tessa—arcane knowledge about the forests, the weather and elemental storms, and about the many mysteries that lay within rivers, lakes, and seas. But when Tessa pressed Ganna for the deeper mysteries, the old Druid told her to use her own magic— her senses, awareness, and intuition, and telling her that Nature will teach her everything she needs to know if she will pay attention.

Suddenly the back of Tessa's neck prickled. She turned to see Matron Mitchell's rotund face peering through the watch-window. A click of the lock and the heavy door swung wide. The Matron set down Tessa's bag and writing case. "I let you have your pencils, but I had to keep your letter opener. You won't be getting much mail. Your door will remain locked until Dr. Mayer tells me otherwise, so you'll be taking your meals in your room for the time being."

When the matron left, Tessa opened the suitcase to find her clothes twisted and crushed. Pushing the grip aside, she snatched the writing case and carried it to a far corner and dumped the contents on the floor. Feeling along the inside edge of the case, she held her breath as she pulled up the false bottom. The sketch Mr. Holmes had given her was still there. And yes, the drawing did look like Mrs. Mayer and the portrait above her desk.

That night Tessa lay awake listening to a woman's sobs reverberating in the hallway. Finally, as dawn's roseate light filtered into the room, she set about putting her belongings in order. There was more than enough room in the wardrobe but surveying the space with her writing case in hand; it was clear she lacked a desk. There was a side-table by the chair, but it offered only a writing surface. She finally found a place to hide Mr. Holmes's sketch and her notes within the brown paper backing behind the dresser mirror.

Opening the case, she took a pencil in hand and made her first notes for Mr. Holmes. At the top of the list was Beatrice Mayer, who bore a strong resemblance to the mystery woman Bauer. Her notes on Matron Mitchell were sparse, but she made it clear that the Matron was more a jailer than a nurse. Tessa also shared details about her surroundings, including the tall fence, the gate, and the gatekeeper. She turned over the page and began a rough floor plan of the front of the building and her ward. To find Mr. Holmes's manuscript, she knew that she might have to explore the entire grounds.

A knock came just as Tessa secreted her notes away behind the mirror. "Yes," she called out. The door opened to reveal a pale and ascetic old man in a wheeled-chair. He was thin, clean-shaven, and wore an open white laboratory jacket over a well-cut suit. His forehead was domed. His deep-set brown eyes scrutinized Tessa through gold *pince-nez*. Tessa's heart raced, and her breathing became rapid. Her body knew, even before her mind, that there was a darkness about the man. He rolled into the room and, patting a file in his lap, introduced himself: "I am Dr. Mayer. I want to learn all about you," he said. Faint anxiety underplayed his tone. Tessa expected a Germanic accent, but it was not forthcoming. "Would you like to go for a stroll?"

"I would love to get some air," she replied, retrieving a sweater from the wardrobe.

Matron Mitchell led the way, opening the door to the gallery that connected the ward to the main building. Mayer paused and grabbed Tessa's wrist. "Will you help me along, Miss Wiggins." Tessa pulled her arm away, took hold of the chair back, and pushed him along until they exited the gallery through a door that opened into an ill-kempt garden in the central common. The doctor pointed to a bench, and Tessa sat.

He wheeled his heavy oaken chair toward her. "Tell me, what brought you here?" he asked, turning his beetling brow upon her.

"I am not certain I should be here," she answered. "I simply need time to get past a horrible experience that occurred some months ago."

"What happened, Miss Wiggins?"

"I rescued a young woman . . . several young women from a dangerous situation. The leader of these women was trapped by her pursuers and she took her own life with a sword." Tears pooled in Tessa's eyes. "I held it—the blade she ran onto."

"Some might call that proper justice."

"That is what others say, but they were not holding the sword that killed Maeve. They don't understand."

"Here at Hellingford we help people release what they hold inside: guilt, hatred, regret, anger. Every human being carries within them negative energies—I call them orgone. By releasing orgone we restore health and balance. If we can purge the orgone within you, you will get well. I harbor great hope for you, Miss Wiggins."

The walk back to Tessa's ward was slow because the doctor's wheeled-chair was heavy and cumbersome. When she saw them coming, Matron Mitchell opened the door to the ward. Leading the way, she took the ring of keys from her belt and stood obediently at the entrance to Tessa's room. Dr. Mayer stayed the Matron's hand: "That will not be necessary, Mrs. Mitchell. Good day, Miss Wiggins."

Tessa closed the door behind her and waited to satisfy herself that the door had not been locked.

Beware," Ganna warned.

"Yes, he seems kind but—"

His ignorance is dangerous. You can heal yourself. Most heartfelt pain is self-inflicted.

"Is it?"

You told the doctor about Maeve, but what of your mother, Rory, and Benjie? Tessa's eyes flitted about the room. "They're dead and gone."

Departed, but not dead, I would say.

Tessa trembled, fell onto her bed, and sobbed.

TWELVE

TESSA WAS EAGER TO EXPLORE Hellingford but was shrewd enough to wait several days before testing the bounds of her independence. There was no map of the sprawling facility, but that afternoon Tessa found the next best thing—Jack.

Jack was one of a handful of patients who worked in the asylum. He pushed a four-wheeled wicker cart stacked with clean sheets, towels, and uniforms from the laundry, delivering them to the various wards and gathering soiled linens. If there were more than three pounds of fat on the man, he hid it well. He walked with a pronounced limp, moving about noiselessly day after day on the same repetitive rounds. This made him akin to invisible.

Today Tessa left the door to her room open and waited for Jack. When he approached her room, she motioned for him to step inside. "Thank you, I'm Tessa," she said, taking the clean sheets from his hands.

He nodded. "Jack."

She chuckled. "Asking what brought you to Hellingford doesn't seem proper."

"Haven't you heard? I'm not fit for civil society—that's what my father will tell you."

"Why would your father say such a thing?"

"He would say that of any sodomite," Jack said, with his chin held high.

Tessa was speechless.

He laughed. "I've shocked you."

She nodded. "You have. This explains why you are the only man allowed on the women's wards."

He held out the red card looped around his neck with a cord. "My job gives me the run of the place—almost all of it."

Jack seemed to enjoy being with Tessa, and they chatted for several minutes. He hailed from Sussex, and it struck Tessa that he led an unusually adventurous life for a country-born man in his mid-thirties. Jack had gone to sea, toiled on a plantation in Peru, and worked his way around the world's great ports: Callao, Manzanillo, Shanghai, and Istanbul, before returning to his home several months ago. The homecoming was a poor decision, for his father learned that he was a homosexual and sent him away again. "Hellingford is where they put you when they want you out of the way," he remarked matter-of-factly. A distant rumble of thunder outside brought his eyes to the window. "I must be on my way."

When Jack was gone, Tessa marched to Matron Mitchell's desk near the entrance to Ward. She was reading and seemed unaware of Tessa's approach.

"Excuse me, Mrs. Mitchell, I must have a word with Mrs. Mayer."

The matron's eyes peered over the top of her magazine. "What about?"

"Visitors and something to do—a job."

As Tessa followed Mitchell through the windowed gallery toward the asylum's front entrance, her eyes lingered on the vanishing rays of the sun. Her spirits rose as the waning amber rays peeked through the gathering clouds and warmed her cheeks. Ganna often remarked that soul-smothering brick and mortar dwellings are too high a price to pay for comfort and the illusion of safety. Tessa felt the truth of that now.

Once in the main building, Mitchell marched Tessa toward the director's office and pointed to a bench near the door. Tessa sat. Mitchell knocked and, receiving no answer, stepped just inside the office. Nurse Halper rounded the corner and scowled. Mitchell immediately jumped back and began to blabber. "Miss Wiggins here, she wishes a word with the . . . with Mrs. Mayer."

"The Director is out, but she will be back shortly. You can go now, Mrs. Mitchell."

The Matron cast a wary eye on Tessa as she marched off. Halper told Tessa she could wait in the office and left the door ajar after Tessa entered.

Tessa's eyes immediately went to the print above Mayer's desk. It was an exceptional etching. Moving closer, she made a note of the signature: M. Menpes, 1880. She imagined a broad-brimmed hat and eyeglasses on the subject. *Yes,* she thought. Mayer *was the mystery lady. Holmes's manuscript could be in this very office.*

"Miss Wiggins!" the Director's entrance surprised Tessa.

"I couldn't help admiring this portrait," she said, hurriedly making her way around to the front of the desk.

"Take a seat." The Director shook her umbrella, closed it, set it by the door, and took her place behind the desk. "What can I do for you?"

"I was wondering when I might receive visitors?"

"That's up to Dr. Mayer."

"Clark was told . . . well, it's been more than a week since I arrived."

Beatrice Mayer opened a file on her desk and slowly turned the pages. There was something wily in her manner. Each page turned yielded "hm-m's" or an "o-oh," as if she were teasing Tessa. "In his last report, Dr. Mayer noted a concern that visits from your friends might complicate your therapy."

Tessa felt her Irish come up but quickly calmed herself. "Then I will talk to Dr. Mayer about visitors and about finding something to help me pass the time."

"What can you do?"

"Gardening, laundry. I was a housekeeper, you know."

The Director's brow lifted. "I need more help in the laundry, but only if Dr. Mayer agrees. Now, if you don't mind, I have a busy day."

On her way out, Tessa stepped around a puddle of water pooled around the tip of Mayer's umbrella—an umbrella with a gold knob.

Nurse Halper was unusually chatty as she escorted Tessa back to her ward, commenting on the damp autumn season, the first women admitted to Oxford, and the funny hand signals that were now compulsory for automobile drivers. The nurse's sociable manner encouraged Tessa to make an appeal: "I'm expecting my friend Mr. Button to call. If he comes, could you deliver a letter for me?"

Halper's cool eyes gave her the answer even before she spoke: "I'm sorry, I'm not allowed." The response made Tessa sad for Halper because she understood that blind obedience is the master-link in the chains of slavery.

A loud bang stopped them in their tracks. It was Jack pushing his laundry cart through the doorway behind them. He nodded hello as he limped past. Following, Halper leaned closer to Tessa and whispered: "I think Jack may be able to help you."

Tessa smiled. That minor act of disobedience revealed Nurse Halper had momentarily slipped her shackles, and in so doing, helped Tessa realize a strategy for finding Holmes's manuscript. *I'll garner allies inside of Hellingford, starting with Jack.*

Halper went on to offer a caveat: "Jack is one of the more amiable patients in Hellingford, but he's prone to fits of anger. He rages whenever a family member seeks permission to visit."

"So, it's true then; his own father committed him."

The Nurse glanced about. "Yes. The only visitor he will see is a former shipmate."

As she approached her room, she saw Jack's cart outside the ward bathroom and casually strolled in that direction. He startled when she entered. "Are we alone?" she asked.

He smiled. "What do *you* think?"

Tessa laughed. "I wanted you to know that I've requested a job in the laundry."

Jack winked. "I knew you were up to something. You want the run of the place."

Tessa smiled. "I hope I was less obvious to Mrs. Mayer."

"Even if you push a laundry cart, there are places you cannot go."

"Everyone needs clean linens."

"Not those that come and go."

"The staff?"

Jack shook his head. "No. Women . . . mostly young from the city. I'm told to stay away from their building—Ward E."

"Where is it?"

He pointed toward the central common and attempted to give directions. As there were more than a dozen buildings, Tessa became confused. "Jack, will you draw a map of Hellingford for me?" He agreed.

Tessa's hopes were soaring as she returned to her room. Dr. Mayer held the key to Tessa's plan, and the key to Dr. Mayer, Tessa surmised, was being a fascinating and compliant patient. She found herself looking forward to her appointment the following day.

Tessa fidgeted in her chair outside Dr. Mayer's office as the matron knocked on the door and called out: "Miss Wiggins is here, Doctor."

"Come," he ordered.

Mitchell showed Tessa to a chair facing Mayer, but his eyes did not move from the open file on his desk. Mitchell closed the door. Tessa remained standing until Mayer looked up and motioned for her to be seated. His eyes roamed over her face—hunter's eyes, looking for a vulnerable spot. When she could no longer bear the weight of his scrutiny, she spoke. "I haven't been completely honest with you, Dr. Mayer."

He leaned forward. "Is this about Ganna?"

Tessa scowled. "Mitchell! The busybody!"

"Now, now Mrs. Mitchell was simply doing her job. Tell me, who is this Ganna that you are having conversations with?" he asked. His eyes never left hers as he swung his chair around the desk. Then he pushed slowly toward her until she could smell tobacco on his clothing.

Her hopeful strategy began to crumble under her mounting dread, but the eager look in Mayer's eyes told her it was too late to turn back. "She is a woman I met a year ago when I was on Maeve Murtagh's trail—a druid priestess. She is dead now."

"A druid? Rather uncommon in this day and age."

"She claimed to be two thousand years old."

The doctor removed his *pince-nez* and began cleaning them with his handkerchief. "Do *you* believe Ganna was two thousand years old?"

"I don't know."

"How did she die?"

Memories of the grisly Imbolc ritual suddenly rose up . . . Holmes and Clark pushing their way through the throng amidst shouts . . . Maeve's blade slicing into Clark's shoulder . . . Ganna's hand falling limp on the altar. In that moment, Tessa realized where she had seen the gatekeeper. He was the mountain of a man who had wrestled Mr. Holmes to the ground the night of her anointing.

"Cian," she muttered.

"Tessa, Tessa. Miss Wiggins!"

Tessa startled. "I'm sorry, Doctor."

"You were mumbling—troubled by a memory, I might conclude."

"It's not the memory that haunts me but Ganna."

Dr. Mayer's brows rose. "How so?"

Tessa deliberately spoke in a halting manner: "Her spirit offers advice . . . teaches me . . . protects me."

"From what?"

"Mistakes . . . danger."

"So Ganna is your guardian angel?"

Tessa's head swiveled. She glared. "You're making fun of me."

Mayer held up his hands in supplication. "No, no. It all makes sense, given what happened. You feel the need for a strong and wise protector."

"But you believe I'm imagining it—that Ganna's presence isn't real."

He shrugged. "Many people believe in such things." He leaned back in his chair and held up the file. "You have surrounded yourself with protectors: Dr. Watson, Ganna, Mr. Button, and even Sherlock Holmes."

Tessa stiffened. Her heart raced. She did not recall mentioning Holmes's name.

THIRTEEN

TESSA'S RED BADGE ARRIVED, granting her relative freedom and the ability to explore Hellingford's rambling complex. There were thirteen buildings. In addition to the patient wards, there was a small residential cottage, a kitchen, a laundry, and the maintenance shed behind the common area. Some of the wards were linked with hallways so that staff and patients could move from building to building without having to go out of doors. Tessa was prepared to walk every hall and building.

Four mornings a week, she washed, dried, ironed, and folded linens. Each day Tessa took a different route to the laundry to reconnoiter the buildings and grounds. When she returned for her midday meal, she carried towels for the bathroom on her ward. This stack of linens and her badge allowed her access to all patient wards except the mysterious Ward E that Jack had told her about. The cottage and maintenance building would prove to be more problematic. However, she was determined to look everywhere until she found Mr. Holmes's manuscript. Each evening she made notes on the map Jack had drawn for her with the aim of passing it on to Mr. Holmes with her first report.

From the road, Hellingford's stately buildings gave a passerby the impression it was a completely legitimate enterprise. Thirty years ago, it was one of forty model asylums built to comply with the Lunacy Act of 1890. However, funding and political interest waned in the time that intervened. More recently, when the doctors and nurses left to care for the wounded during the war, asylums were left in the unqualified and incompetent hands. Hellingford soon found itself unable to care for its patients and was scheduled to close when an anonymous benefactor came to the rescue. He promised to restore

Hellingford to its former prominence with the stipulation that it be run as a private institution. Any doubts about the benefactor's intentions vanished when he promised to engage the world-famous psychiatrist, Dr. Hermann Mayer, as superintendent—bringing him over from the famous Burgholzli psychiatric hospital in Switzerland.

Private, rate-paid sanatoriums and asylums were common, but the mingling of rate-paid and public wards was unprecedented. Hellingford's private wards were meager yet luxurious as compared to the public ones. Nonetheless, the inmates in both were virtual prisoners.

Like Jack and Tessa, the patients in the women's and men's rate-paid wards had been committed by their families who ostensibly sought treatment for their loved ones. However, Tessa was quick to learn that the families' motives were not always loving.

Lady Pamela Fritzwaller resided in the room next to Tessa. She, in particular, touched Tessa's heart because Fritzwaller reminded Tessa of her sainted mother and the sorrow her mother felt when she lost a child at birth. But unlike Tessa's mother, a devout Catholic who prayed for the soul of her innocent child, Pamela Fritzwaller was a spiritualist who sought to fetch the forsaken spirit of her dead baby to her.

Tessa was impressed with the woman's intelligence and mental acuity. Pamela Fritzwaller was drowning in grief, but she wasn't mad. When she told Tessa about a phantom that roamed near her home in Warwick, she was calm, clear, and rational. She shared a scrapbook of newspaper clippings reporting a nocturnal prowler in her town. If she was hallucinating, Pamela wasn't alone. Some eyewitnesses described the prowler as a child, but others said it was a beast.

"It wasn't an animal. He's trying to come to me." Pamela told Tessa. "My boy only comes at night because he knows I am alone then."

"You call the specter 'my boy," Tessa said. "Did he have a name?"

"No. He died at birth."

"But at the funeral—"

"There was no funeral. My husband buried him on our estate the day he died—the day of his birth. Henry was protecting me." Tears flowed down her cheeks. "My boy would have carried our family name and title, but that's gone now."

Tessa's heart sank as she realized that not only had Lady Fritzwaller lost a child but also the hopes for what that child would become and a future she imagined for herself.

Taking the woman's hand, Tessa made a promise: "You have my word that when we both leave this place, I will help you."

Pamela turned her teary eyes toward Tessa. "Then, you believe me?"

"I believe you don't belong here," Tessa told her—for she understood the pitiless power of old ghosts.

Many patients in Hellingford were haunted in a similar fashion by fears, guilt, or regrets. Most living human beings are, and the line that separates those inside an asylum from those outside is indiscernible. Tessa wondered how many of Hellingford's almost five hundred residents did not belong here—including those in the public wards who, for the most part, were suffering from alcohol or drug addiction.

Tessa's red badge was a boon, but it did not grant her complete access to the heavily barred public wards. Her deliveries went only to the Matron at the entrance. Approaching the public wards, she would feel as though she were walking with Virgil and Dante. Muffled screams and shrieks were heard yards away. Then, as the door was opened, the stench of human excrement enveloped her, roiling her stomach and causing her to make her delivery and hurry on.

Making a morning delivery to public Ward F, Tessa encountered an old woman sitting on a step at the entrance. Her hands were working with something in her lap. Her snowy hair was covered in a red kerchief, and a faded emerald shawl was wrapped over the shoulders of a tattered dress. She had a quixotic face and a pleasant smile. In counterpoint to her deeply lined face, the crone's eyes were clear and bright. Tessa heeded her intuition and spoke to the woman.

The old lady looked up. "There you are," she said. Moving her knitting bag aside, she patted a place next to her.

"Do I know you?" Tessa asked. The woman again motioned for Tessa to sit. "What's your name?"

"Beara."

"What are you doing?"

"Honoring the last of the garden," the woman replied. Her hands, corded in blue veins, were deftly twisting dried flowers, brown stems, and vines into a lovely basket. She hummed as her fingers worked the shoots and stems. Tessa recognized the tune: *Will Ye Go Lassie Go.*

"Why are you here, Beara?"

Her hands never paused. "In a mad world, the sane are caged."

Tessa watched in awe as the woman's hands fashioned a delicate vessel—a last gift from the plants and shrubs before they slumber beneath a blanket of snow. There was a wonderful tranquility about the old one. The drift of time was caught up in her weave and Tessa sat quietly, entranced by Beara's sacred act.

When the basket was done, she held it up. "This is for you."

Tessa took it. "What shall I put in it?"

"Gifts for Cailleach."

"Cailleach?"

Beara leaned closer and whispered: "They want to steal Cailleach's treasure."

"Treasure?" Tessa repeated. "Who? What kind of treasure?"

"Offerings to Cailleach."

"Do you know where this treasure is?"

"It is written that it waits in *Ynys Môn.*"

"Anglesey?"

"It has been said that it lies in a cromlech." Beara's eyes closed:
"Paulinus the offering missed,

Still it waits, o'r the straits.

In the cromlech of *Manawydan* will it be found,

thrust into water underground."

Her eyes opened, and she grinned. "My grandmother taught me that, and I taught it to my daughter—as I did all the *geiriau'r Cymry*—the words of our people. Only Ganna knows for sure where the treasure is."

Tessa's breath caught. "How do you know Ganna?"

"I do not know Ganna, but I know *about* Ganna because she is also in the *geiriau'r Cymry*." Again, her eyes closed:

"Ganna fled for those who bled,

Giving on and living on the lives of the *Cymry* sisters."

Tessa clutched Beara's hand: "What does that mean—giving on and living on?"

Beara placed a comforting hand over Tessa's. "It is about protecting the offerings of our earth mother . . . living on with the help of others who gave themselves to this sacred cause."

Something stabbed at Tessa's gut. Forgetting the laundry, she went to her room and curled up on her bed.

She dozed for a time before she came fully awake and saw Beara's basket next to her. Then she was aware of Ganna's presence. "Are you here?" she whispered.

Tell me about this basket.

Tessa went to her door and reassured herself that the Matron was at her desk before describing her encounter with Beara. "Do you know her?"

Beara may be the gray-haired woman from the craggy shores.

"You're being vague. Beara knew you."

There was a long pause before Ganna replied: *How could she know anything about me?*

"Then you think she's mad?"

She may be. People sometimes seek safety in madness, protection from being known or understood. Those who know us put us within the prison of their beliefs.

Tessa sat on the edge of her bed and turned the basket in her hands, remembering how Ganna once told her that profound wisdom is often mistaken for madness. "I think Beara is not mad, and I believe she told the truth about Cailleach, and the treasure, and you. I can see through lies that people tell, but there is no pretense in Beara. She is cold honesty itself."

What did she say about me?

Ganna's apprehension alarmed Tessa. For the first time since they met, she held back: "She said she remembered a poem from her childhood about you or someone called Ganna."

The Druid remained quiet.

"Do you know anything of a treasure, Ganna? Have you ever heard of Cailleach's treasure?"

Cailleach is an ancestor deity. Gifts for Cailleach were votive offerings made long ago in wells, rivers, and other watery places. That is likely what Beara speaks of.

"That must be it!" Tessa cried. "The Mayer's learned about the treasure from Beara and heard about you as well. And Mayer plans to steal Cailleach's treasure."

If that is so, then why take the manuscript?

"Blackmail," Tessa answered. "They plan to use it to get information from Mr. Holmes. I must get a report to him."

They must never find the offerings.

"So, the treasure is offerings?"

Many gave their lives to protect it. It is blessed with blood!

Ganna had never spoken so passionately before.

"What is this treasure to you?"

It is everything to me.

"So, I ask again: What do you know of this treasure, Ganna?"

Don't let this fool's errand divert you from your destiny.

Tessa did not reply.

You're being foolish, so I will leave you to remember who you are.

Ganna was gone, but Tessa's budding doubts remained. And knowing doubt multiplies faster than rabbits, she was wise enough not to worry alone.

FOURTEEN

BEARA SHUFFLED SLOWLY, tugged along by a brawny matron. Tessa hurried to catch them as they climbed the stairs to Beara's ward.

"Stop," Tessa called.

The outsized matron twirled about and eyed Tessa as she approached. "Beara?"

The old woman was unresponsive.

"I'm her friend. What happened to her?"

Beara looked up—her red-rimmed eyes finally widening in recognition. "Please, matron, leave me to take some air."

"Five minutes," the matron said, releasing her grip on Beara and stepping inside.

Tessa wrapped her arms around the old woman, who could only let out a low moan as she fell into Tessa's embrace. "What happened?"

"The treatment . . . the booth."

"Booth?"

"Ah-h-h, you have not been in the booth. I pray you never shall."

The two women sat quietly on the top step outside the ward, and after a few minutes, Beara regained her senses. "Doctor Mayer thinks me a Celtic witch. I suppose I should count myself fortunate. In another time, I might have been lathered in pig fat and burnt at the stake."

"Why is he doing this?"

"I told you. They seek the treasure of Cailleach and believe I know more than I do."

Tessa caught Beara's gaze. "Who are you that they believe you? You're in a madhouse."

"Some know me as an *icidhe*—a healer. Healer indeed," she chortled. "Born and bred in Risca, I practiced the herb craft as did my grandmother and mother before me. We served our people, but they died anyway, not of disease, but coal dust, starvation, and hopelessness. My father, brother, and husband went to their deaths in the Black Vein mine."

"Did you fight with the Federation?"

Beara shook her head. "No. I found my own way. My people thought they were digging coal, but they were digging their own graves. One day I had enough and walked to the entrance of the mine with a sign." She traced the words in the air as she spoke: "Coal—is —death."

"And they put you away for that?"

"Not at first. They tore my signs and mocked me. Some said I was a witch and that my healing book—the *Red Book of Hergest* was the devil's bible. Father McLaren wouldn't go so far, but he barred me from the sacraments and openly called me unchristian. That was all the excuse the villagers needed. The good people of Risca put my home to fire. I wanted to leave when that happened, but that would have been a lie." Beara's eyes were dark and empty as she looked at Tessa. "Hellingford is where they put you when you can't lie anymore. In the end, nothing I did or tried to do mattered. The Black Vein still operates. Men and boys die below, women grieve, and I lost my home."

Tessa took the old woman's hand. "You could hardly call that place home. I once told someone that home is where place, purpose, and peace come together."

"Maybe so, but I think you make it more complicated than it is, my child. Home is where love rests."

"And it rests here with you and me, Beara."

The old woman cupped Tessa's cheek in her hand. "So, you don't believe I am a mad Celtic witch?"

"To the contrary, I believe you *are* a Celtic witch, one with great wisdom."

Tears filled Beara's eyes as she wrapped her arms around Tessa. "My heart called out the moment I saw you."

"And mine too, Beara. I knew you were one of my tribe."

"Demetae? I am of the Demetae."

"No. My tribe is who I am attracted to and who is attracted to me."

"Well said, but why did you come to me now?"

"I wanted to satisfy myself that my instincts were right? I will need help in the coming days, and I need to know if I can count you as a friend."

"Now you know."

❋ ❋ ❋ ❋ ❋

First Jack, now Beara, possibly Nurse Halper—Tessa was confident she would be able to enlist friends to help her in her search for Mr. Holmes's manuscript. She had a plan. It was time for her first report:

October 22

Mr. Holmes,

Please find some way to tell me that you have received this letter. I am sorry it has taken so long for me to report, but I have only recently been allowed outside my room.

I am pleased to validate your suspicions and confirm that the mystery lady that visited Professor

Stone resides in Hellingford. She is Mrs. Beatrice Mayer, the Director here, and the wife of Dr. Mayer, superintendent. Her umbrella has a gold knob, and her face matches your sketch. Interestingly, it also matches an etching that hangs in her office. This artwork is signed by Menpes and dated 1880. She claims it is a portrait of her mother.

I have not yet been able to find your manuscript, but I believe it is here. I am making friends, and they will assist me in the search.

On a related matter, I believe the Celtic treasure Professor Stone is seeking may be real. One of the patients here shared ancient teachings—poems she calls _geiriau'r Cymry_. The professor may know more about this. It is reasonable to think that my friend Beara's information got to Mrs. Mayer by way of her husband, who is treating her. I believe they are both seeking the treasure and might be holding your manuscript as a ransom for more information.

However, burglary may be the least of their crimes. I am certain that they are selling beds in Hellingford to families who wish to lock away troublesome members. One striking example is Pamela Fritzwaller, who is confined in my ward. She, among others, does not belong in Hellingford. When your manuscript is restored, I would ask that you help me put an end to this vile practice.

I have enclosed a map of Hellingford showing my room and circled the places I have already searched. I suspect the residential cottage on the common might be the most likely place to look, but I have not been able to gain entry. My friends and I will continue hunting. Do not worry. It is only a matter of time before we find it.

Please let Eva and Clark know that I am well and that they should soon be able to visit. I will communicate through them in the future.

With affection,

Tessa

FIFTEEN

CIAN DUCKED OUT OF THE GATEHOUSE as Tessa walked toward the front gate. He smiled and held up a hand in greeting when she called out. Then, as she came near, he began waving her off. Tessa halted. Cian marched toward her, took her by the arm, and swung her about. Nurse Halper and Angus were trotting toward them.

"Fight agin' me," the gatekeeper said *sotto voce*. Tessa pretended to struggle. As she did, she rasped: "Has the man from Ceridwen come?"

"Aye," he replied.

Taking the letter to Holmes from her work apron, she reached out as though resisting Cian and slide the note into his pocket. "Give this to him when he returns."

"Now you calm down, missy!" he barked.

Nurse Halper was shaking her head when she and Angus reached them. "What was she saying, Cian?"

He shrugged. "Want'd to know if her people from Ceridwen had come."

"And what did you tell her?"

"Told her one time, but they weren't allowed."

That seemed to satisfy Nurse Halper, but not Director Mayer, who waited at the entrance when they reached the front stairs. "You know that you are not permitted outside the grounds."

"I just wanted to learn if visitors had come," Tessa protested. Mayer ripped the red badge from around her neck. "The doctor has not approved visitors for you. I could have told you that. Maybe, after your treatments—maybe then you may have visitors." Then, turning to Angus, added, "Take her to her room."

Tessa twisted in the hands of the attendant as he dragged her through the door into the asylum and down the corridor to her ward before tossing her into her room.

Tessa's anxiety melted away when she saw Matron Mitchell standing at her door, dangling her red badge from a finger. "I don't know why, but you've been given another chance. Mind your manners, or you'll be confined to this room."

Tessa placed the lanyard and badge around her neck. "I understand. Thank you, Mrs. Mitchell."

"Now off with you to the laundry," the Matron said. "You have an appointment with Dr. Mayer after the midday meal. I'll take you to him."

"I can find my way," Tessa countered.

"You're going to treatment. I must escort you."

"I understand, Mrs. Mitchell," Tessa answered, wishing to seem compliant.

Setting out for the laundry, Tessa speculated as to the reason her badge had been returned, and why an escort was required going to treatment. For Tessa, there was something pompous in the whole notion of a 'treatment'—as if the pieces of a confused mind or broken heart could be put back together and made new. Surely, they would forever be prone to break again along the same fault lines.

With the realization that her investigation was yielding more questions than answers, she decided to take a roundabout path to the laundry, heading to the back of the property toward the enigmatic Ward E. Approaching the building, Tessa heard music—a popular song: "A pretty girl is like a melody." Radios were common in Hellingford, but the guard posted there was not. She kept her distance, promising herself that she would again reconnoiter when she returned for her mid-day meal and appointment.

Hellingford's laundry was fifty years behind the times because labor was free. Lined along a windowless wall were six wooden washtubs with attached hand-wringers. Tessa did not mind washing sheets and blankets by hand. She enjoyed helping water work its magic—cleansing not only linens and clothing but bodies and spirits. Today, the water also brought her little sister's baptism to mind.

Tessa was nine when her family arrived at the church that day. Her mother placed Evangeline in her little arms. "You're her big sister, Tessa. You must watch over Evangeline when I am gone. I want *you* to present your sister to the priest." Her mother went on to explain how the holy water would wash away Evangeline's original sin. Tessa was thankful the *imbas forosnai* had expunged her darker memories of her little sister. She had tried to blame poverty for forcing her to leave her sick sister on the steps of the London Orphan Asylum, but she knew it was a choice *she* made, and no ceremony or sacrament would change the sad thought that Evangeline died alone.

Tessa scrubbed mechanically and placed a sheet in the ringer. As she cranked it, she watched the water flow back into the tub. The gush of water made her think of Clark and something he said. *What was it?* Tessa had been coming to believe that Clark couldn't fit with the new life she was being called to. She had taken him aside to declare that a relationship wouldn't work for them. He had listened thoughtfully. Then Clark looked into her eyes: "Tess, you're a raging river. Me, I'm the lazy stream. But we're made of the same stuff, and we're headin' the same way." He had tried to persuade her not to come to Hellingford. He cared. He loved her. But she kept him at a distance as she had all men since Benjie. She loved men's energy but feared being damaged by it. Men who balance strength with tenderness are rare. Then again, Clark's way with the gardens at Ceridwen showed that he possessed that uncommon trait.

Such nomadic thoughts and strange daydreams have a way of quickening time, and Tessa was suddenly aware that her shift was over. Returning for her midday meal, as was her custom, she took a stack of clean towels and bid good-day to the other ladies and the laundry matron.

Although it was a long way around, she headed to her room by way of Ward E. A guard was still there, slumped in a chair by the door, enjoying a cup. He popped to attention as Tessa drew near. She held up the linens to explain her presence. He waved her off. "Didn't they tell ya, we have our own here? Be on your way now."

Tessa nodded dutifully and continued past the ward and storage building. Then, when she was certain no one was about, she doubled back and ducked into an alleyway between the ward and the maintenance shed. Pulling herself up to the windowsill of the ward, she found an opening in the curtains wide enough to see into a large parlor. Young women in various forms of dress and undress were busy in a variety of goings-on. Some played cards and drank beer, one lay in a cot smoking, others danced to radio tunes. Tess ducked away when one of the residents approached the window. Then, keeping low, she continued on along the ward's outer wall and peered over a fence that connected the ward and shed. There she observed that both the ward and shed had their own outside doors. Just as Jack had surmised, these women came and went. And, just beyond the exit sat a silver-grey Crossley automobile. The number plate was LY-1089. She repeated the number to herself to commit it to memory.

Hellingford was beginning to give up its secrets, but further investigation would have to wait until after her treatment.

Mitchell walked ahead of Tessa toward a small brick building tucked among bushes in the corner of the common. She was surprised to see Dr. Mayer outside because he seemed a man who shuns the sun. His skin was beyond pale, almost translucent, like that of insects that burrow underground.

He thanked Matron Mitchell, who promised to return in an hour's time.

"Why are we meeting here?" Tessa asked.

Mayer tapped his pipe on the side of the building scattering the embers. "Do you recall our conversation about negative energy?"

"Orgoon?"

"Orgone, yes. By releasing orgone we can restore the balance in the mind. That is what we will do today. The machine inside removes orgone. It's my own invention."

He tucked his pipe in his coat pocket and opened the door—gesturing inside. "If you would be so kind . . . a little help."

Tessa pushed his chair over the threshold, squinting as she entered. A glaring electric light splattered across the white walls and tile floor. A wooden booth, half-again as large as a phone box, sat in the corner. The booth had a door with a glass window at the top. The exterior was polished oak, but the inside—even the floor—was covered with galvanized metal. There was a chair inside that faced a speaking-horn similar to those found on an Ericsson telephone. Rubber tubes the size of fingers sprouted from the booth along with a multitude of electrical wires—all attaching to a metal box on the table. A green metal tank bearing the name Draeger sat under the table. Next to it was an apparatus connected to what she thought was an electric motor.

Dr. Mayer rocked back in his chair admiring the bizarre apparatus. "One of a kind," he said. "The first machine that can capture and remove orgone."

Tessa put on a practiced smile. "I suppose you want me inside that booth?"

"No need to worry, Miss Wiggins. You will sit comfortably inside while we converse through the phone box. Our exchange will stimulate and activate your emotions and release your orgone. The machine does the rest."

"Can I breathe in there?"

"The booth is tightly sealed, but the air is pumped in continuously. If you feel uncomfortable, you can knock, and I will unlatch and open the door. Come along now."

Tessa did as she was told and sat down inside. When Dr. Mayer closed the door, everything fell silent. "Can you hear me, Dr. Mayer? Dr. Mayer! " Her heart raced, and she was about to pound on the door when a strong vibration rattled the booth and buzzed in her ears. Suddenly air gushed in from a small round vent above. She took a deep breath.

A crackling sound came from the horn on the wall opposite her: "Miss Wiggins."

"Yes. I'm here," Tessa gasped.

"Today, I wish to talk about your early life and home, about Ganna and your other guardians."

SIXTEEN

IT WAS LIKE A DREAM. Being in the orgone booth lightened Tessa's spirits. She rambled on about her life in Spitalfields, her brother Rory and the other irregulars, and how Mr. Holmes had helped her family. She also told Dr. Mayer about Benjie and her life as a 'slum sister' in the Salvation Army. The doctor showed little interest until she began talking about Ganna—how they met and spent their time together. He asked many questions—some repeatedly. Everything about Ganna, Maeve, and the Sisters of Scáthach came pouring out in a torrent of jumbled memories mingled with tears.

Then it stopped.

Dr. Mayer wheeled over to the booth, unlatched the door, and opened it. "How do you feel?"

Tessa took a deep breath. "Wonderful. Relaxed . . . sleepy."

"You did well." He held the door open. "Do you think you can find your way to your room?"

As Tessa walked out of the treatment room, her euphoria receded. Coming fully to her senses, she realized she had an opportunity to explore two remaining buildings in the complex—the cottage residence and the maintenance shed. Reasoning that the maintenance shed might be another likely place to hide Mr. Holmes's manuscript, she headed in that direction.

A nurse pushing a patient in a wheeled-chair eyed Tessa warily as she approached. Sherlock Holmes, a master at manipulating appearances, had taught Tessa that deception is the art of distraction—it's overt, not covert. As the nurse came close, Tessa tucked her red badge into her pocket and called out: "Oh, thank heaven, nurse. I've lost my pass." Then, pointing over the nurse's shoulder, "A red badge. Did you see it?"

"No." the nurse answered.

Tessa fretted and wrung her hands. "I had it at the laundry. It must be here somewhere."

The nurse told Tessa to calm down and report to the laundry matron—precisely the direction she wished to go.

She returned to the dim, narrow alleyway that lay between Ward E and the maintenance building. Bending lower, Tessa ducked under a window and made her way to the small fence that connected the two buildings and peeked over it. The Crossley was still parked outside. Jocular voices inside the shed brought her back to the window to listen. More than one man was there.

The oaky scent of cigar smoke tickled her nose as she crept toward a broken window in the shed. Bringing her eyes up to the jagged opening, she saw five men seated around a table playing cards. A sixth was hunched over a small table positioned under a skylight.

"Blast you," one of the men exclaimed, slapping his cards down. He was speaking to a tall, slender fellow who was raking bills and coins toward him and stacking them in neat piles along the edge of the table.

"Quit whinging, Jakes," the winner said. When he turned toward the man at the table, Tessa could see the gentleman's deeply furrowed face and deep-sunk eyes. "What's taking so long, Carnaby?"

The spectacled man jerked to attention and patted a ledger. "It's a big haul, sir. Five minutes more."

The aged man turned back to the table and began shuffling the cards. "Another hand, gentlemen?"

"Ya think we're wonky?" Jakes exclaimed, pushing back his chair. "I'm gettin' some air." He plucked a pack of cigarettes from his pocket and headed toward an open back door that led outside the shed and away from Tessa's window.

The old man held up the deck of cards and looked questioningly at the other men. "Another round?" One man groaned and left the table. The others shook their heads. Scraping the piles of coins into his palm, he held his jacket pocket wide and let the coins slowly tinkle in. He placed both hands on the edge of the table and slowly pushed himself up to his feet. One of the players reached over and took his elbow when he wobbled. Steadying himself on the back of his chair, he turned and shuffled toward the table. The accountant's eyes grew wider as the old man approached and bent over his shoulder. "What's the haul, Carnaby?"

"Here's the total," he said, pointing with the tip of his pen at the ledger. "Look, look at that," the man stuttered. "A record week, sir."

A humming sound vibrated from the old man and blossomed into a broad closed-lipped grin as he turned to the others. "Gentleman, I am sorry for your losses. Let me make it up to you." He spread his arms magnanimously. "You may have your pick of anything here before we pack it up—one thing, mind you—one."

"Aces, gov'nor," one of the men barked as they scurried to the shelves lining the walls.

The light from the dirty skylights was poor, but Tessa could see items and articles you would only expect to find in cases on Bond Street. Glimmering on the shelves were watches, necklaces, buckles, and belts. There were also posh scarves, fur collars, and leather gloves.

The old man chuckled as he watched the greedy melee. "One now—one item," he repeated, wagging a finger. He patted Carnaby's shoulder, "Look after things, will you? The lorry will soon be here to pack up. I must have something to eat. Be certain the ledger goes with the shipment. You know where."

"Yes, sir," the bookkeeper said as he stood and took the arm of the old gentleman. They trundled to the door where Carnaby took a sweater from a hook and draped it over the man's shoulders. Then he took a cane hanging on the doorknob. Hefting it in his hand, he noticed its light weight. "What's this made of?" Carnaby asked.

"It's called aluminum. Light and strong," the old man said, clanking the tip on the door handle.

"Ah-h, the stuff in Verne's space-ship."

The old man chortled. "Not in space-ships, but airplanes, engines, and electrical wires."

"Ah-h," Carnaby nodded as he opened the door.

Tessa crouched lower and crept from the window to the corner of the shed to watch the old guy toddle off—her excitement mounting as more pieces of the 'Hellingford puzzle' came together. Tessa wondered if the manuscript might have already been shipped off. She would make a note of that possibility in her next report.

Caught up in these thoughts, she gave the old gent time to move on before tiptoeing from the shadowy passageway that led back to the common. Cautiously she stepped into the daylight. Cane and all, the old man moved swiftly. Tessa momentarily lost sight of him among the bushes before again catching sight of him near the door to the cottage. He entered without knocking.

She turned back toward the public wards and the stoop where she had met Beara. The old woman wasn't there. Tessa was past due in her room and was about to turn back when she heard a sharp tapping sound. Looking around, she saw Beara's smiling face through a dirty window in the ward.

Tessa came closer. "Can you come out?" Beara nodded and held up a finger. A short while later, Beara emerged with her knitting bag in hand. Without a word, the old woman sat down on the step, pulled a small rock from her bag, and began burrowing in it with a crude awl.

Tessa wanted to ask about the stone but had more urgent questions. "Ever since we met, my mind has been spinning with questions about Cailleach's treasure, your word-songs, and another mystery—Hellingford."

"Young people always want answers, even when there are none to be had. Even if I could answer all your questions, you would not be content. The questions you really need answers to are those you haven't thought to ask."

Beara's pedagogical words reminded Tessa of Ganna's teachings, and she regretted she had not told the old Druid the whole truth about Beara. Maybe she would when Ganna returned.

"Do you remember your poem about Ganna?"

"It is not my poem, but yes."

"You said it was about sacrifice. Is it wrong to give yourself to a greater purpose?"

"Only if it is not *your* purpose."

"How do I know my cause—my reason for being?"

Beara chuckled. "My dear, it's a waste of time to ask *me* such a question. Only you know the answer."

Tessa became quiet as she watched Beara grinding a hole into the soft rock. "You said there were questions about this place."

Tessa nodded. "How long have you been in Hellingford?"

"Long enough."

"What do you know of the women in Ward E?"

"Alice's girls," she answered. She went on to tell about Alice Diamond, a rough young woman who the courts sent to Hellingford just after it reopened. The judge had sentenced her to a year, but she was discharged after a month. After her release, Beara saw Alice go into Ward E with Mrs. Mayer. The building had been vacant until

103

Alice returned with a gaggle of young women from the city. "They are said to be members of the Forty Elephants. Maybe you've heard of them."

Indeed, Tessa had. Everyone in Britain knew of the notorious all-woman gang operating from the Elephant and Castle District in London. They marauded the city with impunity. Dressing in expensive clothes, they entered fine shops *en masse*, filling hidden pockets and capes with stolen goods and departing before besieged store clerks could stop them—£200,000 worth per year, according to the newspapers.

"This would explain the items in the maintenance building," Tessa remarked when Beara told her story. She wondered if one of the Forty Elephants had stolen Holmes's manuscript but later discounted that notion because the manuscript would have little value to a street merchant or pawnbroker.

Tessa waited for Beara's attention, but the old woman remained intent on drilling a hole in the stone. "Beara, what do you think about the old man who lives in the cottage?"

"He's too old for me," Beara quipped with a chuckle. "I know only that he comes and goes. He commands respect from the doctor and his wife, or maybe it's fear."

Tessa nodded. "Well, I am due in my room, Beara. I must be on my way."

"Wait," the old woman said. "I have something for you." Beara took a long leather thong from her bag and pulled it through the small hole she had drilled in the stone. Then, tying both the ends of the cord in a knot, she held the necklace out over a finger. The stone was the size of a walnut, rough-cut, hard, and rose-colored on the outside, soft and white inside. She handed the necklace to Tessa. "It is a *glain neidr*—druid's glass. Some call it an adder stone. It is a rare and wonderful mineral forged in the fires of inner earth and cooled and shaped by the waters of a river." Tessa looked dubious. "It's a shield."

Tessa's eyes widened. "Do you believe I need protection?"

"I think so. This stone has been with me for many years. Only today I felt a compelling need to give it to you." Beara placed the thong over Tessa's neck. "When intuition speaks, we must obey."

SEVENTEEN

MATRON MITCHELL STOOD WITH HANDS ON HIPS as Tessa entered her room. "I'm sorry," Tessa began, "I know I should have —"

Before she could complete a sentence, Mitchell held up Holmes's sketch and several sheets of stationery.

"I didn't know you were an artist," Mitchell said. "It's lovely. It should be on the wall and not in some dingy place behind your mirror."

"It was personal and—"

"Your mother, I suppose," the Matron said. "If it were not for the eyeglasses and hat, I would say it looked like Director Mayer. And why hide the writing paper? We are not barbarians here. You can write letters." She went nose to nose with Tessa. "Of course, you may not be able to send them." She took the keys from her belt and walked to the door. "You are confined to your room. I'm certain Mrs. Mayer will wish to chat with you about this."

Tessa's eyes bounced about the room, self-judgment storming her mind as the matron left. She had been careless and naive. Grasping the rock pendant Beara had given her, she mumbled: "I do need protection."

Who gave you the adder stone? Ganna asked.

"Ganna!" She took a breath. "An old woman I met."

And you know what it is?

"Yes, I scoffed at the notion I needed a shield but . . ."

But you accepted the stone because you need protection from Mitchell . . . or me?

Tessa went to the window in the hope of keeping her face from betraying her as she recalled Beara's troubling verse about Ganna. "You are quick to impart knowledge, but share little about yourself, Ganna . . . how precisely I will serve."

My teachings are all that is important.

"That's not true. As you took your last breath, I felt your spirit come into me. I gave it shelter without fully understanding what that means. While I wanted to help Mr. Holmes, I also came to Hellingford because I truly feared I might be losing my mind." She turned from the window. "Should I be frightened about that?"

Not if you believe in our cause. The union with the Divine Mother must remain unbroken.

"And what of me?"

Ganna did not answer. With each second that ticked, dread trickled into Tessa's heart. She clenched Beara's crystal, and Ganna was gone.

One thing was clear, Tessa needed to leave Hellingford. Then, as if in answer to her resolution, the sound of an auto brought her gaze outside. Through the bars beyond the glass, Tessa could see a burgundy Daimler limousine driving in. She called out: "Clark!"

Tessa pressed her hands against the window as the auto pulled to a stop. Rapping frantically on the glass, she called, but Clark couldn't hear her. She desperately yanked the window up, but Clark had already gone through the front door before she could raise it. Running to her door, she pounded, yelled, and twisted the knob over and over.

Minutes later, Mitchell's face popped into the window. "Pipe down."

"Clark—Mr. Button is here for me. I must see him. Call up front—see for yourself."

Just then, Tessa heard the limousine's motor start. She ran back to the window and watched in dismay as Clark drove off, pausing only for a moment at the gate. As the automobile continued down the road, she prayed that Cian had passed on her letter.

Hearing the clank of her lock, Tessa twisted toward the door fully prepared to lambaste Mitchell. Her shoulders relaxed when Jack entered carrying linens. She put her finger to her lips and motioned for him to come in and close the door. He asked: "What's wrong?"

"I must get a message to Cian." Then, after calming herself, she laid out a plan for getting word out of Hellingford. Without hesitation, Jack agreed to bring paper and pencil with the next delivery of sheets, promising he would take her letter to the gatekeeper.

"Thank you, Jack, you're a godsend."

Jack blushed. "I do what I can."

As Jack was leaving, Matron Mitchell entered. "I'm to take you to the doctor and Mrs. Mayer."

No words were exchanged as Tessa was walked to the front office. Mitchell pointed to the bench next to the door. "Wait here," she told her.

Tessa heard two voices inside the office—hushed but strident. Dr. Mayer was one of the voices, and she recognized the other as that of his wife. The doctor's voice grew in volume and intensity: "I fear you've lost sight of our objective, caught up in this nonsense about buried treasure."

"Do you think I could forget? Tessa Wiggins is one of his minions, and we have her firmly in our grasp. Don't worry. He'll come. But we can also find the—"

"Alice's girls provide all the treasure we require. I put the hospital's administration in your hands so I could put my attention elsewhere, but it may be time I take the role of superintendent more seriously."

"Superintendent indeed," she laughed.

Tessa slid along the bench closer to the door. As she did so, Nurse Halper rounded the corner and cast a wary eye. "Wait quietly.

They will come for you." Tessa nodded and straightened upright. Halper moved on.

Tessa listened intently, but the fiery exchange had cooled, and she could only pick out an occasional sentence or word. She heard Beara's name and 'treasure' spoken several more times. Hearing footsteps near the door, Tessa sat up and folded her hands in her lap. "Come in, Miss Wiggins," Beatrice Mayer said, holding the door open.

The doctor and his wife put on smiles as Tessa took a seat. "Do you know why you are here?" Mrs. Mayer began.

"Why was I not allowed to see Mr. Button?" Tessa demanded.

"You violated our trust!" Beatrice Mayer shot back.

"You can confine me to my room, but you have no right to keep visitors from me."

A sly smile spread across the Director's face. "Is it possible that it has not yet occurred to you that here at Hellingford, you have only the rights given to you—the privileges you earn?"

Tessa turned to the doctor, "I accommodated your treatment. You said—"

"Yes, Miss Wiggins," the doctor agreed. "One treatment. You have had but one treatment. It is our opinion that your visitors, those who may have contributed to your condition, will not be allowed to see you until you are better. You will be receiving *daily* treatments from now on. If you cooperate and get well, you will be permitted to have visitors."

"But Mr. Button—"

"Mr. Button was disappointed that he was not able to see you," Mrs. Mayer said, "but he understood." She picked up a small object from her desk. "He asked me to give this to you." She held out a penny and then dropped it into Tessa's hand. "He said he wanted you to know he is thinking of you."

Tessa contained a smile. "May I continue working in the laundry?"

"You may, but you must return to your room straight away at the end of your shift. It's been reported that you wander about."

Tessa nodded.

Dr. Mayer smiled. "Very good, Miss Wiggins. Return to your room. After your meal, you and I will have another treatment."

Nurse Halper was waiting outside as Tessa left the office. Walking back to her room, Tessa saw the old man from the cottage scuttling toward them—the tip of his metallic cane clinking on the tile floor. As they passed, Halper smiled and nodded: "Good morning, sir."

Tessa's eyes followed him as he passed. "I take it he's not a patient."

"Far from it," the nurse said. "He's Hellingford's benefactor—saved this hospital from ruin. You and many others are the recipients of his largess."

"Is he from these parts?"

"I've never been introduced, but I think not. He comes and goes from London but keeps a residence here, the cottage in the common. He brought the Mayers here. A truly extraordinary gentleman."

KIM KRISCO

EIGHTEEN

TESSA WAS STUNNED by the realization that she had been playing the damsel in distress. It was not a role she had ever cast herself in. When the burgundy limousine drove up Hellingford's lane, she had imagined a knight's white charger, and she was crestfallen when Sir Clark did not slay the dragon lady—but more than that, surprised. Her awareness blossomed into dismay as she began to wonder if she might be holding Holmes in similar regard. He rescued her and her family decades ago, and later her brother Rory when he became tangled in Maeve Murtagh's illicit schemes. The storybook belief around the rescued damsel had somehow slinked into her psyche and fashioned an unwelcome feeling of helplessness. Now the truth was laid plain before her, and she knew that, if she was to escape Hellingford, it was up to her.

Tessa answered the knock she had been waiting for and opened the door to find Jack wearing a sly grin. He handed her the bedsheets with a wink. She put her hand on his as she accepted the linens with a smile and nod. When he left, Tessa scanned the room for a place to hide the paper and pencil. Once again, the sparsely appointed room offered few hiding places. Then, her eyes settled on the very linens in her arms. *Of course*, she thought. She made her bed and hid the stationery and pencil in the dirty linens. Her timing was impeccable—for Matron Mitchell came to escort her to treatment.

It was a short walk to the small red brick treatment building. As before, Dr. Mayer was waiting outside with a pipe in hand. He told Mitchell to return in an hour. He nodded toward the door, and Tessa opened it. The antiseptic white room still held its cloying metallic scent, but the room felt more ominous than she remembered. Crimson tubes and black wires sprouted from the control box, fastening themselves to the airless booth like a sinister sea beast. The motor under the table was already humming, and next to it the green metal tank with N2O stenciled upon it. She hesitated at the door to the booth.

"Nothing to fear, Miss Wiggins. Just as before, take a seat. We will talk and—"

"About what?"

He frowned. "Just as before, I will ask you to tell me about your life and the people and events in your life. I urge you to be forthcoming and not hold back. We will start where we left of."

"I can't remember what we talked about. Why is it my memory is so poor?"

"As the orgone is extracted, bad memories vanish with it. That is precisely what needs to happen if you are to get well. Now step inside." When she hesitated again, he wheeled his chair closer and narrowed his eyes.

Tessa stepped in. The booth door closed and clanked as the doctor latch took hold.

Bound in silence, Tessa could barely hear the motor, but she felt the rush of cool air from the vent above. Then came a cracking sound from the horn on the wall followed by the doctor's nasal voice. "We will begin where we left off. You said a rather interesting thing. Yes, here it is. You said: 'I often feel as though death is stalking me.' When did these feelings about death begin?"

"Early," Tessa said. "Death is an intimate neighbor in Spitalfields."

She went on to recount the day her father left home and how her mother, who picked rags and sold penny bunches of violets, died of pneumonia shortly after, how Rory died freeing his friends from the clutches of Maeve Murtagh. She also told him that her sister Evangeline died in the orphanage and Benjie in the war. The doctor listened impatiently before urging her to talk about more recent

THE MAGNIFICENT MADNESS OF TESSA WIGGINS

events and deaths. His interest peaked when Tessa recalled her clash with Maeve in a cave not far from Hellingford.

"You say this cave held ceremonies, Celtic ceremonies," he noted. "Tell me about this cavern?"

The motor grew louder, and that metallic smell became more pungent as Tessa struggled to recount how, after Ganna died, she chased Maeve into a grotto deep within the sea-cliffs and, in the end, how Maeve twisted in agony on a sword that Tessa held.

"Tell me again about Ganna's teachings," Dr. Mayer said. "Did she say anything about a treasure?" His questions came faster now—her answers tangled, her thoughts twisted and jumbled. It was as if her body was purging itself—disjointed words and horrid feelings churned in her gut. Dr. Mayer's questioning became louder and more frantic. "Tell me about Mr. Holmes, Tessa. When was the last time you saw him?"

"I don't want to talk about him," she said.

The booth vibrated and shook. The torrent of air from the vent above became noticeably stronger. The coppery odor was overpowering. Her eyes watered.

"You *must* answer my questions," the doctor said, his voice becoming harsher, his words blending with the whirling sound of the electric motor that was spinning, and spinning, and spinning everything into a ghastly tangle in her gut.

Then the vibrations stopped. Silence.

Slowly coming to her senses, Tessa was dizzy and disoriented. She had sweated through her dress. Her eyes were swollen, making it difficult to see.

The doctor opened the door to the booth and waited. Tessa wanted to bolt but was too weak to stand. The doctor cursed and told her to come out. She rose and wobbled on her feet for a moment before she took a step. Dr. Mayer wheeled backward to let her pass. She stepped around him and out of the booth. Turning back, she saw

115

him framed in the doorway of the booth with a loathsome grin on his face.

"I won't do this anymore! I won't go into that horrible box again. The air. I couldn't breathe."

"Nonsense," he said. "You will—"

Tessa grabbed the arms of his chair and pushed back hard. It slammed through the doorway, crashing into the back of the booth. As he struggled to right himself, Tessa closed and latched the air-tight door.

The doctor pounded on the window and shouted—his cries muffled. His breath fogged the window as his efforts became more emphatic and desperate. As she turned to leave, Tessa relished the sheer panic in his eyes.

Still disoriented, Tessa walked aimlessly in the common before Matron Mitchell found her. "You were to wait for me. Now come along." Tessa did not object when Mitchell took her arm. As they walked toward her ward, she saw the old man in the cottage staring at them from his window. He was smiling.

✻ ✻ ✻ ✻ ✻

Tessa was dozing in her room after dinner when she was startled by the sound of an automobile outside. She leaped to her feet and hurried to the window. She groaned when she saw it was a Model T hearse with black curtained windows. It was not unusual to see a hearse at Hellingford, but they usually came at dusk so as not to alarm patients. As it pulled up to the main entrance, Nurse Halper stepped outside. Two men took a stretcher from the back of the vehicle and marched through the door Halper held open for them.

Tessa went to her door and looked through the small window toward Mitchell's desk. The matron was leaning against the ward's open door—her hand covering her mouth as she stared intently down the hallway. Jack wheeled his cart onto the ward as Mitchell pointed toward the commotion at the entrance. Huddling together, they exchanged whispered words. Mitchell finally closed the ward door, and Jack went about making deliveries. Tessa turned away and sat on the edge of her bed anxiously waiting for Jack's knock.

When it came, she hurried to let him in. "Who died, Jack?" Tessa asked the moment he caught her eye.

His usually amiable demeanor was absent. He glanced over his shoulder before he spoke: "Dr. Mayer."

NINETEEN

TESSA LAY CURLED in her bed, trying to recall what she said during her treatment session. It came not as recollections but as fractured images, the echo of words, and queer feelings. Her effort produced more questions than clarity, and Tessa was left to wonder what she had imagined and what was real. Had she locked Mayer in the booth, or was that something she fancied? *Jack didn't say how or where the doctor died.* The longer she thought on it, the more convinced she became that her confrontation with Dr. Mayer was a fantasy—until Mitchell came.

"I suppose you heard about Dr. Mayer?"

Tessa rolled onto the edge of her bed and sat up. "What happened?"

The Matron hesitated, then closed the door and pulled up a chair. Looking back to ensure the door was closed, she spoke in a half-whisper. "They found him in the treatment room—a heart attack."

Tessa remained quiet, her body trembling. "Natural causes then?"

"It would seem so."

"How is Mrs. Mayer?"

"Halper says she is sitting in her office as calm as a cat in sunshine."

Hearing voices outside, Tessa rose and walked to the window. Mitchell followed. They watched two men slide a canvas-covered stretcher into the back of the hearse and close the doors. Then someone must have called out because one of the men waved, opened the rear doors again, and stepped back. Mrs. Mayer appeared, pushing an empty wheeled-chair toward the attendant. He placed it inside and latched the doors. Mrs. Mayer was stoic. No tears.

"You may have been the last person to see him alive," Mitchell remarked.

Just then, a brief knock came to the door before it swung open to reveal Nurse Halper. She scowled at Mitchell. "You weren't at your post. You're to lock down the ward. Director Mayer wants the staff upfront." The Matron nodded and pulled the chair back into place. Before leaving, she turned toward Tessa. "You will be confined to the ward for now, but you will be able to go to the laundry tomorrow. Remember, return straightway."

"I will. I won't wander, Mrs. Mitchell."

* * * * *

The laundry room was the hub of Hellingford gossip, and the next day, Tessa was eager to have more details about Dr. Mayer's death. As she made her way, she again noticed the old man peering from his cottage window. If there were inquiries about Dr. Mayer's death, he might say that he had seen her leave the treatment building just before the doctor was found. She moved quickly along, determined not to look over her shoulder, hurrying past the public wards to the laundry.

"What are you running from?" It was Beara. She was sitting on the steps of her ward sorting through a basket of dried herbs.

"It's terrible, isn't it?" Tessa remarked.

Beara continued plucking leaves and stems, placing them in small cloth bags. Tessa had observed Ganna doing the same many times, herb-craft being an integral part of living in the olde way. "What's terrible?"

"Beara, I assume you heard about Dr. Mayer. Did you see anything?"

Beara laughed. "Why are you asking me—you were with him."

"Yes, in that dreadful place . . . that horrible machine."

"Aye, a beastly machine." Beara agreed. "He would question me over and over about the treasure."

"What did you tell him?"

"Everything, nothing. I don't know." She looked Tessa in the eye. "I don't know what I said." Beara shuddered. "He deserved to die."

Tessa stiffened. "Why do you say that?"

The old woman set the basket down and looked hard at her. "You know why, and I fear that your lies will not serve you."

Tessa clutched the druid's glass hanging around her neck.

"Aye, cling to that stone, but know that it will serve only the truth!"

Tessa's eyes widened as she felt the stone growing warm in her hand. "I must get on to the laundry."

Tessa hurried to the laundry building where she hoped the warm water, fragrant soap, and the joyful chatter of the women would lift her spirits and clear her mind, and at first, the water seemed to work its magic.

As she hung out the last sheet to dry, she knew exactly what to do. The first part of her escape required that she write an urgent letter to Mr. Holmes.

The single piece of paper Jack had brought could barely contain everything Tessa wanted to report. Some details were murky because Mayer's orgone booth still fogged her memory. Her experience confirmed what Beara had shared, that the orgone treatments were being used to extract information from unwitting patients. Hellingford could be embroiled in a blackmail scheme. Most certainly they were harboring thieves—the Forty Elephants gang in Ward E. It was likely their stolen goods were being shipped out from the maintenance shed. She knew Holmes would make sense of it all.

Tessa folded her report and tucked it into the soiled sheets for Jack. That done, she turned her attention to the escape itself. She had allies now, and she considered how each might help her. Her survey of the complex was paying off, for she knew where the weak links in security lay. The buildings' outside windows were barred with two exceptions: the maintenance shed and Ward E. Her way out had to be through one of those two buildings.

That night Tessa had difficulty dropping off to sleep. The moon was nearly full, and its radiance painted the walls and ceilings of her room in shades of cornflower blue. She knew the moon's energy might bring Ganna. In the dead of night, it did.

What troubles you? Ganna asked.

"I think I may have killed a man," she said without emotion.

Much has happened since I was last with you.

"Indeed." She went on to tell Ganna about her treatment and how she locked the doctor in his own vile apparatus and then shared other details that led to her decision to escape.

Ganna listened patiently before she spoke: *Yes, it's time to leave this place. You should never have come.*

"I did it for—"

Mr. Holmes, I know. But Tessa, the only debt you owe is to the goddess who sustains our life. As for any obligation you owe Mr. Holmes, that debt is best paid to those whose lives you will touch by using what he has taught you.

"I can't do what Mr. Holmes does."

Ganna laughed. *You say the same to me. Have you thought about why I chose you?*

"It's because I have Iceni blood—the proper lineage."

That makes you one of hundreds. I chose you because you have a warrior's heart that's been tempered in battle—battles in which you defeated the greatest foe: fear. Most flinch from fear, but a warrior awakens to it—moves toward it.

"It's not courage so much as avoiding regret that motivates me."

Regret and fear are fabrics made from the same yarn. Every night you do battle, and each morning, you arise with renewed resolve.

As Tessa allowed herself to embrace Ganna's words, tears came to her eyes.

Ganna was content to let Tessa be with her feelings and bid her goodnight.

When Tessa woke at dawn, her plan was clear. She would make her escape tomorrow. Each of her allies played a role with Jack at the center of her scheme. She wondered if, in the end, he would risk his freedom and safety to help her. She would know soon, but now she needed to pay a call on Beara.

Careful not to deviate from her routine, Tessa went to her job after a meager breakfast. Along the way, she noticed that the old man in the cottage was not at his window, and the brick treatment building was padlocked.

The chatter in the laundry room hushed when Tessa entered and donned her apron. Wheeling a cart of dirty linens toward a waiting washtub, she noticed the women and girls were paying undue attention. As she filled her tub with hot water and placed the washboard inside, she was halted by a remark: "Blood shall be sprinkled upon my garments and stain all my raiment." Tessa wheeled about to find the ladies huddled together—staring. She turned a sharp eye on them. "Don't hide behind bible verses. If you have something to say, speak plainly."

A woman of great height and thin limbs walked toward her. "You're a nosy one. All questions, poking into everything high and mighty like." Her nose tilted up, and her eyes narrowed. "Poor Dr. Mayer was on to you, and he paid the price."

"You best forget fairy tales and stay to the bible." Tessa kicked over a bucket of water, tossed her apron aside, and marched out of the building.

If the ladies in the laundry were casting an accusing finger, it would not be long before others would call her to account. Escaping tomorrow may be too late.

TWENTY

PANIC DROVE TESSA'S STEPS as she made her way to Beara. Her doubts loomed large as she studied the guard posted outside the Forty Elephants ward. *He will be a serious obstacle*, she thought. Turning toward the maintenance shed, she noticed smoke wafting from the stovepipe and wondered how many men were inside today.

There had been frost the evening before, but the sun was already warming the air when Tessa came to the entrance of Beara's ward. As usual, the old woman sat motionless on the top step, this time with something cupped in her hand—a twitching bird. Beara stroked the soft yellow feathers of the swift. "I was afraid this would happen," Beara said as Tessa came near. "The frost got her. She waited too long; now she's suffering."

"Let me have her," Tessa said. The little bird fluttered as Beara tenderly slid the bird into the palm of Tessa's hand. Closing her eyes, Tessa covered the creature with her other hand. Her lips spoke in hushed words Beara could not understand. When Tessa removed her hand, the swift lay motionless. "She's passed on."

As Tessa returned the bird, Beara nodded: "I will bury her in the garden." Stroking the dead bird with her finger, she added: "I'm sorry little one. It's the best I can do."

"If it troubles you, I will do it."

"Death does not trouble me; it is graves. What creature wants to be put into the ground? No, put my dead body in water that knows no bounds."

Tessa smiled. "Indeed, put me in a mighty river that knows no bounds," she echoed.

Beara looked up. "Why are you here?"

"I should have told you. I think I killed the doctor," Tessa said.

"I know," Beara answered.

"It wasn't murder though. I don't know what happened, but I will not find answers here. I must get away, and I need your help."

Beara held her arms wide. "Look at me. I can barely get out of bed in the morning."

"It's not your strength I need, Beara. Do you have something among your herbs that will weaken or confuse a person—just for a while?"

"How so?"

"Awake and moving, but muddled," Tessa said.

Beara grinned. "Salvia."

Matron Mitchell was surprised by Tessa's seeming return from the laundry but was satisfied with the excuse that Tessa was ill. Often patients were after their treatments. "Rest," the Matron told her on her way out.

With each tick of the clock, Tessa's anxiety mounted. She jumped when her door suddenly opened. "Director Mayer wants to see us," Mitchell told her.

The women exchanged no words as they walked in tandem to the front office. Mitchell knocked, waited, and then cautiously looked in. Mrs. Mayer waved them inside.

Beatrice Mayer straightened in her chair and neatly folded her hands on the desk. Her cheeks were not tear-stained, nor her eyes red. Her face was resolute and devoid of color. She gestured to the chairs, and Tessa and Mitchell sat.

"As you know, Dr. Mayer passes away yesterday." She bowed her head for an instant before looking up again bearing a resolute expression. "Rumors are swirling about. I won't gratify the gossip mongers by repeating them, but it is important to put a stop to wild talk—for the benefit of the hospital, you understand." She leaned forward and eyed both of them. "Will you help me quash this gossip?"

Mitchell nodded. "Certainly."

Mayer turned to Tessa, whose head then bobbed in agreement.

"Very good. Miss Wiggins, you were in the treatment room with Dr. Mayer yesterday afternoon just before he passed away." Tessa grew pale and her lips trembled. "When you saw him . . . when you were with him, I imagine you noticed how poorly he looked."

Tessa's momentary stillness caused the Director to restate her question. "Surely now, you must have noticed how poorly he looked. Yesterday morning my husband told me he was feeling unwell. I encouraged him to postpone your treatment, but he declined. You must have seen how ill he looked."

Tessa's wordless response caused Mayer's eyes to widen. She pursed her lips, and her head swiveled toward Mitchell, who began nodding nervously. "Yes, yes, now that you mention it," Mitchell replied, "Dr. Mayer did appear off-color when I brought Miss Wiggins to the treatment room."

Mayer turned to Tessa, who followed Mitchell's cue. "Yes, he was not himself, to be sure."

The Director's shoulder's relaxed, and her lips turned up, and her entire demeanor lightened. "So, there's the truth of it. I would appreciate it if both of you would add this grist to the rumor mill. If you should be asked about my husband, will you mention how very ill he was yesterday?"

"If I may ask, when is the funeral?" Mitchell inquired.

"There will be no funeral. No wake either. You can share that as well," Mrs. Mayer said as she stood. "Thank you both. That is all."

Tessa's mind whirled as she made her way back to the ward. Her plan to escape Hellingford was now less desperate but still necessary. Any relief she had felt about being accused of murder was overshadowed by Beatrice Mayer's perplexing effort to ensure that her husband's death appears to be natural. She must add this news to the report she had prepared for Mr. Holmes.

Using a mostly blank page from the bible in her dresser, she added the update, then folded it into the letter she had already prepared. Sealing it tightly, she tucked it into the stack of dirty laundry awaiting Jack.

Like clockwork, Jack knocked and entered. Lowering his voice, he asked if she had the 'package' for him. She pointed to the linens on the dresser and took the fresh ones from his hands. "Take my letter to Cian. He will get it to a friend." She put her hand on his. "Thank you, Jack. I hesitate to ask more of you, but I need your help in another way."

"Of course," Jack replied.

Tessa sat him down on the edge of the bed and shared her plan to escape. When she concluded, she asked if he thought her plan would work.

He looked dubious. "I can only do *my* part."

"I trust the others will do theirs as well." Taking his hand, she added: "You're very brave."

"No more than you," he replied, rising and taking the soiled sheets and letter. At the door, he turned to reassure her, "Cian will have your letter today and Mr. Holmes soon after."

"Thank you. I'll never forget what you've done."

After he left, a strange feeling arose within her. She must have told Jack about Mr. Holmes but couldn't recall doing so.

TWENTY-ONE

TESSA PRESSED HER FACE against the iron bars on the window and let the cool, moist air uplift her. A gust of wind shook the trees and, Tessa caught the scent of a storm. Sure enough, the raindrops came, slowly at first, splashing on her face and trickling down her cheeks—*The Mother's blessing*, she thought. The cool water washed away her unease, and a dusky gauze settled over the horizon and held back dawn's golden promise. Tessa's doubts were soon swallowed up by storm clouds as they billowed, churned, and reached for the heavens.

Patience is power, Ganna reminded her. *Waiting is the most difficult action. Watch . . . sense. Can you feel the tension in the air, Tessa?*

"Yes."

Lightning in the making. Reach out your hand and invite it. Call to it.

She did. It struck, and thunder rumbled nearby. Tessa giggled. "I didn't do that?"

Ganna laughed. *I think you did.*

Then, it struck again just beyond the perimeter fence. Her hand jerked backward, tingling, hot. She flexed her fingers, examining them for burns as she watched water drip from her fingertips.

Water is the greatest teacher, the old Druid told her. *It falls and flows freely. It does not resist, and yet it overcomes everything. Water only becomes foul when it ceases to flow.*

Tessa nodded, closed her eyes, and listened.

Water is timeless—everywhere at once. The river flows from the hills, through canyons, and into the sea, in the same moment. It has no past or future. It flows with and within us, as it does above and below us. Water is our connection with The Mother, and it is through water that we are able to commune with her—remember this.

"Ganna, can others bond with The Mother?"

Long ago, most creatures lived in communion with her, but human beings broke this bond and left the garden. The Mother grieves for the loss.

"How do I commune and restore that bond?"

You will know soon. It requires three things: that you be in swift water, that your heart is open, and that you bring a precious offering. To receive, you must give. It is the way of all things. The Mother requires that you offer something of great value. Now, listen and call out to the storm as I have taught you.

Then Ganna was gone.

Tessa reached through the bars, lifted her hands, and began rocking slowly from foot to foot as a fervent chant rose from deep within her belly. As she called to the eye of the storm, lightning flickered high in the clouds coming closer, CRACKING and SIZZLING as it STRUCK the iron fence at the perimeter of Hellingford. This time she didn't pull away when it burned but waited for the sensation to pass.

Tessa did not know how long she stayed at the window, but noises in the hallway, and the smell of coffee, announced that the ward had awakened to a new day. Her plan was about to unfold.

Tessa's doubts began again to mount with each tick of the clock. She realized she had put herself in the hands of people she barely knew. Time makes the rules that govern relationships, and Tessa wondered if she had given time its due.

She had but one task, to dress warmly in layers of clothing, making certain she wore her best shoes, and take an extra pair of socks. It was a long walk through the hills and forests back to Ceridwen, and it was raining. Reaching for a scarf in her dresser, she saw Mr. Holmes's penny—the one Clark had left for her. She found herself wishing Clark was here now.

Sitting on the edge of her bed, Tessa refused to look at the clock, knowing time would pass more slowly if she did. She closed her eyes, listened to her breath, and felt her heart beating its proud cadence: 'I am, I am, I am.'

Her waiting ended mid-morning. Jack rolled his laundry cart to Tessa's door and knocked. Without waiting, he went to Matron Mitchell's desk and engaged her in a hushed conversation—no doubt sharing some titillating piece of gossip. Tessa opened her door and, moving quickly and quietly, lifted the soiled laundry in the wicker cart, climbed in, and pulled the linens over her. She was overcome by the musk of human bodies but then quickly found a strange comfort in it.

Suddenly the cart moved. As the wheels bumped and rumbled on the tile floor, Tessa watched light filtering through the sheets as the cart moved under the gallery windows. She gasped when the handcart struck the door to the common and bounced outside. "How are you doing?" Jack whispered. "Fine," she answered, trying to peek through the twisted fabric. "Keep your head down," he warned.

In her mind, she could picture the cart moving along the crushed-stone pathway. *We must be near the cottage*, she thought. Just ahead were the public wards—Beara's ward. She wondered if the old woman was able to get the salvia-tainted tea to the guard in Ward E. "Jack?" she whispered. "Sh-h-h, wait. Yes, he has a cup in his hand, but I don't see Beara about."

"Go to him," Tessa bade.

Jack rolled the cart to a stop and walked toward the guard sitting outside the Forty Elephant's Ward. "Ello, gov'nor," he called.

The man struggled as he rose from his chair. "What? Who?" He swayed as he stood, squinting at Jack. "What do you want?" Almost toppling over, he dropped back into his chair.

131

Jack approached and knocked on the door of the ward. "Bloody hell," a voice inside barked. The door swung open. A husky young woman smeared with thick crimson lipstick scrutinized Jack. "What's all this then?" she asked.

"This fellow here seems to be ill," Jack said as he brought the guard to his feet.

The woman laughed. "Hey, Alice, there's a couple'a gents here." An older, pale woman yanked the door wider. "Ha! I get the young one," she quipped. "Come in for a drink, why don't you?"

The guard's eyes widened, and a lecherous grin spread across his face. He tore his arm away from Jack and stumbled into the arms of the burly woman. She screamed with laughter and let him fall to the ground. Other women rushed out toward the commotion, shouting and taunting the poor fellow. The guard tried to right himself, but like a beetle on its back, he could not get atop his legs. Streaks of laughter erupted as the ladies teased him with a shapely leg or pursed lips. "Come on, lover-boy," one said as she held out her hand. He pulled on it and sent her plummeting on top of him.

Jack stepped back from the tumult as the crowd of women clustered around the entrance to the ward. The ruckus grew louder, and just down the way, the door to the maintenance shed opened. Several ruffs emerged from the shed and began walking toward the uproar.

Jack went to the cart and casually moved it closer to the shed. One large fellow remained wedged in the doorway to the outbuilding. "I think they could use your help over there," Jack told him. Seeing the scantily dressed women in the distance, the man agreed.

As the fellow passed him, Jack pushed the cart up to the door. "Here you go, Tessa. Good luck," he said and walked away.

Tessa carefully brushed the linens aside and peeked over the rim of the cart. *Perfect.* The door to the shed was open, and no one was about. She climbed from the cart, stopping only a moment when her foot tangled in the sheets. Head down, Tessa slipped silently into the maintenance shed.

As Tessa's eyes adjusted to the dim light, she looked around carefully to make sure she was alone, then hurried across the shed to the far door and freedom. As her hand touched the knob, the door suddenly swung wide, pushing her back onto her heels. Framed in the exit was Beatrice Mayer—Angus behind her.

Tessa pivoted only to find two more goons blocking her retreat.

"Abandon all hope, ye who enter," the Director jested.

There were no words for Tessa. There was nothing to be said.

Mrs. Mayer smirked. "Miss Wiggins, it appears Hellingford is unable to meet your needs. However, there is a special incurable ward in Bedlam that will suit you and your friend Beara."

Tessa grew faint and fell to her knees.

"You needn't worry about your letter to Mr. Sherlock Holmes— your missive was sent. Let us hope he comes soon."

"Jack!" Tessa cried.

"Yes, little limping Jack," she laughed. "Lunatics make poor friends."

TWENTY-TWO

THE THREE-HOUR TRAIN RIDE from London to Blaenau Ffestiniog offered Watson a rare opportunity to have a long chat with his friend. In earlier days at 221b, they spent countless hours together, but since retirement, their conversations were abridged and seldom ventured into intimate realms. Holmes had been absentmindedly tamping his pipe for some time, which told Watson his friend was troubled.

"Clark's telegram is disturbing, but I would not put too much into it," Watson remarked.

Holmes did not look up. "He said Tessa was in danger."

"He said she *might* be in danger. He was unable to visit her. You are usually the one to remind me to stay to the facts. Good advice, that. We will know more when we have Tessa's second letter in hand."

Holmes did not rejoin.

"Blast it, Holmes, light the damn thing or put it in your pocket. I'm—"

"It's all right, Watson. We're both out of sorts. I should have acted when I received her first letter."

"As I recall, she was making good progress then. There was no hint of danger in her first letter."

"None of which you were aware," Holmes rejoined. "Tessa reported that the mystery lady was a woman named Mayer—Mrs. Mayer. I know her husband, Hermann Mayer."

"The psychiatrist?"

"We met in a hospital in Zurich—Burgholzli by name."

"A psychiatric hospital!" Watson exclaimed. "So, is that the 'scruffy cat' referred to in your blackmail letter?"

Holmes nodded. "Thirty years ago, I was taken to Burgholzli after two fishermen found me on the shores of Brienz Lake—raving like a madman, I was told. The doctor who treated me was—"

"Mayer," Watson said.

"I apologize, my friend. I should have told you long ago that my grand hiatus began with treatment in a mental institution." His eyes conveyed regret. "Now is not the time for this tale, but you need to know that Tessa may be a pawn in an effort to strike at me. It never occurred to me that Dr. Mayer was the villainous sort. He didn't seem so when I knew him."

"He may have fallen on hard times and turned to blackmail," Watson said. "In any case, you may be putting the cart before the horse. We'll know more when we have Tessa's report."

Clark waved off Elis when he came to the door and was waiting in the hallway for Holmes and Watson. "My apologies, gentleman," he said, lowering his voice. "I'm struggling to keep the Davis sisters at bay."

Elis was waiting at the entrance to the parlor as Clark led the way. "This way, gentleman."

As he stepped into the room, Holmes transformed himself into the epitome of graciousness. He walked directly to the settee' where Gwendoline and Margaret Davis waited. Gwendoline extended a hand, and Holmes took it. "The doctor and I pledge ourselves to Tessa's safe return."

Gwendoline frowned. "I would hope as much. She's in Hellingford because of you."

He cocked his head. "I have always seen Tessa as a canny woman who makes her own choices." As he turned, he noticed a large strapping man standing off to one side. The man held his head low, but Holmes knew why he laid back when the big fellow looked up.

Following Holmes's intense gaze, Clark said: "This is Cian, Mr. Holmes."

"Cian and I have met," the detective said. "A man of exceptional strength."

The outsized man grimaced. "Sorry I am, sir, for the wee tussle in the cave."

"Cian is a friend," Margaret said.

"And a good one, I am certain," Holmes agreed. "Tessa will need all her friends." As he took a seat, Clark winked and handed over Tessa's letter.

"Can I assume you have all read this letter?" Holmes asked.

They nodded.

Holmes read silently.

October 27

Mr. Holmes,

I cannot express my joy upon receiving the penny Clark passed on when he attempted to visit. This report necessarily comes by way of Cian, the gatekeeper. You can count him as a friend.

Your stolen manuscript brought us to Hellingford, and I can report that, while it is a functioning asylum, it houses criminal enterprises, the scope of which I have not completely ascertained.

My survey of the complex revealed two singular buildings: One houses two dozen young women who, I was told, are associates of Alice

Diamond. If my friend Beara is correct, these ladies are members of the Forty Elephants gang.

The second building is a maintenance shed that appears to hold stolen goods—most probably from the Forty Elephants. An old man in his seventies manages it. He comes and goes but has a cottage on the grounds. He is said to be the one responsible for restoring Hellingford. A clue to his identity might be a grey Crossley automobile parked behind the shed. The number plate is LY-1089. I am not certain it is his, but it is here when he is and gone when he's not.

Hellingford has pushed me to my limits. In particular, Dr. Mayer's orgone treatment is a trial. This apparatus consists of a small booth in which I sit while being interviewed. A motor pumps in metallic smelling air to remove so-called orgone. The treatment makes me light-headed and confused while I'm in the booth. As you might deduce, the orgone machine may present opportunities for a blackmail scheme. I make this point because I was specifically asked about you, and I am uncertain if I ever mentioned your name. I would not knowingly do so, but I may have unwittingly. My friend Beara, who hails from Anglesey, has similar experiences in the booth, and that is where she likely told the doctor about Celtic treasure. If there is a treasure, Beara will be the key to finding it.

More recently, I heard the doctor and his wife arguing about you. She claims that you did something dreadful to her family. The quarrel ended with him deciding to play a larger role in the running of Hellingford. This would be *difficult, as Dr. Mayer is bound to a wheeled-chair.*

More to come,

Tessa

October 28 - Addendum

> *For reasons that will become clear, I plan to escape from Hellingford and hopefully arrive at Ceridwen by the time you read this letter.*
>
> *Something shocking has occurred. Dr. Mayer is dead. And what is worse, I may be the cause. I was the last to see him alive. After an orgone treatment, we had a row, and I pushed his chair into the booth and locked the door. As he is a cripple, I fear I may have caused a fatal injury.*
>
> *Shortly afterward, my ward matron and I were called to Mrs. Mayer's office, where we were told to lie about her husband's demise. She appears to be concealing the cause of his death, and there is to be no funeral.*
>
> *All my instincts tell me to flee this place, and so I go tomorrow. If I am not at Ceridwen in two days' time, my plan has failed.*

Holmes handed the letter to Watson and lit his pipe.

Margaret pointed at Holmes. "This is not one of your cases, sir. We here are all agreed that it is time to call in the authorities. At Clark's urging, we have waited for you and Dr. Watson to arrive before doing so."

Holmes took a long drag on his pipe and slowly blew the smoke through pursed lips. It curled before him, momentarily obscuring his placid expression. "And what will the authorities find, do you think?

Tessa's failed attempt to escape will have the entire place on alert. Any evidence of crimes will be hidden. And on our side, we have two letters written by a woman who has been legally committed."

"But Dr. Mayer's death—" Margaret began.

"An investigation of which will surely put Tessa in the docket— maybe on the gallows. No, no—justice may have to find its own accord concerning any crimes. We need to bring Tessa home." He paused. "*I* need to bring Tessa home. For as you so aptly noted, Miss Davis, she was acting on my appeal. I suggest we have a spot of tea and consider our next move with care."

As the group went to the dining room, Watson called Holmes to the side. Reaching in his coat pocket, he removed an envelope. "This note from Dr. Kraepelin was waiting for me when I got home. I hadn't thought much about it as it seemed irrelevant until now." He opened it and handed it to Holmes.

> *Dr. Watson,*
>
> *I felt it incumbent on me to write and tell you that I will make myself available to conduct an evaluation of your patient Miss Wiggins as a professional courtesy.*
>
> *I recently attempted to contact Dr. Mayer at Hellingford with plans to make a professional call and enjoy a round of golf if the season permitted. He is a consummate player.*
>
> *I just received a call telling me that Dr. Mayer has died of a heart attack. A great loss. I had looked forward to introducing his orgone therapy to a larger professional community in London.*
>
> *Please make an appointment at your convenience.*
>
> *Yours respectfully,*
> *Elias Kraepelin M.D.*

"What do you make of it, Holmes?"

He folded the note and handed it back. "Keep this to yourself for the moment. Tessa's instincts are good, but she is in greater danger than even she imagines."

TWENTY-THREE

TESSA HAD NOT LOST HER MIND, but she knew she might if she remained locked in a dank cell on the public ward, surrounded as she was by raging alcoholics, drug addicts, and incurables.

There were no chairs, tables, or lamps in her cell. A grimy canvas cot that smelled of urine was the lone piece of furniture. The life-giving elements of air, light, and sound came through one small, barred opening in a steel-reinforced door. A sardonic grin mirrored a stray thought: *Maybe I was too quick to discharge the white knight.*

Instinctively, Tessa's lips moved in a hushed prayer to fend off a growing feeling of helplessness. She was reluctant to call on Ganna or maybe afraid. Suspicions about how the old Druid had extended her life had plagued Tessa's mind ever since she heard Beara's rhyme about the *Cymry* sisters. What had been a small sliver of doubt was growing and wedging itself ever deeper into Tessa's heart.

Suddenly the door swung wide. A large woman appeared in the doorway. She held Beara up by one arm. The colossus of a woman had shaggy, ruff-cut hair. and her lips were pursed tightly. "I'm Matron Lyn," she barked. "Mrs. Mayer thought you might be lonely." As if she were tossing a hat, the Matron flung Beara inside and slammed the door.

The old woman righted herself and pulled her sweater back onto her shoulders. Beara smiled. "Just when I think I'm immune to life's disappointments, I find myself amazed."

"I'm sorry, Beara. It was a mistake to include you in my plan."

"It's never a mistake to do what is right," she answered. Then, seeing the lone cot in the corner, added: "Although I may feel differently tonight."

Tessa embraced her. They stayed in each other's arms for some time before Tessa sat the old woman down on the canvas bed. "The cot is yours," she said.

"How sweet," the matron said through the cell window before opening the door again. "The Director wants a word with you two. Come along."

As Tessa and Beara walked out onto the ward, their senses and sensibilities were immediately assaulted. Unkempt women huddled around windows and lay sprawled on grimy straw mats on the floor. Some of them wandered about trance-like, arms extended, reaching out for . . . what? Strange drawings you might expect to see in a primordial cave covered one of the walls along with scribbled warnings: "Don't come here." "Not in my house." The acrid ammonia smell of urine turned her stomach. But what most sickened Tessa was the look of hopelessness in the women's eyes. They were cast-offs—the embodiment of unwelcome tribulation, the symbol of something gone wrong in the world. These women were no longer sisters, wives, daughters, or mothers. They were things—burdens to be hidden away and forgotten. As Matron Lyn led them outside, Tessa and Beara took a deep breath, welcoming the cool air and sunlight.

Mayer stiffened to attention behind her desk when Tessa and Beara entered her office. Both she and her framed look-alike behind the desk stared at them. "Attempted escape is a serious matter, ladies," Beatrice Mayer began. "As you are painfully aware, our public wards are crowded, so I will need to transfer you to Bethlehem Royal Hospital in London. The high rate of mortality creates frequent openings, so I am certain I can find a place for you both. But before I send you on, I wonder if either of you might have something to say that might alter my decision?"

"What do you want?" Tessa shouted.

"The treasure—the 'blood of the slaughtered."

"We don't know where the treasure is or if there is a treasure!"

"Beara knows the treasure exists, don't you?"

"I know only the rhymes I was taught," Beara said.

"Yes, I know: 'Ganna fled for those who bled, giving on and living on the lives of the *Cymry* sisters.' But that is not all of it, is it old woman?" She opened a notebook on her desk and poked a finger into a page. "The whole verse is:

'Ganna fled from those who bled on Mam,

Giving on and living on the lives of the *Cymry* sisters.

The offerings she will hide, until her death is bona fide,

and Ewryd can be satisfied."

Beara's eyes grew wide. Her worst fear had come to pass. She had betrayed her sacred trust in the orgone booth. "If you know, then why ask?" Beara said.

Mayer stood and leaned over her desk. "Because I don't know what it means!" Her head swiveled to Tessa. "But you may, or Professor Stone, or Sherlock Holmes, or Ganna."

"Ganna is dead!" Tessa said.

"Maybe so, but she was with you before she died. I'm certain she told you about the treasure."

"We don't know anything," Tessa repeated.

Beatrice shook her head and returned to her chair. "If that is so then I have no use for you. After you bring Holmes here, you're off to Bedlam."

"*You* took his manuscript!"

"Not me, but yes. And all the better that you came instead."

"Where is it?"

Beatrice Mayer laughed. "I hope you don't think me that foolish."

"What is Mr. Holmes to you?"

Mayer bolted from her chair as her face twisted into an angry mask. "He killed my father and took our home and wealth. My mother's life became a nightmare. I've waited long for this moment. The great Sherlock Holmes will soon know what it's like to lose everything and everyone he holds dear." When her breath became more even, she sat down and neatly folded her hands. "You have this night to think about what I have said. After Holmes comes, you're both going to Bedlam."

Tessa and Beara were returned to their cell. Their situation was bad, but the realization that Holmes, and probably Clark, may be rushing into danger, maybe to their deaths, was crushing. Jack had fooled her. Tessa's instincts had failed her. *How did this happen?* Tessa wondered. Her brother Rory raised her to believe that trust in others is always misplaced. In Spitalfields, that was true.

"I'm sorry," Beara said. Tessa did not reply. "The *geiriau'r Cymry* are sacred. They're not for *o'r tu allan rs*—outlanders. I babbled during the treatments, mixing Welsh with English, but Dr. Mayer relentlessly questioned me about the treasure. I tried to change the *cynghanedd*—the poem, but . . ."

Tessa turned. "Then there is a treasure?"

Beara nodded.

"And you know where it is?

She bobbed her head. "In a way, but it's a large area."

Tessa took Beara by the shoulders. And Ganna? Is Mayer right?"

Beara nodded again. "Yes, the poem is as Mrs. Mayer said."

"Living on the lives of the Cymry sisters," Tessa mumbled in a daze.

Beara put her hand on Tessa's. "Ganna is living through you, isn't she?"

"I was afraid to tell you—afraid you'd think me mad."

Beara's brows lifted, and her lips pursed, "So we're in the right place, aren't we?" she said as she erupted into laughter. Tessa joined her, and soon Matron Lyn was looking in wonder through the window in the door.

"What does that say about us, Beara, that we can laugh in the midst of this trouble?"

"It's tears or laughter. We're wise enough to laugh. It's cheap medicine."

"You *are* wise, Beara."

"Wise? No, but I've learned to give my instincts free range and to heed the advice of dying people. It has served me well until now."

Matron Lyn soon yielded to their contagious laughter and was heard chuckling to herself. Their laughs became fitful giggles and then quit shoulder shaking before Tessa walked to the Matron at the window. "Tell Mrs. Mayer we will take her to the treasure." Lyn looked perplexed. "Just tell her."

TWENTY-FOUR

"LET US BRING REASON TO THE TABLE," Holmes implored as he fended off anxious plans and pleas from the Davis sisters and Clark. "Hellingford is at best corrupt, and at worst, a criminal enterprise. It would be fool hearty to charge in like the proverbial bull in Thomas Goode's. Tessa sent us valuable information, and we must use it."

Holmes then went about giving instructions in the manner of General Haig. Clark and Cian were to review the map of Hellingford that Tessa sent, adding more details and noting all entrances and exits. Watson would accompany Holmes on the next train to the city where the doctor would engage Professor Stone and seek information about the Crossley parked at Hellingford. Holmes would make a side trip, disembarking at Pangbourne and proceeding to Purley-on-Thames to learn more about their adversary.

"What's in Pangbourne?" Watson asked.

"Not what, who," Holmes told him, putting his finger to one side of his nose. "I'll join you on your return trip from London," he added.

Knowing they were champing at the bit for something to do, Holmes asked the Davis sisters if they would loan their auto and locate a recent map of the island of Anglesey. When Margaret asked: "Why," he answered: "because the treasure is there."

"Watson, I, and hopefully Professor Stone, will be back late this evening. We will burn the midnight oil and be on our way to extricate Tessa at dawn."

"I'll make plenty of coffee," Gwenda said, happy to have some part to play. Elis, the butler, seemed content to have no assignment.

* * * * *

The train bore Holmes and Watson past mounds of slate tailings, belching chimneys, and pastures glinting with autumn color. Holmes knew that the mutual trust that Watson and he held was in jeopardy, and he intended to put it right during this trip.

What is it about train rides that cause friends, or even strangers, to open the door to their deepest selves? Maybe it's the unbroken rhythm of steel wheels reminding us that we are pursued by time or the illusion that we know where we are going.

Watson appeared to be enjoying the countryside, but Holmes knew better. "Well, Watson, the pieces are coming together," he said to breach the silence.

The doctor turned to him. "More in your mind than mine."

He nodded. "We all have our secrets, Watson. I say this not as an excuse but knowing that when I expose this skeleton in my cupboard, my excuses will appear feeble—or even ugly—the truth having been held captive for so long in the dark."

Watson's heart sank upon seeing the mortification in his friend's eyes.

"So, Watson, let me tell the story of Dr. Mayer. It began thirty years ago at Reichenbach Falls. You were with me, but that was before Moriarty and I grappled at the edge of the falls. I bid a hasty farewell to life in that final struggle, but it was Moriarty who toppled first. I skidded down the slippery wall of the abyss in a less dramatic fashion. I was amazed when I came to my senses on the shores of Brienz Lake. It's curious how the mind works in moments such as that. Time slows, and your senses burst with clarity." Holmes paused in thought. "In any case, after Moriarty and I tumbled over the falls, I found myself on the shore of the lake with broken ribs, a fractured tibia, and deep cuts on my back and scalp. I was barely conscious, undoubtedly suffering from shock. I cannot recall precisely what happened, but the upshot was that two fishermen from Ringgenberg found me and took me to Burgholzli Hospital in Zurich. As you noted, it is a psychiatric hospital, but it also has a medical clinic that serves the local community.

"My physical wounds were tended, but the trauma to my psyche was not as easily mended. The moment I regained my faculties, my thoughts turned to Moriarty. If I had survived, possibly he had as well. This vague fear intensified when one of the nurses told me that an English gentleman inquired about patients recently admitted. As I was only a day out of surgery, visitors had not been allowed. So, there I lay, leg in a cast, twenty stitches, weak, and helpless."

Watson looked wide-eyed at his friend. "But Holmes—"

"Why didn't I contact you in Meirengen? For the same reason, I allowed Moriarty's ruse to take you away from Reichenbach Falls. If the Professor had survived, or Moran was in the vicinity, your life would have been worthless. So, you see my predicament. I was in no shape to run, so I did the next best thing—hid."

Holmes chuckled. "Even now, I laugh. I put on quite a show feigning a mental disorder. Alternating between German and English, I raved day and night. It worked. I was transferred to the mental hospital where I was treated by—yes—Dr. Hermann Mayer.

"I won't bore you with the details, except to say that my treatment became more complicated when I found my way to a drug cabinet in Mayer's office. Cocaine had been useful as an anesthetic on my wounds, and I found it worked wonders internally as well. As always, it was a temporary relief, and once discovered, my addiction caused Dr. Mayer to keep me at Burgholzli for several more weeks.

"I let the doctor think his treatments were working. I even endured his ridiculous orgone machine—the same treatment Tessa wrote about. However, she did not understand that orgone treatments involved pumping nitrous oxide into the patient's booth to relax the mind. I knew from the start that his orgone apparatus was a farce, but I played along.

"When I felt it was safe, and after my cast was removed, I shared my true identity with the doctor. Shortly afterward, I was released with the agreement to continue treatments when I returned home. I thought I had seen the last of the man until Tessa wrote. So, there you have it, my friend."

"Then Dr. Mayer is hoping to blackmail you about your stay in a mental hospital?" Watson concluded.

"One might think so. But with Tessa's most recent letter and your note from Kraepelin, I am left to wonder if Dr. Hermann Mayer is the real culprit. He was not a cripple when I knew him."

"That was thirty years ago, Holmes."

"Kraepelin was expecting to go golfing with the fellow. Let us simply say that the true identity of Hellingford's superintendent is in question. Nonetheless, either he or his accomplices hope that news regarding my stay at Burgholzli might be a *coup de grâce*, as they would simultaneously blackmail my former clients."

Holmes paused and turned to his friend. "Can you forgive me?"

Watson smiled. "Thirty years ago, like Lazarus, you came back from the dead with fantastic tales of Tibet, Persia, Mecca, and Khartoum. I will simply add Zurich to your itinerary. However, I hope you will share those adventures with me after Tessa is safely home."

"Agreed," Holmes promised, taking his friend's outstretched hand.

The train went on to London after delivering Holmes to Pangbourne. As they parted, Holmes promised to rejoin Watson on his return trip four hours later.

The detective's first stop was The Herd, an inn where he had a quick bite to eat and secured transport to Purley-on-Thames—only a few miles away.

Holmes recalled that Pangbourne had been the subject of literary inspiration—good and otherwise. D. H. Lawrence was uncomplimentary about the village and its people. To the contrary,

Kenneth Grahame and Jerome K. Jerome held more positive opinions.

As the jaunting car took Holmes to Purley-on-Thames, Holmes could see why writers and artists like Mortimer Menpes would be attracted to the place. Nature's fall finale was in full play along the tree-line roadway. Glimmering lights on the distant horizon prompted the driver to announce: "Up ahead, sir, there's the Menpes place—Mort and Rose Mary."

As they came closer, Holmes saw that the shimmering lights above the tree line were reflections from the glass rooftops of large greenhouses. "A gardener extraordinaire," the driver explained. "Menpes raises strawberries and carnations."

"Does he still do art?"

The driver laughed. "You will see, sir. You'll see."

TWENTY-FIVE

MORTIMER LUDDINGTON MENPES greeted Holmes's unannounced visit with joy. His reputation preceding him, the detective was immediately ushered into the drawing-room and offered tea. He explained that his visit was a matter of urgent business and that he must forgo an invitation to tour the estate as he had to catch the train in Pangbourne in two hours' time. Mempes's initial disappointment was assuaged when Holmes explained he was seeking information about an etching or dry-point portrait. The artist's brows arched as he twirled the end of his mustache with two fingers. "Well, sir, purely as a matter of information, I believe I have created over five hundred etchings. A few are in my studio. Shall we look?"

Menpes's studio was enormous. The ceiling was vaulted, and all the walls but one were devoid of windows. In the center of the ceiling was a square frosted glass box that radiated a soft glow into the room from a skylight above it. It bathed the room in an iridescent light that evenly illuminated the paintings on the walls. "Some of my etchings are over here," Menpes said, strolling to the south wall. Holmes recognized Sir Charles Todd from the Greenwich Observatory, the artist Whistler, and the author Arthur Conan Doyle, but nowhere among the paintings, street scenes, and cityscapes did he see a portrait of the woman he was looking for.

"You're disappointed," Menpes noted.

"Not in your impressive body of work, but in the subject matter. I was looking for the likeness of a particular woman."

Menpes invited Holmes to sit as he pulled up a stool next to an easel. "Please, tell me what you know about this woman while I do a brief sketch—if you don't mind."

Holmes acquiesced, and the artist pinned a sheet of paper to the easel, rummaged in a small wooden box for a piece of charcoal and began sketching. "Describe her to me."

Holmes struggled to describe the mystery woman from memory. Then, he reached into his coat and retrieved Tessa's letters. "Ah, yes. If this report is correct, you completed this etching in 1880."

"The year I married Rosa. I was on a sketching tour of Brittany when I met my wife." He continued working the charcoal on the paper, smudging areas with the tip of his little finger. "Let me try to recall." Menpes scratched his chin, putting a grey blotch on his cheek. "1880 . . . yes, after our wedding, Rosa and I celebrated in Paris and met up with a friend of mine, James Whistler. We returned with him to London and enjoyed his company for some time." The artist's eyes suddenly opened wide, and his finger pointed upward. "Yes, I recall doing a dry-point portrait of a lovely young woman in Whistler's studio. It was a friend of James's. I remember distinctly because her name was Rosa also, Rosa Corder."

The name Rosa Corder struck a note of familiarity with Holmes, but he could not place it until Menpes went on. "Yes, Mr. Holmes, Rosa Corder was an artist friend of Whistler's and the close friend of Charles Milverton."

Holmes's body tensed at the mention of the man's name.

"It seems you know the fellow," Menpes observed.

There is no finer feeling for Holmes than when a multitude of small details coalesce in his brain, as they did the instant Milverton's name was spoken. A more vile and odious human being Holmes had never encountered. Known as 'the king of blackmailers,' he preyed mostly on defenseless women, using their careless letters to extort money. If his ransom was not paid, he sent the letters to newspapers or loving husbands, destroying lives, loves, and family reputations.

Many years ago, Holmes and Watson were forced to hide in Milverton's study where they witnessed one of his victims shoot and kill him—a murder Holmes never felt obliged to report. Rosa Corder was Milverton's lover, and Beatrice Mayer was Rosa Corder's daughter. At last, Holmes understood why he was targeted and why blackmail was to be the instrument of retribution. Tessa was but a pawn in Beatrice Corder's loathsome ploy.

Holmes rose quickly from his chair. "My apologies, Mr. Menpes. I must hurry. Lives are at stake."

Menpes was both surprised and amused in the same instant. "Happy to be of service," he remarked as Holmes dashed away.

The train from London could not come soon enough for Holmes, and mercifully it arrived on time. Watson waved from the carriage window, and Holmes hurried aboard. Upon entering the compartment, Holmes was pleased to see the cherubic face of Augustus Stone. "I purchased a private compartment so we might not be disturbed," Watson reported as Holmes took his seat.

"Thank you for coming, Professor. I assume I need not tell you that there may be danger associated with your participation."

Stone chuckled. "Nonsense, Sherlock. You know how I feel about Miss Tessa. It appears my mystery lady has led you on a merry chase."

"Mystery no more," Holmes countered as he shared what he had learned from Menpes.

"Milverton's daughter!" Watson exclaimed. "Revenge then?"

"Yes. She's after *me*."

"Did you know Milverton had a daughter?"

"No. I knew of her mother. Rosa Corder was one of several women in Milverton's life. To be honest, I never thought about Corder or any of the others." Holmes paused, absorbed in reflection. Watson looked to Stone, who grimaced and shrugged. Then Holmes suddenly lurched to life again. "If there is any consolation in this situation, it is that Tessa is safe for the moment. She is being used to lure me and will be kept alive until I rise to her bait." He removed his pipe and began filling it from a suede pouch. "We have a lure as well—the Celtic treasure. That's why we need you, Stone."

Augustus put on a look of modesty. "Well, sir, the treasure—"

"I want to hear all you have to share, Professor but spare me a moment." Then he turned to Watson. "Were you able to trace the number plate?"

Watson's chest puffed up as he told a rambling story about his trip to the vehicle-licensing agency. He pulled his notebook from his jacket pocket and read: "The vehicle in question is licensed to a Mr. Farhad Turani who resides on Conduit Street in Mayfair."

"Iranian or Persian," Stone observed.

"A well-to-do Iranian or Persian," Holmes added. "The name is not familiar, but there is something notable about the address." Then, nodding to the professor, he said, "Excuse my anxious divergence. I am most eager to hear what you have to share?" Holmes sat back, preparing himself for one of the Professor's orations.

Stone had Tessa's letters in his lap and perused them momentarily before he began. "Tessa's eye for detail is commendable. I'm speaking of her mention of geiriau'r Cymry—the words of the Celtic people. As you may be aware, the Celts had no written language that we know of. Caesar's *Commentarii de Bello Gallico* reported that the Gauls used the Greek alphabet and Italic script on tombs, altars, and the like. However, most communication was oral—which brings us to Beara. The Celtic people's history, beliefs, practices, and laws were passed down via poems, cynghanedd's actually, a system of alliteration and internal rhyme employed to make the stories and teachings memorable. Beara may be a veritable Celtic library. I'm keen to meet this enigmatic woman. Tessa reports that she hails from Anglesey, the mother of Wales. If there is a treasure, I will venture to say; it will be in Anglesey."

"I concur," Holmes replied. "And with that treasure, we will find Tessa, Milverton's daughter, and my manuscript."

"By George," Watson exclaimed, "I had nearly forgotten about your manuscript."

"Quite so," Holmes replied. "When we have Tessa, I am certain we will have my manuscript as well."

"And possibly a treasure," Stone added.

Holmes checked his watch. "We shall be at Ceridwen before nine. We will finalize our plan, get a few precious hours of sleep, and leave for Hellingford at first light."

TWENTY-SIX

"WHY HAVEN'T THEY COME?" Beara asked.

"They're lying in wait for Mr. Holmes . . . setting a trap, and we must stop them."

"So that's why you promised treasure," Beara said. "But they will wait until after Mr. Holmes comes."

Turn time against them, Ganna said.

"Ganna's here," Tessa announced.

"Aye, I sensed her presence," Beara replied.

Turn time against Mayer.

"How?"

Tell her that the treasure can only be found on the day the Lord of Darkness points the way—on Samhain—a day hence.

"Why would she risk losing Holmes?"

Her avarice is great. The woman sees the treasure as her due. Something owed for her misfortune.

"Then you will help us?"

I don't know that I can.

Beara tugged Tessa's sleeve. "What is Ganna saying?"

"In a moment, Beara. Recite the poem about Ganna."

The old woman closed her eyes:

"Ganna fled from those who bled on Mam.

Giving on and living on

the lives of the *Cymry* sisters,

The offerings she will hide,

until her death is bona fide,

and Ewryd can be satisfied."

"Ganna, those words say that you hid the offerings on Anglesey."

Stillness came over the cell. The light in the room seemed to grow dim, and Tessa felt queasy. Beara felt the energy shift as well and grasped Tessa's hand.

Slowly and painfully, Ganna told a story that took place on Anglesey two thousand years ago.

I can still see Suetonius Paulinus and his garrison attacking Ynys Môn. Word of his march reached us the day before his troops arrived, and our armed men and women prepared to greet him. We druids set about protecting the sacred altars, shrines, and offerings gathered for ceremonies. I was among the youngest of the priests. A novitiate and I were sent to hide the offerings in the countryside.

"So then, it is true, Ganna."

"What?" Beara cried.

When Tessa relayed Ganna's story, Beara's face grew ashen. "She was there at the end—when they burned the sacred groves."

Ganna remained quiet, but Tessa could feel her sadness and something else as well. "So Ganna, you carried out your mission to protect the offerings, plying olde arts to sustain your life." There was no reply. "Ganna?"

A loud knock came from the door—Matron Lyn. "Mrs. Mayer will see you." Swinging the door wide, she added, "You had better have good news. She's in a foul mood."

Beara and Tessa sensed a change the moment they arrived at the Director's office. Muscle-bound Angus was standing outside and held his hand up to halt them. They heard Mayer barking inside. ". . . every exit. And don't be obvious. Go!"

The door swung open, and two burly men walked out. Their white uniforms did not hide the brutes they were.

Angus poked his head inside. "Matron Lyn with two women."

Tessa and Beara were ushered in.

"I hope I understood your message correctly," Mrs. Mayer said. "You will take me to the treasure, is that right?"

Beara nodded.

"Good. I have important business, but in a day or two—"

"We must go *tomorrow*," Tessa blurted.

"What's the hurry? It has waited two thousand years."

Tessa approached the desk. "It can only be found on Samhain."

The Director looked dubious.

Beara was quick with an explanation. "The sun shows the way. That's why the horde has never been found." Beara's fabrication surprised Tessa. Her reason seemed plausible.

The Director slammed her fist on the desk and rocked back in her chair. She eyed Tessa and Beara warily. "Very well, but you are both coming along. If this is a wild scheme, your days will end in an obscure grave in Anglesey."

Matron Lyn was waiting when Beara and Tessa left the office. She grabbed hold of them both, preparing to parade them back to their ward, but then halted and moved to one side. The old man from the cottage was marching toward them, his expression dour. Tessa could see the anger in his eyes. Angus held up his hand, but only momentarily before he unlatched and opened the door. The old man jabbed the tip of his cane into the door and pushed it wide until it banged against the wall.

"What the devil is all this about a treasure?" he yelled. "We have Holmes within our grasp, and you still insist upon running off on a fool's errand."

Mayer looked up sheepishly. "And we need to go tomorrow."

The old man raised his cane. It wavered in his hand as if he were preparing to bring it down on Mayer. She stood and held out a hand. "Colonel, please let me explain."

He pointed his cane. "Sit down."

She sat.

"This elegant office seems to have given you the notion that you are running things. You evidently forget who financed your schemes and rebuilt this derelict hospital. I accommodated your little plans because we all shared a larger purpose . . . to obliterate Sherlock Holmes, his reputation, and his existence. I, for one, have not forgotten that he murdered your father. And he was not content just to kill him. He slandered his good name through the insipid scribbling of John Watson. Sherlock Holmes aggrandized himself in fictional make-believe while trampling the life of you and your mother."

"I could *never* forget! Although it was many years ago, I remember how you and Professor Moriarty took care of us."

"We take care of our own, and Holmes has not made that easy. There seems to be no escaping his dangerous obsession to put an end to us. That's why Holmes must be brought down once and for all."

He smiled as a dark fantasy came to mind. "I have bagged heavy game, the most dangerous beasts in the world, in the Himalayas, Madhya Pradesh, and Zambia, but the trophy I most long to see on my wall is the bloody head of Sherlock Holmes!"

The old man was shaking now, struggling to replenish his breath. "Calm down, sir," Mayer said. "The means to disgrace and dishonor Holmes, as well as his bloody manuscript, is in our grasp. We know he is coming for Tessa Wiggins. Now ask yourself, is this where we wish him to come? If he disappears from here, the police will tear the place apart. We have a good thing here—the Forty Elephants, paid residencies, and blackmail."

The old man's pinched face relaxed. "Beatrice, has it occurred to you that Wiggins and the old woman are leading you on a merry chase?" the Colonel asked.

"Of course," Mayer said. "But they know where the treasure is, and with the right inducement, they will show us."

"Then what? Off to Bedlam?"

Mrs. Mayer smiled. "I think not." She shrugged her shoulders. "It will be a tragic tale: Two crazed patients run off on a wild goose chase seeking treasure, and we find them drowned or dead from exposure. It is getting frightfully cold, you know."

"Yes. The weather is taking a turn."

"So, we can have our cake and eat it too, Colonel."

His eyes widened in delight. "I will have to make a call, but I believe your plan has merit. Of course, we must be careful in its execution. We will leave a hint here, a small object there, to lure him and his entourage into the wilderness."

"And retrieve a Celtic treasure to boot," she added.

The old man was chuckling now. "I have underrated you, Beatrice. I adore the idea of using Holmes's own clockwork brain against him." Suddenly, he whacked the tip of his metal cane on the edge of her desk. "But neither of us must lose sight of who is running this show."

Mayer lowered her head deferentially.

The old man steadied himself over his cane and took a breath. "Very well, we will bring him to Anglesey, or wherever the treasure is, but he will not die there, and you know why."

TWENTY-SEVEN

"HOLMES IS A CAUTIOUS FELLOW," the Colonel said. "He will interrogate everyone he can put his hands on. We must prepare, and this is important," he said, pointing a finger at Mrs. Mayer. "Since we seek both the treasure and Holmes, we must cast our line with the precision of a master angler—hanging a little truth on the hook with the bait. He can spot a scheme at a glance, and we want him to. If he believes he is outwitting us, he will fall into our trap."

The Colonel and Mayer strolled about the asylum, spinning a web they hoped would snare Sherlock Holmes. They moved about the buildings and grounds, saying that they were preparing to leave on a weekend holiday. Stopping at Tessa's room, Mitchell helped them pack a suitcase for Tessa with warmer clothing and serviceable shoes for hiking. Then on to the groundskeeper, requesting digging tools, rope, lantern, and two torches. "Cleaning an old churchyard," they told Earl, making certain he saw a pistol in the Colonel's pocket.

Jack observed all this with curiosity. Always on alert for a juicy piece of gossip, as he moved about with his deliveries, he heard Mayer talking to Nurse Halper about the Stag Inn at Cemaes Bay. He passed on this news to the ladies in the laundry who had already embraced the notion that something odd was afoot at Hellingford.

After leaving Nurse Halper, Mayer went to her office to deposit the last bit of bait. From the back of her desk drawer, she removed an artfully hand-drawn map she had made on the cover page from Holmes's manuscript. Then, she lit a match and carefully burnt the edges so that the remaining scrap revealed only two Welsh place names. Placing the bogus map into the fireplace, she sprinkled ashes on top. The stage was set—the curtain would go up tomorrow morning.

Later that day, the Colonel greeted Jack as he entered his cottage. Parking the laundry cart out of sight, Jack furtively made his way to the bedroom window. There he saw the old man packing an overnight bag and putting a Mauser in his coat pocket. This puzzled Jack because another revolver also lay on the bed next to the bag. A knock at the cottage door announced that Buddy, one of the maintenance shed fellows, entered. The Colonel strapped-up the suitcase and pointed. "Take this to the auto." As Buddy picked up the suitcase, the old man handed him the Webley revolver. "This is for you. Pack whatever you need for overnight and be ready to leave at dawn."

Buddy flipped open the cylinder to ensure it was loaded. Snapping it closed, he asked: "Are we expecting trouble?"

"It will help *avoid* trouble."

"As you say, Colonel."

"Get some sleep, Buddy. Until the morning, then."

✻ ✻ ✻ ✻ ✻

Beara often remarked that her snoring kept the devil away, and Tessa believed it—not that she would have been able to sleep. She knew Holmes and Clark would likely come in the morning, and her plan to lure Mayer away bought them only a little time. She and Beara would have to find a way to escape on the way to Anglesey. They would travel by road, and if Angus or someone else came along, it would be difficult to get away. The many unknowns, chief among them being their final destination, made planning impossible. Ganna would have to show the way—but would she be willing to do so? The old Druid had hidden parts of herself. Over and over in her mind, Tessa examined past conversations with Ganna, for if the old priestess was anything, she was scrupulous with her words. She had said that her spirit was tethered to the world for millennia, and she seemed to say that the body Tessa had seen take its last breath in the cavern near

Ceridwen was not hers. Also, there was Beara's poem: 'others of the *Cymry* sisters.' Tessa was a *Cymry* sister. Ganna told her this when they first met. Tessa was chosen because she had tribal blood and was a descendent of Queen Boudicca. As she recalled this, Tessa felt the cold hand of caution tap her shoulder, for Boudicca had sacrificed herself for her people.

✳ ✳ ✳ ✳ ✳

When Holmes, Watson, and Stone arrived that evening, the windows of Ceridwen Manor were aglow. Clark, Cian, and the sisters were waiting for them in the drawing-room. Holmes began by introducing Augustus Stone, adding that they would be setting out for Hellingford at first light. Clark showed Holmes Tessa's hand-drawn map of Hellingford and pointed out the additions he and Cian had made showing the roads to, from, and near the hospital. Margaret Davis announced that the limousine was fueled and offered the help of the staff.

"I will go," Cian declared.

Watson grimaced at that suggestion, but Holmes saw the wisdom in it. "Thank you, Cian. Your help in negotiating Hellingford will be invaluable, and your command of Welsh may be useful."

"As will his muscle," Stone added admiringly.

Holmes stood at the hearth. "Before we finalize our plan to rescue Tessa, it behooves me to offer an apology." Addressing himself to Gwendoline Davis, he said: "Madam, you rightly pointed out that I am the reason Tessa is trapped at Hellingford. But more than that, I am the cause of this entire debacle." He went on to share what he learned during his visit to Mortimer Menpes. "Also, I have reason to believe this mysterious Mrs. Mayer is not acting alone." Holmes paused, bowed his head, and–brought his fingers together under his chin. "I've been naïve. I've fallen into a trap set by a woman who believes I wronged her. To her way of thinking, she was.

However, she is not in command of all the facts regarding her father's death. Nonetheless, a trap set for *me* has snared Tessa."

Gwendoline, touched by his sincerity, rose from her chair and approached him. "Sir, we accept your apology. We think no less of you as a detective and a man. You are the epitome of humility and honor." She placed her hand on his shoulder, "Tessa is fortunate to have you as a friend."

He nodded. "Thank you, all of you. Now let us review the plan and get some sleep."

When the briefing was complete, Holmes asked Watson to stay behind and share a brandy with him. The two old friends sat silently before the hearth. Colleagues for over thirty years they had faced death countless times. What always made it bearable was that they faced it together.

Ellis was securing the manor for the night and came into the drawing-room with a small tray. He approached Holmes. "Sir, a telegram came for you earlier this evening, but I did not wish to interrupt your meeting,"

Upon taking it, Holmes noticed it came from his housekeeper Mrs. Thornton. It was not like her to contact him while he was away, but he understood why she had upon reading it.

S. HOLMES –

R. FERGUSON CAME TO COTTAGE TWICE. VEXED, ANGRY, REGARDING CASE IN 1896. IS BEING THREATENED. CONTACT HIM AT MINCING LANE IMMEDIATELY.

THORTON

Watson saw the despair in Holmes's eyes when he looked up. "More news?" Watson inquired as Holmes laid the telegram aside.

"The undoing of my life and legacy has begun."

TWENTY-EIGHT

SAMHAIN WAS A DAY AWAY. Tessa recalled last year's celebration when she whirled around the bonfire with the Sisters of Scáthach—Ganna chanting: *"Sireadh Thall"*—seek beyond. That night Maeve was wounded trying to save the sisters, and Holmes was nearly crippled for life in his attempt to save her. In this recollection, Tessa felt the full power of sacrifice as a measure of love.

"Where are your thoughts, Tessa?" Beara asked.

"Samhain."

"Calan gaeaf," Beara repeated.

"That's what Ganna called it."

"Aye, a reminder that we all walk between light and dark. You should know that I did not make up a complete lie for Mayer. Many olde tombs are aligned with the rising of the sun on *Calan gaeaf* because it is the time when the veil between this world and the next is thinnest—making it easier for the departed to cross over."

"And for those in the otherworld to come here," Tessa added.

"You've learned much from Ganna."

"But I am not Ganna," Tessa stated. "I don't know what she knows."

"Don't worry; she will come," Beara said.

I am here, Ganna announced.

"Ganna is here, Beara." Once again, Tessa found it strange she did not feel Ganna's presence before hearing her voice, possibly because Ganna had been gone for longer and longer periods.

"If you can hear me Ganna," Beara said, "where is it we should lead the others?"

171

The answer is in the words of our people that you know well.

When Tessa relayed Ganna's answer, Beara calmed herself, closed her eyes, and recited:

"Ganna fled from those who bled on Mam.

Giving on and living on the lives of the *Cymry* sisters.

The offerings she will hide,

until her death is bona fide,

and Ewryd can be satisfied."

Beara put her finger to her chin. "*Mam* is Welsh for mother—and *Ynys Môn* is the mother of Wales," Beara noted.

Tessa seized on the last lines: "Until her death is bona fide and Ewryd can be satisfied." Her breath caught. "Are we going to your true grave?"

And where might that be?

"Ewryd can be satisfied," Tessa repeated.

Beara chuckled. "Be satisfied . . . *bodlon.* Bodlon means 'satisfied,' and Ewryd is a celebrated Welsh saint. The place we seek is a cunning combination of words that craft the name of a town in Anglesey—Bodewryd."

Tessa laughed. "That is why no one found the treasure. It's in Bodewryd."

Nearby, Ganna confirmed. *But they shall never have it.*

* * * * *

Holmes enjoyed his pipe as he stood before the fireplace. Only a few embers glowed among the ashes. The room had grown cool, mirroring an uneasy awareness that had been mounting within him. With the exception of a few boring, dry spells, he had moved from one client to another his entire career—picking his cases, choosing only those that tantalized or challenged him. He was successful if one counts success as mysteries solved. Only three cases were never brought to a fruitful conclusion. However, recent events begged him to reconsider the meaning of success. For within the tangled web of life, every intention, action, and reaction pull on threads that radiate in a multitude of directions. Every touch, thought, step, breath, smile, tear, word, and every moment of delight or fear, ripples out to countless others as it had for Beatrice Mayer and her mother, Rosa Corder. Someone had put an end to Milverton, but that was not the end of the story. Such thoughts weighed on the detective's mind.

Elis entered, holding a cup and saucer. "I thought you might do with some coffee, sir," he said, setting it on the table next to Holmes. "Thank you, Elis."

The butler remained there for a moment and then spoke again. "Sir, it may not be my place, but I wish to personally thank you for coming to the aid of Miss Wiggins. I have grown quite fond of the young lady. All of us at Ceridwen have, and we pray you will bring her back safely."

Holmes nodded. "I will do whatever is necessary to see that she returns home, Ellis."

He bowed slightly. "Dress warmly, sir. As we like to say in these parts, it is getting too cold for the angels to fly. I fear a storm is brewing."

"Thank you, Elis."

The butler moved on as Watson entered with his nose twitching to the bittersweet smell of hot coffee. "Here you are, Holmes." As Elis passed, he turned to the butler. "Might I have a cup as well, Ellis?"

Watson took the chair opposite his friend. "Have you slept at all, Holmes?"

"What I could grab in this chair."

"I understand that Thornton's telegram is unsettling, but we can quickly put a stop to all this when we have Mayer and the manuscript in hand."

"I'm certain that Mayer or Corder, as I am inclined to call her, is not acting alone. I've been thinking about the number plate you tracked down."

"Farhad Turani's auto? Should I have recalled that name, Holmes?"

"Not the name, Watson, the address—Conduit Street. Do you recall anyone we knew who once lived on Conduit Street?"

Watson scratched his chin. "No one comes to mind."

"Yes, well, I don't like to read too much into coincidences, but I've learned not to discount them either. Everything that has transpired since the theft of my manuscript seems to be dragging me back into a past I'd as soon disremember. An old adversary had a residence on Conduit."

"Who?"

Holmes shook his head. "As I say, I must not read too much into coincidences."

The look in Holmes's eyes caused Watson to fear that his friend was slipping into one of his dark moods.

Ellis entered with a cup for Watson and offered another to Holmes. "Gwenda is preparing a hearty breakfast, gentlemen."

Indeed, the hope-giving smells of breakfast on the stove awakened the others, and Clark and Cian could be heard coming down the stairs.

There was little talk as people made their breakfast plates and took a chair around the dining table. Holmes was the last to enter. He served himself a triangle of dry toast and sat down at the head of the table.

Holmes reviewed the plan they had made the evening before and then turned to Cian. "Regarding the old man Tessa mentioned in her last letter, what can you tell us about him?"

The burly man's face pinched up. "I kept to the gatehouse, sir. The only time I sees the old gent is when he's huntin'."

"What does he hunt, Cian?"

"Bout anythin', sir. But he is partial to bigger game. A crack shot he is. I once helped to carry out a great stag he bagged. Who'd a thought it of the old fellow . . . one shot straight to the heart."

TWENTY-NINE

THE WAILING WIND BEFITTED TESSA'S MOOD. She worried and wondered why it was that she was no longer able to sense Ganna's presence. She had reached out to Ganna during the night, but the old Druid did not come. Now she feared the priestess might not help them. She had no such doubts about Clark and Holmes, who she knew were heading into a trap. She prayed that Holmes's vigilant nature would be enough to protect them. A part of her wanted Holmes to follow; another part hoped he wouldn't. Regardless, the approaching tempest could make it impossible for Holmes to track her. Yesterday she noticed the seagulls flying low and gathering on the rooftops. A storm was brewing at sea and would soon be whipping the coastline. Even if she had scraps of paper or something else to mark their way, the gale would obscure any signs she may try to leave.

Matron Lyn opened the cell door and tossed in two raggedy men's coats. "They'll be coming for you soon."

Tessa donned the coat and held her out arms to show Lyn that the coat sleeves hung below her fingertips. "That'll be the least of your worries, missy," the matron told her. Beara buttoned her sweater, pulled on the coat, and gathered up her knitting bag without a word or whimper. She not only accepted her fate but seemed to embrace it. It wasn't resignation but an uncommon trust.

Ten minutes later, Angus and Buddy marched them out of the ward and down the path toward the maintenance shed. Jack watched from the door of the laundry room as they passed. Looking hard at Jack, Tessa thought she saw remorse in his eyes.

As they approached the shed, Angus turned back for the luggage while Buddy continued on with the two women. The leaden sky smothered the dawn, and dark clouds formed on the western horizon. As Tessa had anticipated, they were being taken to the grey Crossley parked just outside the shed's open rear door. "I've never traveled in such a grand automobile," Beara exclaimed when she saw it. *Most folks in Wales would say the same*, Tessa thought. The automobile would be noticed but—*how might it be remembered?*

As Buddy prodded them through the doorway, Tessa twisted from his grasp and pushed him backward with both hands. He went down on his back. Running to a workbench, Tessa's hands swept the surface, looking for something hard. Her fingers seized on a spanner just as Buddy got to his feet. She held the heavy wrench high over her shoulder, halting Buddy mid-stride. "Now, missy, you're gonna get yourself in a heap of trouble." She swiped the hefty wrench back and forth, causing him to step back. As she dashed for the outer door, Buddy's arm wrapped around her waist and twisted her onto the hood of the auto. He reached for the wrench but wasn't quick enough. Tessa brought it down hard on a headlamp. "Ah, lady!" the brute cried as he heard glass break. Wrestling her to the ground, he took the wrench from her grip, stood, and pointed it at her. "Any more of that, and you'll have a taste of this," he warned.

"Very well," Tessa huffed as she came to her feet. Buddy glanced at the smashed headlamp shaking his head and stuck the spanner in his back pocket.

The women were inside the auto by the time Angus arrived with two bags. He grinned when he noticed Buddy's dusty suit and tousled hair. "Too much for ya?" he chuckled. Buddy grunted.

Five minutes went by before the Colonel and Mrs. Mayer arrived. The Colonel handed a briefcase to Angus. "Put this in the boot." As he walked on, he reached into his coat pocket, removed the Mauser, and slammed his palm against the clip to ensure it was in place. Tessa's fears rose when she saw this.

Mrs. Mayer got into the back seat with Beara and Tessa. The Colonel sat in front next to Buddy, who was waiting in the driver's seat. When the motor started, the Colonel beckoned Angus to his window. "If Brady calls, tell him we are on our way. Remember, no trouble when Holmes arrives. Don't help. Don't hinder." Angus offered a perfunctory salute: "Right ya are, gov'nor." The Colonel then turned to the back seat. "Buddy can find his way to Cemaes; then you will lead the way from there." He pointed the pistol at Tessa, his face sinister and dark. "Miss Wiggins, I know you are a loyal disciple of Sherlock Holmes but trust me, you do not have his talents. I suggest you do what you're told if you want to live."

"Who *are* you?" Tessa demanded.

"I am the man who missed his mark twice. But trust me, young lady," he said, "I will not miss again."

Tessa did not know all of Holmes's history, but it was clear the Colonel was a long-time adversary. She wondered if Holmes had written about the old man in his manuscript.

Diffused light flashed and pulsed on the horizon—lightning at sea. The answering thunder faintly growled in the distance. A great storm was building.

Within the hour, they were approaching the narrow strait that separates Anglesey from the mainland.

"The Menai Bridge," the old man said. "Do you know it, Buddy?"

"Aye, sir."

Suddenly, Tessa was shaken by a vision . . . a memory— Ganna's memory: Roman invaders fording this strait. Soldiers huddled on barges, clanging on shields with their swords as they crossed the white-capped waters. Mounted centurions desperately clinging to saddles as they fought the twisting tides, pushing through the cold blue currents toward a dense array of warriors. And there, among the fighters on the opposite shore, were the druids in their green robes, dashing among the warriors waving firebrands and imploring the heavens to rain lightning down upon their enemies.

"Damn," Buddy mumbled as the first raindrops pelted the windshield. The wind smeared the droplets sideways across the glass. Then, just as they were across the bridge and on the isle, it was as if Zeus himself opened a flood-gate. Rain began pouring in a torrent, and what had been a difficult road was quickly becoming a punishing one.

The auto swayed as the mud on the road thickened. Tension seized the travelers. The Colonel pulled his collar up and braced himself. Mayer stiffened and clutched the door handle, but Beara nary dropped stitch as the auto made its way through an alphabet of towns: Amlwch, Llanallgo, Pentraeth—finally stopping for gas at Llanbadrig. When the attendant reported the broken headlamp, the Colonel turned a dreary eye on Buddy, who could but grimace. "You're welcome to stay and wait out the storm," the attendant offered. Buddy shook his head and rolled up the window.

As the storm strengthened, more lightning splintered the horizon. With each flash, the travelers waited for the thunder's confirmation. The temperature was dropping. Cold water sprayed from cervices and seams in the auto's canvas top, chilling one and all, but none would gratify the others with a word or shiver. Glancing at Beara, Tessa wished she had the old woman's serenity. Beara seemed to find the still-point in the eye of any storm—including this one. Tessa tugged on Beara's sleeve. "I imagine you never thought you're be leaving Hellingford like this," she whispered.

Beara paused as her needles dropped into her lap and her head angled to one side. "I thought I'd be going out in a coffin having died in a putrefying place with cold people. So, if I am to go now, it will be a blessing to die in the land of my people—my home." She gripped Tessa's hand. "where love rests."

Buddy suddenly let out a whoop of delight when he saw the road sign announcing their destination was seven miles away. "Cemaes ahead, sir."

The Colonel straightened in his seat and wiped the moisture from the barrel of his pistol with the lining of his coat. "Buddy, stop at the first place of business you encounter and ask directions to The Stag Inn."

"I'm certain I can find—"

"That's not the point. Ask directions at your first opportunity and drive on to The Stag."

"Do we have time to eat, sir?"

"It will have to be sandwiches. You must watch our precious cargo. I will attend to business inside."

When they arrived at The Stag, the old man pulled the collar of his coat up around his ears, tugged his hat tighter over his head, and took his cane in hand. As he opened the door to leave, a gust of rain blew into the car.

Upon entering the inn, the Colonel shook the water from his hat, stomped his feet, and hobbled into the barroom. There was but one patron at the bar, staring into an empty glass.

"What brings you out in this nastiness?" the barkeep asked.

The Colonel wiped the water from his brow with a finger. "I'm writing a history of smuggling and—"

"Aye," the bartender cackled. "and you've come to the right place, ya have. Cemaes was at the heart of it fifty year ago—and fifty afore that."

"So, I understand," the Colonel answered. "I had heard that the cave of the blue horse was where the longboats waited for the ships carrying contraband. I wondered if you would be kind enough to point the way?" The proprietor looked dubious as he glanced out a window. "I have a sturdy vehicle outside," the Colonel added.

The lone customer, who had been listening to the interchange, remarked: "I'll take ya, sir, for the paltry price of a pint." Extending his hand, he added: "Brady's the name, sir."

Without hesitation, the Colonel ordered a pint for the patron and five ploughman's sandwiches. When the barkeep went to the kitchen, Brady locked eyes with the Colonel.

"Admirable, Brady. You're quite an actor."

"What's the plan, sir?"

"You will leave with us. After an appropriate amount of time, you'll return here, wetter than you are now, and wait for our friends. Of course, you will offer your help to them as well." He laughed and poked a boney finger into Brady's vest. "And there'll be more than a pint in it for you when we get Holmes."

THIRTY

CERIDWEN'S CHAUFFEUR AND GARDENER grew up on the docks, and he still possessed the manner and vibrato of a docker, so Holmes knew that Clark Button was the obvious choice to storm Hellingford's front door if one wished to create a distraction—and that was the plan. But more than that, Clark's affection for Tessa would make him unstoppable. He was to burst into the front office demanding to see Tessa Wiggins. Watson would follow and, avoiding the ruckus, go directly to Tessa's Ward. As this was happening, Cian would skirt the outer perimeter of Hellingford toward the garden shed to thwart an attempted abduction. Using these diversions, Holmes hoped he would have unimpeded access to other areas of the hospital. Stone would remain in the auto as a guard.

As the Daimler rolled to a stop at the front gate, Holmes reviewed everyone's assignment. "We may catch Mayer and the others by surprise, but we will focus solely on Tessa's rescue—that is our priority. Grant no quarter, and question everyone you encounter in your search. Gather what information you can. Remember, Tessa's life hangs in the balance." Clark Button's chest tightened at those words. Cian patted Clark's shoulder, jumped out of the vehicle, and waved to the others as the auto drove through the gate.

The assault worked flawlessly. As the Daimler lurched to a halt at the front stairs, Clark marched into Hellingford and pounded on Mayer's office door bellowing at the top of his lungs. Watson followed, donning a white jacket and placing a stethoscope about his neck. With some well-chosen words, he expected easy passage onto Tessa's ward.

Initially, Matron Mitchell stood like walls of Jericho when Watson knocked at the door to the ward. But when the doctor invoked Dr. Mayer's name, Mitchell's 'walls' tumbled. Once her defenses were breached, the Matron became a veritable fount of information. She showed him to Tessa's room and told him about the suitcase she had prepared—making a note of the stout shoes she was asked to pack. "I was led to believe that Miss Wiggins would be in the countryside," she told Watson.

Cian found no resistance upon entering the garden shed because he was a familiar face. Indeed, few had been aware that he had left his post at the gate. After confirming that the Crossley was absent, he questioned Owen Davies, the groundskeeper, who was putting away tools. "A *ffestiniog* rain will soon be upon us," Owen said. "*Ydw*," Cian agreed. The gardener had much to say about the weather. When he paused, Cian asked about the absent Crossley. It was Owen's opinion that there was "odd goings-on that morning," as he described the entourage that assembled and left a little more than an hour ago. He told Cian that he had provided them with rope, shovel, pick, and several torches. He guffawed: "They sez they were cleaning a churchyard—and in this weather!" He squinted one eye and lowered his voice. "More likely they're puttin' someone *in* the churchyard," reporting that the old Colonel had a pistol with him.

After waiting several minutes, Holmes walked through the front entrance around the gaggle of persons who had assembled to confront Clark and slipped unnoticed into Mayer's office. His eyes quickly surveyed the room, pausing only for a moment to observe the etching above Mayer's desk. Searching the desk drawers yielded nothing. As he turned to leave, he noticed smoldering embers in the fireplace. Taking a poker, he prodded a scrap of chard paper onto the floor. It was a page from his manuscript with a drawing on the back. He smiled as he examined it.

As planned, Watson and Cian made their way back to Mayer's office near the entrance just as Holmes was ducking outside to help Clark, who was now fending off an irate Nurse Halper and a ham-fisted Angus. Cian, a man of action, quickly had Angus by the collar. Watson was the last to rendezvous. With a shake of the head, he offered a disappointing report to Holmes.

The situation was tottering on the edge of violence when Holmes shouted: "Stop this! I am Sherlock Holmes. The authorities will be here soon. I suggest you share all the information you have about the whereabouts of Tessa Wiggins."

This pronouncement, together with the reputation of Sherlock Holmes, ended the *melee*. However, stories and opinions from the staff members able to help differed greatly. When it became clear that Tessa and her abductors had fled, Holmes put an end to the interrogations.

Watson shook his head. "We don't have any good idea where they are headed, Holmes."

"To the contrary," he answered, dangling the scrap of chard paper from his fingertips.

"What is it, Holmes?"

"A dainty piece of cheese," he said, handing it to Watson. "Please locate the two towns on this would-be map and wait for me in the auto—all of you. I'll be out soon. There is one more place I must inspect." The band returned to the Daimler, and Holmes hurried on to the cottage.

Making quick work of the feeble lock, he entered. There were but three rooms, bedroom, sitting room, and office. He went immediately to a shelf of books behind the desk and ran a finger along the spines. Two volumes piqued his interest, *Three Months in the Jungle*, and next to it a leather-bound edition of *The Dynamics of An Asteroid*.

Rifling through the drawers of the large mahogany desk yielded nothing of interest. Turning to leave, Holmes's eye caught sight of the heads of two beasts mounted over the desk—not the common deer or boar, but those of a Bengal tiger and Cape buffalo. *The two most dangerous animals in the bush*, Holmes noted. There was a space left between the two trophies as if it were being saved for another head. He grinned. What had been vague suspicion suddenly blossomed into an astounding certainty—Colonel Sebastian Moran was alive and well.

Approaching eighty, Moran might appear to be a minor threat, but Holmes knew better. The Colonel had made two attempts on his life—one at Reichenbach and the other at Baker Street. No doubt Moran had taken a page from his biographical journal that warned: "Knowing the habits of your prey is no guarantee of success, but it will put you well on the track to bagging your trophy." This insight troubled Holmes, for he knew that his actions, thus far, had been predictable.

Checking his watch, he hurried off to meet the others but no sooner had he opened the cottage door than he found his exit blocked by a wicker pushcart. Holmes eyed the red badge around the neck of the fellow standing behind the cart. Their eyes met for only a moment before Holmes stepped aside. As the fellow's stare became unwavering and intense, it became apparent he would not move. Holmes started to walk around the cart when the man spoke: "You don't remember me, do you?"

"Should I?" Holmes answered.

"I suppose not. Our paths crossed when I was a lad."

Holmes's eyes flashed upward for a moment before they narrowed again on the young man. "I have no recollection, and I must be on my way."

Holmes made but one step before the man spoke again: "I wonder if you will as conveniently forget Tessa."

Holmes swiveled. "Where is she?"

Jack stood unmoving. "It would be a shame if Tessa had to pay for your sins."

Holmes startled at this but before he could reply, the stranger added: "She and an old woman are on their way to Anglesey. The

Colonel and Mayer wait for you and your people at The Stag Inn at Cemaes Bay."

"And 'they' are?"

"The Colonel, Mrs. Mayer, and a scoundrel from the Colonel's tribe. They have pistols."

Holmes stepped back and bowed his head. "Thank you—"

"Jack," the man answered. "Jack Ferguson." He turned to his cart and muttered: "Don't thank me. I'm not doing this for you."

Holmes hurried back to the entrance and down the stairs.

"Whither are we bound, Captain?" Stone asked as Holmes took his place in the front seat next to Clark.

"To Cemaes Bay with haste," Holmes told Clark. Turning to Watson, "I take it that the other towns on that charred scrap of paper is also in Anglesey."

"Yes, Cemaes Bay and Llanbadrig," Clark said. "Llanbadrig is on the way to Cemaes."

Stone's eyes grew wide. "So, they're going after the treasure?"

"Yes, and after me as well," the detective said. "Colonel Sebastian Moran appears to be the puppet master."

"He's alive!" Watson gasped. "How did he escape the hangman's noose? Never mind, we will soon have him in our grasp. That scrap of a map was an excellent find, Holmes."

"Not a find," Holmes retorted. "Moran wants me to know he has the manuscript and that Tessa is on her way to Cemaes Bay by way of Llanbadrig."

"*Wants* you to know?" Watson exclaimed.

"Moran's gigantic ego demands that I know it is him putting it over on me."

"Then this pursuit is a trap?" Watson rejoined.

"I was told as much by one of the patients—Jack Ferguson, an old case you might recall Watson."

"Jack Ferguson," Watson repeated. "I don't recollect—"

"The Sussex vampire. How could you forget? It was I who suggested to Jack's father that he be sent off to sea."

"That was better than the alternative," Watson pronounced.

"Obviously not, Watson. Look what poor Jack has come to."

As they went on, Holmes did not join in the banter generated by Watson and Stone in the back seat. He pitied Cian, a man of few words, who was trapped between the two loquacious curmudgeons.

The rain's pattering suddenly became a drumbeat, and speculation about Tessa and the treasure shifted to nervous thoughts about the storm and the road ahead. The caterwauling wind seemed determined to outrun the auto, and ditches were fast turning into swirling brown streams. Clark was hunched over the steering wheel, his eyes locked on the road—knuckles white.

A stop at the gas station in Llanbadrig told them they were on the right trail. "Good luck, that," Watson remarked.

"My dear Watson, they wanted us to stop at Llanbadrig, and so we obliged. However, we've now confirmed what Jack Ferguson told me and that an old woman travels with Tessa, no doubt the one called Beara. He also mentioned their driver is a full-bodied fellow."

Minutes later, Clark nudged Holmes, who seemed to be in a daze, announcing that Cemaes Bay was just ahead. Holmes cleared his throat and turned to Watson and Stone. "I believe a little preparation is in order, given we are headed into a trap."

THIRTY-ONE

THE PROPRIETOR WAS DUMBFOUNDED. "Sherlock Holmes from *The Strand*?"

Holmes grimaced.

"Of all days," he exclaimed, "when the storm has kept even the thirstiest man away." Then he turned to the lone gentleman at the bar. "What do ya think, Brady? Mr. Sherlock Holmes here at The Stag!"

Brady touched a finger to his cap and summoned his most congenial nature to the fore. "Pleased to make your acquaintance, Mr. Holmes. What brings you to Cemaes?"

The barkeep nodded as Holmes described the automobile and persons he was seeking. "Pleased to say I can help ya there, sir. Less than an hour ago, Brady here was kind enough to show those folks to the cave they were seeking. The elderly gent was a writer who—"

"An hour—is that so?" Holmes rejoined, turning to the man at the bar.

Brady cringed. "Thing is, sir, I was asked not to say where I took them. I don't know as I can betray a confidence, 'specially when the gentleman was so generous."

Holmes put a £5 note on the bar. "Well, the cat is out of the bag. Where is this cave?"

Brady snatched the money. "A small jaunt, but we best not go on foot."

"And ya best go quickly afore the tides come in," the innkeeper added.

The roiling charcoal sky signaled the storm was getting worse. Holmes returned to the auto to make a report and wait for Brady to come alongside.

"Can the fellow be trusted?" Clark asked.

"The barkeep knows him, so he hails from these parts. Of course, we will exercise caution when we get to the cave."

"Cave is it?" Stone chimed in.

"*Ogof y ceffyl glas*," Cian said. "The cave of the blue horse, it is."

"Ah!" Stone replied. "So named after a young man who tumbled over the cliffs on his dapple-grey horse. What was it, Cian, two hundred years ago? The cave is said to be haunted."

"That tale was likely spread to protect smugglers from busybodies and beachcombers," Holmes noted.

A Model T pulled up next to the limousine. Brady pointed and moved ahead. Clark followed, halting for a moment when their guide turned onto a narrow lane going down to the beach. "We'll get below well enough," Clark said. "Not certain about up."

When they reached the beach, the Model T stopped. Brady got out and walked to Holmes's window. "Ya, I can see their auto up ahead. We best go on foot from 'ere, gov'nor."

"Give us a moment," Holmes told him. Brady nodded, pulled his cap over his ears, and walked in the direction of the cave.

Holmes turned to the back seat. "I am certain Moran and Mayer know we are following, so we have lost the element of surprise. Our best defense is to separate. Watson, you Cian and Stone will lay back."

"Nonsense," Watson said. "I'm going with you."

"Not this time. We have but two pistols, and yours will be needed if Clark and I fail to get the upper hand. If shots are fired, go into the rocks above, wait, and watch." Then he turned to Clark. "I will lead. Stay back a judicious distance and run at the first sign of trouble."

"I'm ready," Clark said.

Brady waved when the two men stepped out of the Daimler, and the three of them moved down the stony beach toward the cave. As they passed the Crossley, Holmes glanced inside, turned back toward Clark, and shook his head in the negative.

As they got closer to the cave, Holmes could see a faint light tracing the edges of the entrance. Brady pointed. "There inside, sir," he said.

Holmes pulled the pistol from his pocket and cocked it. Brady stepped backward behind Holmes and poked a pistol into the detective's back. "I'll take that," he said, reaching around for Holmes's weapon. "Now, signal your friend to come forward."

When Holmes remained motionless, Brady waved Clark forward. Squinting into the rain, Clark cautiously approached. When he saw Brady's pistol, he spun and ran—until a shot rang out.

Moran was giddy as he hobbled to and fro before his catch, Mauser in hand. Mayer stood just out of the rain at the cave's entrance holding a lantern, and Buddy shined his torch on the faces of their captives lined against the cave wall—Tessa, Beara, Stone, Watson, Clark, and Sherlock Holmes. Moran came nose to nose with the detective whose arms were bound with a rope. "To be honest, Holmes, I had some doubts this scheme would work."

"It hasn't," Holmes answered. "One got away."

Moran laughed, "That lumbering oaf. We will be long gone before he can do any harm."

Holmes glanced around until his eyes settled on Tessa, offering a reassuring nod. "If I were you, I'd give the credit to Brady here, " He smiled. "Any chance of getting my fiver back?"

The Colonel laughed and turned to his grinning accomplice. "Not to take anything from Brady's acting talent, but putting a local fellow at the bar was my idea. However, I do feel the need to share the credit with Miss Tessa. She is the reason you and your associates find yourself here." He cocked his head in an artificially quizzical manner. "Could it be that your great brain was muddled with emotion? That's one for the books, but unfortunately, you will make no further entries in your memoir." He leaned closer to Holmes. "I was rather disappointed that I only received one mention in your *magnum opus*."

"I suggest we have our fun later," Brady said. "We should be on our way if we want to beat the incoming tide."

Moran turned to those lined up against the wall of the cave. "Brady is right. We must be going." Glancing over his shoulder: "Holmes, you, Tessa, and the old woman will be joining me." He waved his pistol at Clark, Stone, and Watson. "The rest of you will remain here to greet the tide. Brady will be in the rocks above to see that you don't swim too far—should you choose to try. Bullets or the tide—decisions, decisions," Moran said with a chuckle.

The Colonel stepped behind Holmes, checked the bonds on his hands, and poked his pistol hard against Holmes's spine. "Move along."

Buddy followed, prodding Tessa and Beara along. Mayer walked behind.

The tide was already creeping in as they left, and the wind-blown spray from the waves stung their faces as they moved toward the Crossley.

Tessa's eyes moved along the rocks above the beach, hoping to catch a glimpse of Cian, but the storm was conspiring with Moran and Mayer, the downpour and wind making it impossible to see.

Mayer threw her lantern aside and ducked into the auto, followed by Tessa and Beara.

"Keep your pistol handy, Buddy," Moran ordered as he pushed Holmes into the front seat and climbed in next to him. "If the two ladies exhibit any nonsense, shoot them." Moran turned back toward them. "Miss Wiggins, you and your friend will show the way now."

Tessa leaned closer to Moran. "In this storm, I am not—"

Moran pointed the pistol at Holmes's head. "Miss Wiggins, if you and this old hag cannot show the way to the treasure, you are not much use to me. *All* of your lives will end on this stormy beach. Now, where do we go from here?"

Tessa had not sensed Ganna's presence since yesterday, and she feared that the old Druid was committed to keeping the offerings hidden, even if it cost their lives.

"Yes, well . . ." Tessa said, turning to Beara. "Recite the *cynghanedd* again."

"The whole thing," Mayer added.

Beara hesitated. Tessa nodded in reassurance. Beara's eyes closed, and she spoke in a monotone:

"Ganna fled from those who bled on Mam.

Giving on and living on

the lives of the *Cymry* sisters.

The offerings she will hide,

until her death is bona fide,

and Ewryd can be satisfied."

Tessa put her hand on Beara's. "Be satisfied . . . Bodewryd, right?"

Beara offered only a worried look.

"Bodewryd," Tessa said. "That's the way."

"That turnoff is just before Cemaes," Buddy said.

"Of course," Mayer said. "I should have guessed. I can't believe it's finally happening. Justice has finally seen fit to restore my fortune."

"Onward to Bodewryd," Moran said. Then to Holmes: "I can hear that clockwork mind of yours even in this maelstrom: 'Where will be my best opportunity?' That's what you are thinking, isn't it?"

"You will make a mistake," Holmes replied.

"Ah, psychological combat." Moran laughed as the auto's tires spun, flinging stones that pelted the fenders. The Crossley fishtailed as Buddy maneuvered the auto onto the lane that was fast becoming a bog.

As they ascended from the beach, the wind sang a howling song, and Tessa looked back to see the tidewaters surging into the cave.

THIRTY-TWO

"BLOODY HELL," Buddy bellowed when the Crossley skidded sideways into a ditch. Mayer's head hit the window, and she slumped forward in a daze. Beara and Tessa knocked heads, but the impact only served to push Moran's pistol deeper into Holmes's ribs. "Get those notions out of your head," he warned, checking the rope binding the detective's hands.

The tires whizzed, and the rear end swayed, but the Crossley didn't budge. Buddy threw open his door and stepped out. "Mingin' mud," he growled as his boot sank ankle-deep into the muck. He made his way to the rear end of the auto. After a number of expletives, he came back to report. "Good and proper stuck, Colonel. Gonna need a push."

Holmes lurched to attention. "Not you," Moran said. "The two ladies will do."

Buddy opened the rear door, and pulling his pistol from his belt, motioned for Tessa and Beara to exit. They moved to the back of the auto, and Buddy showed them where to push on the boot when the tires spun. "Bullets travel faster than you can run." He reminded them.

As the driver climbed into his seat, Beara pointed to Tessa and then to a field on their left. Tessa shook her head 'no.' Beara nodded 'yes'.

Suddenly the tires spun, and Ganna's voice burst in Tessa's head: *Run!*

Tessa swallowed hard and darted into the heath. The old woman leaned on the boot, pretending to push. The tires whirred, and the muddy water-drenched Beara from the waist down before they finally stopped. "We need Holmes too," the driver said, stepping outside.

Shots rang out. "It's Wiggins!" he yelled. He could barely make out Tessa slogging through the bog twenty yards off.

Moran shouted. "What's happened?"

Buddy grabbed Beara by her sweater, pulled her around to the back door, and pushed her inside. Moran's head swiveled.

Holmes chuckled. "Looks as though Miss Wiggins got the best of you."

Moran's mouth twisted in a snarl as he turned to Beara. "Where's she going?" Beara shrugged. Then he motioned to Buddy: "Help me with Holmes and grab the torches. We can't let her get away."

Tessa pushed through the deer grass and juniper, pausing only a moment to catch her breath. Her nose picked up the beguiling scent of sea lavender, and her heartbeat slowed. The rain slackened and a phantom fog rose up from the ground. It climbed ever higher, swallowing up distant objects.

Breathe it in, Ganna told her. *You are on the land of our people.*

"I was afraid you wouldn't come. I must go back for—"

They are safe. Hurry on.

Tessa pushed forward at a brisk pace. As she did, the fog-filled her lungs—calming and cleansing her. It felt as if she were moving through an enchanted snowfall.

"Beara and Holmes are—"

Safe. Avarice and hatred will bring them to us, but you must hurry. There is something we must do before they find you.

Ganna guided Tessa, directing her further and further from the road. The gorse tore at Tessa's coat and scratched her ankles as she pushed deeper toward the remote sea cliffs. Shrouded in hoary fog, Tessa moved cautiously with her hands outstretched before her. "Where are we going?"

Not much farther.

Tessa heard something and stopped. Voices. Moran and the others.

Hurry, Ganna urged.

Tessa pressed on blindly, moving as Ganna instructed. Then her chest suddenly tightened. She was short of breath, weak. "What's happening, Ganna?"

We're here, Ganna said. *The abode of Manawydan, the rightful king of Britain. His burial chamber lies ahead. It is sacred ground— the altar of The Mother.*

"Is that where the treasure is?"

Aye. On your left, follow the hedgerow down.

The ground sloped lower into a deep swale. Mud was ankle-deep and getting thicker, sucking Tessa in. Each foot had to be pried from the greedy sludge before she could move on. She was already exhausted.

Stopping again, she turned to listen. No sounds, but she could see a wavering glow behind her. *Torches*, she reckoned. The fog began disappearing like ghostly wisps of a dream, but it still clutched at the hem of her dress.

Hurry, Ganna urged. *The cromlech is just ahead.*

Within a few yards, Tessa saw a huge flat rock resting in a pool of water. Smaller stones poked through the water's surface along the edge of the pond. Moving toward the massive stone, Tessa found herself knee-deep in the middle of a stream that flowed rapidly downhill.

The entrance has fallen in, Ganna said. *There is another way— they're connected. Follow the water now.*

Less than twelve yards ahead, a massive stone slab the size of an automobile sat atop smaller stones that surrounded and encapsulated it. Tessa could see an opening at the end nearest her. The rushing water from the gully flowed into the gap between the stones and disappeared.

There! Ganna confirmed. *Stay in the water.*

The rain continued, but the miasma of fog was fading fast and was now only inches above the ground. Faint shouts in the distance told Tessa her pursuers remained undaunted. She moved frantically toward the cromlech—the burial tomb. The water was getting deeper, and Tessa moved to the shallower edge of the stream. A faint glow in the western sky promised the end of the storm, but the ground could hold no more, and rushing water flowed past her into the tomb.

Stay in *the water and enter*, Ganna commanded.

Tessa reached the gap in the standing stones, bent lower, and stared wide-eyed at the water rushing past her into the cavern. "I'll drown," Tessa said.

There is a ledge inside.

Tessa gripped the rocks on either side of the cromlech entrance, ducked her head, and entered. A pungent arboreal odor of lost ages and things long dead greeted her nose.

Struggling on with both arms extended, Tessa inched her way forward in water that was now above her knees. It whooshed and swirled around her. The current was strong, and she struggled to stay on her feet. Then she slipped and tumbled into the torrent. It was only two feet deep but intense enough to force her forward.

Move to your right toward the wall! Ganna yelled.

Tessa shrugged off her heavy wet coat and began swimming and kicking her way toward the wall. Finally, she found purchase on a rocky ledge and pulled herself up onto it. She huddled against the wall, shivering. Her breath was short. Sliding down, she wrapped her arms around her legs to warm herself.

A voice echoed: "Wiggins! Wiggins, come out." It was Buddy.

BANG! A gunshot reverberated, and she heard a bullet ricochet off a rock near her head. Then came a cry and a splash. "Help!"

Tessa saw a small light bobbing in the water toward her—*his torch.* Tessa caught it and directed the beam toward the entrance, where she saw Buddy tumbling and splashing helplessly in what was now a roaring stream. "Help me!" he screamed again as he cascaded toward her. He caught sight of the torchlight and reached for it. She stood and pressed herself flat against the wall as his hand grasped at her ankles. She swatted his wrist with the torch—his fingers recoiled. He plunged on, his shouts growing fainter with every second. When she could no longer hear him, she shined the light into the gloom ahead and saw nothing but swirling dark water.

"What's lies down there?" Tessa asked.

You will see, Ganna answered. *Stay on the ledge.*

Torch in hand, Tessa side-stepped along the rocky shelf until the tunnel widened and the water slowed.

Shine the light to the other side, Ganna ordered.

Tessa swung the torch slowly across the water until the beam revealed an opening carved into the opposite wall. It was about four feet square. Above the hollow was a female figure with her legs apart, her hands resting high on her inner thighs.

"What is it, Ganna?"

It is the place I hid while my people died.

Tessa's body shivered. "What do you mean?"

Ganna gave a low moan that trailed off into silence.

"Tell me!"

Ahead is the altar where we brought the offerings. Catrin and I brought them here before Paulinus attacked.

"So, you were able to keep the offerings from the Romans."

Ganna sighed. *We waited, but Catrin was impatient and returned to fight.*

"And you stayed here to guard the offerings."

I cringed in that cranny like a craven coward. The Romans slaughtered our people and set fire to our groves. When I crawled out a day later, I stumbled among the charred bones of those who had sacrificed themselves. The stench of their burnt flesh was horrible.

Ganna let out a low, deep moan that grew into a desolate wail. It tore at Tessa's heart. "But you preserved your body in the olde way and maintained the connection with The Mother for two thousand years."

My spirit carried on but not my body. Beara's poem told you as much. That was not my body at Imbolc, but that of one of our sisters.

Tessa's heart was racing—her thoughts and feelings muddled.

I believed a body could hold two spirits, but I was wrong.

"What of us . . . what of me?"

Only one spirit can remain.

Tessa's eyes hardened. "Yours."

THIRTY-THREE

"YOU LIED, GANNA."

I believed I could tether my spirit to your body until you were ready, but . . .

"That's not possible."

You know it yourself, even when I am with you for a brief time . . .

Tessa completed her thought: "Your spirit takes command."

Tessa was numb. There was no panic, anger, or even fear. Somehow, she had known this all along. Maybe in her heart, she had had already begun to surrender to her sacrifice as she doubted that she could take Ganna's place.

You are troubled.

"Less than I might have expected. I am not ready to accept your mantle."

Please believe me; I always intended for you to carry on.

"When I was prepared. But I am not ready, and there is no more time."

"Buddy!" It was Mrs. Mayer's voice echoing. "Buddy!"

Hurry. We must go to the altar.

"Hear me, Wiggins," Mayer shouted, her voice echoing off the stone walls of the cavern, "You have ten minutes to come out with the treasure. If you don't, Holmes and your friend will be dispatched. Do you hear me?"

Tessa called out. "The treasure's here. I can bring it to you. I need time. The water is treacherous."

A moment of silence ensued.

"Twenty minutes," Mayer shouted. "Twenty minutes and they both die."

Stay to the ledge, Ganna said. *The altar is just ahead.*

Tessa slid along the ledge, the water splashing onto her feet. When her torch began to dim, she repeatedly struck it against the palm of her hand.

Don't worry, Ganna told her. *There is light ahead.*

And there was. What had been a tunnel widened into a vaulted chamber. Light shined through a fissure in the rock above and rippled on a twirling pool of water below. Reflected shards of light glistened on the walls and ceiling of the domed chamber. Tessa shined the torch beam into the pool of water. What she saw froze her in place, and she caught her breath.

The water was twisting in a massive vortex that wound down into a deep fissure in the earth. A crude chain stretched out from one wall to the other in front of the whirlpool. She wondered if Buddy might have clung to it before the waters dragged him into oblivion. As her eyes became accustomed to the light, Tessa saw swords, shields, gold torcs, jewelry, gems, and piles of coins heaped up along the far wall just behind the whirlpool. The cache glittered and flashed as the torchlight swept over it. It was a fortune, but the prayers and intentions each offering embodied were beyond price.

Tessa could not believe her eyes. "The treasure."

The beam of light finally settled on something chiseled into the stone above the whirlpool—a list. The words were in Greek. "What does that say?"

It is the names, Ganna said, *of the sisters . . .*

"The ones who gave their bodies to you?" Tessa muttered in disbelief. Her eyes went from name to name to name. There had to be forty or fifty. Her mind couldn't grasp what she saw. "This is where they gave up their bodies," she mumbled.

Tessa was taught to believe martyrs are holy, that a soldier who dies in battle is brave, yet when a person willingly gives her body and life to a wiser, mightier, and nobler spirit, they think her mad.

"Read them!" Tessa demanded.

Yes, read our names, Ganna. Of all the things on earth that I could miss, hearing my name is the one I pine for the most. I gave my body willingly—we all did. Honor us for our sacrifice, Ganna. For even in the midst of life's tribulations, there is an elemental sweetness. It was hard to leave. I am Agronā . . . Agronā. My mother named me for the goddess of the river. Honor Gwyn, who came before me, her name means blessed, and Ceri, Rhiannon, Arial, Efa, and Dona. Let our names echo again. It is hard to forsake life!

There is no time for this. Quickly, take some of the offerings.

Tessa stood motionless, her heart pounding. She felt a strong presence that she now realized had been growing since the water ceremony.

Tessa, hurry.

Tessa scooped up a handful of coins and a gold necklace.

Hold tight to the chain and make your way to the center of the water.

Caught up in the overpowering madness of the moment, Tessa did not hesitate.

This is at the heart of everything I have been teaching you. It was all to prepare you for this moment that you deserve to know. Hurry.

Tessa stuffed the coins and necklace into a pocket and grasped the chain with both hands. She stepped cautiously into the water and immediately slipped on the slimy bottom. Regaining her balance, she carefully slid each foot along in turn, making her way into the center of what was now a wild river flowing above her knees.

You will feel hollows—cavities where you can place your feet.

"Yes, I feel one now." Tessa moved forward, still holding fast to the chain. Soon both of her feet were resting in hollows carved into the stone below the water. Feeling more secure, she let out a long breath.

You are going to commune with The Mother. Remember what you learned about mutuality and sacrifice. Mutuality was common sense: Getting something requires giving something. Sacrifice required three things: What you give must be of value to you. Your intention must not be self-serving, and you must make the offering without expectations.

Now, prepare your offering.

Tessa struggled to calm her mind amid the menacing sound of the swirling water. Suddenly she saw her distorted reflection on the surface—the image twirling round and down.

The offering!

Tessa brought her mind to the present moment and took the coins and necklace in one hand and held them over the whirlpool. Closing her eyes, she slowed her breathing. The water rushing around her legs was the only sensation. Eyes wide and fixed on the center of the vortex, she opened her hand. The coins and necklace glistened for a moment before disappearing into the shadowy water.

Put yourself in the hands of The Mother. There is nothing to be said.

Her mind was fighting her, wanting to go to Beara and Mr. Holmes. Her heart pounded and blood pulsed in her temples. Closing her eyes, she let herself feel each heartbeat. Her body shuttered. "I'm going to die," she murmured.

In that simple thought, everything stopped.

She let go.

Tessa felt her heart split open and thought it might burst through her chest. She heard a great sigh rush from her lungs, and Tessa waited for her knees to buckle—but they didn't. Opening her eyes, she looked down, expecting to see blood pouring from her, but there was only the black swirling water.

She suddenly became aware of the cold in her body. "Beara. Holmes," she muttered, praying she wouldn't hear a gunshot. " I can't do this."

You can. You were nearly there. Imagine you are newly dead. Your spirit is reaching out for the last earthly sensation. Reach!

Tessa took a long deep breath uncoiling her body.

What do you feel?

Nothing. Floating. Even the cold was gone now.

Then, her body jolted, and her chest heaved violently—a burning in her belly.

Open yourself.

She was shaking and breathing in small gasps as the wonderful warmth spread to every part of her body.

Good.

Tessa's hands relaxed and dropped away from the chain. She reached out over the water. "Hold me!" she sobbed, leaning over the vortex. "Oh-h-h," she moaned. "Sadness." Tears streamed down Tessa's face. "She is suffering . . . bereft. Oh, my god!"

Tessa's tears seemed endless.

A gunshot rang and echoed—the bullet zinging as it ricocheted off a nearby rock.

As Tessa swiveled, the water seized her legs and dragged her toward the whirlpool. Falling backward, her hands caught hold of the chain just as the swirling vortex seized her.

Another shot rang in her ears. She pulled herself up and found the hollows again. "I'm coming! I've got the treasure."

Tessa put the chain under her arms and slid her way to the ledge. "I don't understand what happened, Ganna. It was torment."

The sadness is that of a Mother whose children have forsaken her. The sorrow is yours too, for the destruction of the fields, forests, and mountains reflect what people are doing to each other.

Tessa struggled onto the ledge again and collapsed. "I cannot bear this sorrow." She reached out and grabbed a handful of coins and a glistening golden neckpiece, a torc, and pushed herself to her feet. "I can't do this. I must save my friends."

The offerings are important, but this place is sacred. It must be protected!

"If you want my body Ganna, take it now, but I will not forsake them."

THIRTY-FOUR

FEAR HAD TESSA FULLY IN ITS GRIP as she rushed back toward the entrance of the cromlech. Water flowed in a torrent now, splashing higher onto the ledge. Each step required pushing against an ever more powerful current, trying to sweep her back to the altar and below.

Think about what you are doing. Ganna said. *We can find a way—"*

"There is no time."

Tessa pushed on until she saw light from the entrance and stopped for a breath. "Ganna, I'm sorry."

She put the torc around her neck and patted her pocket to make certain the Roman coins were still there. With her last bit of strength, she pulled herself up and out of the tomb.

Upon seeing Tessa emerge, Mayer shouted: "Do you have it?"

Holmes moved toward Tessa, and Moran thrust his pistol into the detective's back. Beara remained still.

Mayer ran for Tessa and shook her frantically. "Where is it?" she demanded. Then, she saw the torc. "Gold! It's gold." Tessa pulled out the coins and held them in the palms of her hands. As Mayer snatched at them, they tumbled into the mud. The greedy woman went to her knees, frantically sweeping through the muck, but they were gone. She got to her feet and twisted the torc off of Tessa's neck. "There's more, much more, isn't there?" Mayer bellowed.

Tessa nodded. Looking into the woman's covetous eyes, she said: "You're welcome to it if you can find your way."

"What happened to that bally idiot Buddy?" Moran called out.

"The water took him," Tessa said.

The Colonel looked at the surging stream flowing past them into the cromlech and shook his head. "But it didn't take you."

"I won't go in. It's sacred. We don't belong there."

Moran smirked. "I believe you are right. You look the worse for it. Your friends will go."

Mayer became excited. "Yes. Two can carry more." Then she turned to Moran: "Shouldn't we wait for the water to subside?"

The Colonel grimaced. "When the storm passes, bodies will be found on the beach. The authorities will be searching for us—asking questions. Others will find our treasure."

"*Our* treasure!" Mayer cried. "You said you only wanted Holmes."

"I don't believe I used the word 'only.' You owe me. Hellingford has been restored and converted into a lucrative enterprise."

Tessa lurched. "That's why you killed Dr. Mayer."

Moran grinned as a low-pitched cackle resonated in his throat. "You know better, Miss Wiggins," he said with a hiss. "I apologize for my insensitivity; I know his murder weighs heavy on your heart."

"Nonsense, Moran!" Holmes shouted. "The real Dr. Mayer *is* dead, but Tessa didn't murder him. You killed him and his wife shortly after he arrived at Hellingford. I'm not certain who the fellow in the wheeled-chair was, or if he is even dead, but it wasn't Dr. Mayer."

"Is that true? Tessa gasped.

Holmes nodded.

The sides of Moran's dark lips tugged upward, producing a sinister smirk. "And so, another mystery solved—is that it, Holmes? I had come to believe that your mental capacities had diminished."

"Stop it," Beatrice said. "You can deal with Holmes after we have the treasure."

Holmes caught the woman's eye. "Has it not yet occurred to you, Beatrice, that you are as expendable as me? What need has he of you?"

"Awfully clever, Holmes. Sowing the seeds of discord," Moran said.

The woman's giddy expression transformed into a concerned look as she glanced at the Colonel's pistol.

"Come now, don't let this rascal upset you," Moran said.

Her anxious eyes glanced about. "Let's get on with it," she said. "Send them in."

"Do you really think he will give up the pleasure of killing me?" Holmes said.

Moran chortled. "You think too highly of yourself, Holmes. If the waters shallow up you and the old woman, I will take solace in the fact that the great Sherlock Holmes disappeared from this world with nary a grave marker. And rest assured, your legacy will be buried after you."

The Colonel forgot that Nature, the great disrupter of plans, always has the last word. Buddy had already been offered in sacrifice, and more would follow.

Moran nudged Holmes toward the entrance to the cromlech. Beatrice followed his lead, dragging Beara by the arm. "There's no need to send the old woman in," Holmes said. "Give me a sack or a case, and I will fill it with treasure."

"Yes," Beatrice said. "We should get the cases from the auto."

"There is no time," Moran countered.

"I will go," she said, turning back toward the road. "Wait for me."

Moran shook his head. "That damn woman and her treasure!"

Tessa walked toward Holmes and Moran. He stepped back and pointed the pistol. "Stay back, young lady."

"I know the way. I will go with them."

Moran chuckled. "No, you are my guarantee that Holmes and the old woman will come out with the treasure. You were the lure that brought Holmes here. I'm not about to let him slip away now. If you don't wish to be responsible for two more deaths, you had better share your secrets for surviving the waters in that tomb."

Tessa stepped toward the edge of the small river feeding the tomb. It had grown large enough to float a small boat, and the current was fierce. She peered into the water and leered at the Colonel. "I will no longer be used as a pawn in your vengeful game," she spat.

"Really? And what will you do about it, Miss Wiggins?"

Tessa leaped into the raging water, and in a moment, was snatched up into the tomb's dark orifice.

THIRTY-FIVE

MORAN STOOD FLAT-FOOTED—stunned—his mouth agape. Suddenly, Holmes spun and grabbed hold of his pistol and yanked it upward. A shot rang out, and then another. The two men toppled to the ground, wrestling in the mud. The Colonel rolled over and twisted the pistol toward Holmes's chest.

BANG!

The shot turned everyone's head. There stood Beatrice, pistol in hand. "Up gentlemen . . . slowly."

The Colonel crawled toward his cane, jammed it into the mud, and hoisted himself onto his feet. Beara offered the detective her hand, and Holmes rose slowly.

"I love a woman with her own gun," Moran said, using his cane to point to his pistol in the mud. Beatrice retrieved it and wiped the muck off on her sweater. As he reached for it, she shook her head. "I feel safer with both pistols."

"You need me," Moran said.

"I'm not certain I do," Beatrice replied.

"What about the treasure? What about Brady? He'll come for you."

Beatrice grimaced, shrugged, and reluctantly placed the Mauser in Moran's waiting hand. She then threw the suitcase at Beara's feet.

Moran pointed his pistol at Holmes. "I should kill you now."

"Why don't you? Why haven't you?" Holmes questioned.

"I wish to relish this moment a little longer. But, if like Miss Wiggins, you are anxious to end it all now, I'll be happy to oblige." Holmes bristled as Moran chuckled and glanced at the raging water rushing past them. "I never thought to ask if you could swim. Well, we'll soon know."

Beatrice tucked her pistol into her coat, picked up the writing case, and carried it to Moran. "I brought the manuscript by mistake," she said, setting it at the Colonel's feet. "but the suitcase will do." Then she turned to Beara. "Dump the clothes out, old women."

Beara complied and shook the contents of the suitcase into the water.

Moran snickered. "Yes, Miss Wiggins will not be needing a change of clothes." He noticed Holmes's eyes glance at the writing case. "Of course, you're concerned about your masterwork." Help me with the case, Beatrice. I don't want to take my eyes off this fellow.

She hesitated.

"Open it," he ordered.

"The rain—"

"Open it," he repeated.

Holmes's eyes widened as Beatrice lifted the lid. "Empty!" she exclaimed.

Moran laughed. "Just a little more cheese on the trap."

"You're more diabolical than your old master," the detective said.

"A compliment." Moran motioned to Beatrice. "Give Holmes your torch." Holmes took it. "Now, sir, if the life of this old woman is not enough motivation for you to return with a suitcase full of treasure, then consider the possibility that Miss Wiggins may still be alive. You might save her."

A large splash behind him had Moran wheel around, "Bloody hell!" he yelled. Beatrice turned to see Cian charging them like a great highland bull. Close behind was Clark Button, who had Dr. Watson by the elbow.

As Moran trained his pistol at Cian, Holmes kicked his cane, and he toppled like a skittle. Beatrice got off a nervous shot before

Cian wrapped his immense arms around her and lifted her off the ground. He squeezed until her pistol dropped.

The bullet had struck Clark, who was on one knee holding his arm. "Go on," he told Watson. Professor Stone came last, waddling in the distance, torch in hand. Clark picked up Beatrice's pistol with his good hand and showed it to Cian, who set the woman gently down and pointed a cautioning finger at her.

Holmes held the Mauser on Moran, ordering him to remain down. "Where's Tessa?" Clark asked. Holmes pointed toward the cromlech. Beara was already at the entrance.

Clark rushed along the edge of the water toward the cromlech entrance. Beara had to grab his arm to keep him from being swept into the waters. He handed her the pistol and, wedging his feet against rocks at either side of the entrance, prepared to duck inside. Judging the current, he took a deep breath.

Before he could act, something had him by the collar. Cian, up to his thighs in the furious waters, held Beara in one hand and Clark in the other. He dragged them to one side and out of the water.

The big man called for a torch, and Stone brought it. Without a word, Cian plunged into the primordial vault. Clark and Beara regained their footing but could only watch as Cian vanished into the darkness. Drawing closer to the entrance, they could hear the huge man's legs driving through the swift water.

Cian quickly found the ledge running alongside the tunnel and pulled himself onto it. His feet were nearly too large for the narrow pathway, but he was able to make his way slowly. He shined the torch ahead. "Tessa, *ble wyt ti*," —'where are you,' he called.

Watson and Holmes stood guard over Moran and Beatrice Corder. Clark and Beara stood watch at the entrance to the tomb.

Tessa's fingers were getting numb as she clung to the chain at the edge of the whirlpool, her feet battered by the churning water. The cold drove everything from her mind but dread. Letting go would be a simple act, and she was the perfect sacrifice. Her life was the most valuable thing she had—her intention selfless. And truly, she had no expectation as to what would happen. She might have said that she didn't care, but her grip on the chain made that a lie. Maybe it was the thought of a mortal sin that caused her to hold on. Dante would have her believe that her soul would be torn from her body and flung to the seventh circle of hell where it would sprout and grow into a tree that trapped her soul forever. Such was the fate of those who take their life, but what of those who give it?

"No!" Tessa screamed. Her body shook with a renewed vigor. "I want to live," she rasped. Then louder it came: "I want to live, Ganna. I want my life! The Mother spoke to *me*. I am of this age. Your time has passed."

A deep sigh came from Ganna. *Put down your sword. I love you, Tessa.* Ganna was laughing now. *You are more than ready, my dear warrior. Get to your feet.*

Tessa pulled on the chain, but she was too weak and tired.

Cian's booming voice called out: "*Ble wyt ti*, Tessa. *Ble wyt ti*," he called.

Stay with him and the others. This sacrifice is for me to do. Remember this moment born of love for you and The Mother. There was a sound like wind whistling through a crack under a door, and then . . .

Ganna was gone.

Tessa hung on for some time before she could gather enough strength to make one last effort. She wrestled the chain under both arms and, pulling herself backward, found purchase in the footholds. Standing upright again, she closed her eyes and offered a prayer for Ganna: "*Gadewch imi ddod adref at fy mam*" —'Let me come home to my mother.' After two thousand years, Ganna's spirit had gone home.

Suddenly Tessa felt a familiar warmth in her belly that spread throughout her body to her fingertips and toes. Her sight and hearing intensified. "Mother!" Tears rolled down her cheeks.

Cian's voice came again. "W*yt ti yma*—are you here?"

It was fitting he should come. Like his namesake from the primordial past, Cian was descended from the ancient and mysterious *Tuatha De Danann,* who worshiped the elemental Goddess Danu— 'The Mother.'

When Tessa saw the light from Cian's torch shining into the grotto, she called to him. In a moment, he had her by the arm. Cian's loutish face possessed the most astonishing smile she had ever seen. "I've got you," he said, lifting her up past him and setting her safely back onto the ledge. Hoisting himself onto the outcrop, he took her by the hand.

"Wait." Tessa told him, "There's something we must do."

At her direction, Cian shuffled his way along the ledge to the back of the chamber above the whirlpool. As he reached the offerings, he steadied himself, slipped a toe beneath the edge of a shield, and flipped it into the vortex. It clanged against a rock before it was sucked into the boundless darkness below.

As Ganna had taught her, Tessa grabbed the chain and stepped back into the swirling water. She slid along the bottom, hands clasped tightly on the chain until her feet found purchase in the hollows at the center of the stream. Cian continued to toss and throw the offerings into the whirlpool—swords, jewelry, golden plates, coin from every realm, and crystals and gems the size of a fist.

Tessa closed her eyes and slowed her breathing. Her body swayed—at first imperceptibly, then more and more, her lips moving in supplication. Cian tossed the last offerings into the whirlpool, folded his hands in front of his belt, and bowed his head. Tessa remained silent at the edge of the whirlpool staring into the foaming water.

As her head rose, it seemed to Cian that her eyes shone in a new way. They were dark and luminous—and remained so.

Cian smiled and nodded.

Tessa made her way back along the chain to the ledge and Cian's open hand.

"What did she say?" Cian asked.

Tessa squeezed his hand. "Be not troubled. I will abide."

THIRTY-SIX

"DON'T LET THEM OUT OF YOUR SIGHT," Holmes told Watson and Stone, handing his pistol to Stone. Muddied and breathless, Holmes hurried to the entrance of the watery cavern. Clark had put his jacket over Beara's shoulders and was struggling to light a soggy cigarette.

"Anything?" Holmes asked as he came close. Clark shook his head.

The worst of the storm seemed to have passed, but the rain was still falling, and thunder rumbled. As more time passed, a somber mood descended on the trio waiting at the entry.

"I don't know what I shall do if Tessa doesn't come out," Holmes said.

Beara and Clark remained silent.

"Give it up. They're gone!" Moran shouted.

Angrily, Watson thrust his pistol into the Colonel's side. Suddenly, Moran dropped to one knee. Watson reached out to stop the old man's fall. He barely saw Moran's cane before it hit him hard above his ear. Watson reeled back, dropping his pistol. As Stone turned, Beatrice snatched her pistol back and pointed it at him and Watson.

Steadying himself, the Colonel pointed with his cane, "Beatrice, get the one in the mud."

Watson's yelp brought Holmes to attention, but it was too late. Beatrice and Moran had the pistols now. "Come this way," Moran shouted. "All of you—slowly." He balanced himself in the slippery mud and struggled to catch his breath.

217

Soon all five captives were on their knees. Watson was bleeding and dazed. Beara attended him. Moran ordered Beatrice to get the rope from their auto. *Why did he not shoot us?* Holmes wondered.

The Colonel began taunting Holmes: "I can hear that great mind of yours exploding with questions. Answers are forthcoming, but not at this moment or in this place. But do not doubt that your fate is sealed. Enjoy the little time that remains for you."

"What about Tessa and Cian?" Holmes asked.

"You can't really believe they are alive."

"Tessa survived once. Cian's strong."

Moran laughed. "There you go, sowing seeds of doubt and discord again."

Eyeing Beatrice, Holmes asked Moran: "What of the treasure?"

"Ha! I don't give a tinker's damn about the treasure."

"What?" Beatrice shouted.

Moran sighed impatiently.

"I want the treasure!" she bellowed.

The Colonel's shoulders relaxed. "Of course, but we must bind them up first."

"If you do, he'll shoot you," Holmes told Beatrice.

Moran's pistol shook in his hand. "Enough! Mrs. Mayer, I wish—"

"Stop!" she shouted. "Stop calling me Mrs. Mayer. The old woman can bind them. I'll keep my pistol for the moment." She tossed a rope to Beara. Moran handed her his penknife and ordered her to cut the rope and bind the others.

When everyone's hands were tied, Moran satisfied himself that the knots were adequate and took his knife back. Then he turned to Beatrice. "You seemed to think Tessa and that oaf are coming with treasure, but they're not, so . . ." He fired once. Beatrice's eyes held a look of astonishment as her legs buckled, and she crumpled to the ground.

There was a collective gasp, and Beara cried, "No!"

Suddenly the storm surged, and a great gust of wind moved through the trees. Moran shrugged. "Apparently, you were right about me, Holmes. But that offers little comfort, I'm sure." The old Colonel wavered for a moment before he steadied himself on his cane. "Yes, I am a little wobbly Holmes, but as you just witnessed, I am still a crack shot. However, this puts me in a quandary. I fear I am not able to manage all of you by myself."

"Colonel!" a voice called out in the distance.

He blinked his eyes, struggling to focus before seeing two figures—a small one atop the capstone over the cromlech and a larger one to the side—Tessa and Cian.

His jaw dropped. "Ha—they made it! No matter." He turned to the others. "Now, this is precisely why I prefer my Mauser to your Webley. Three shots have been fired. Seven remain. If I had relied upon the bulky Webley, I would be in a fix as there are six of you."

"Drop your pistol!" Tessa shouted. Thunder rumbled, and the air roiled. Tessa closed her eyes, slowly raised her arms, and began chanting in a queer tongue.

Moran laughed. "The Wiggins woman is a delightful amusement. I must kill her last."

Tessa's incantations grew louder. Moran smacked his lips and shook his head. "I thought it a ruse, but she *really is* mad as a hatter."

Lightning flashed, illuminating the gathering. The clouds darkened and churned. A strong gust of wind swatted the rain into their faces and eyes. Then, Tessa lowered her head, went to one knee, and thrust both arms outward, shouting entireties into the wind.

CRACK! A blinding spear of lightning fractured the air above, struck the earth behind Moran, and leaped over the ground to the old man's cane. He shrieked. His body lurched, back arched, eyelids fluttered, and nostrils flared. His mouth jerked open in a noiseless scream. The metal cane sizzled, and flames ran up his arm.

When the lightning released him, his rigid body reeled backward, splashing into the mud like a marble statue.

It was difficult to breathe. The air had been purged from everyone's lungs. Their eyes were open but not really seeing.

In an instant, the tempest was gone. An eerily stillness descended upon the moor. As the rain slowed to a drizzle, the air became pungent with the acrid smell of burnt hair and flesh. Smoke still curled from Moran's gaping mouth.

Holmes rose and approached the body, blinking in an effort to understand. His mind was a tangle of thoughts. He labored to find words as he peered at what remained of Moran's body. The skin was grey and pitted with burnt black holes. And the eyes . . . wide as they could stretch, had no eyelids, and a white pudding-like substance oozed from the sockets and dribbled down his temples.

Watson went to Holmes's side for only a moment before his stomach heaved and he had to turn away. Beara, white as chalk, had already regained her senses and began loosening the bonds on everyone's wrists. As Tessa approached, the old woman turned, lowered her head, and spoke: "*Fy offeiriades*—my priestess."

THIRTY-SEVEN

THE EVENING SKY GLOWED with Samhain bonfires as two mud-spattered autos motored back toward Cemaes Bay. Professor Stone pressed his nose against the window. "They have not forsaken the old ways," he said to Tessa.

"I know Ganna's spirit is dancing among those flames," Beara added.

Cian slowed the Crossley as they all watched the animated silhouettes gaily prancing about the fires. "Ganna's spirit will always be with us," he said.

"And the spirits of all those women who gave Ganna life," Tessa said. The names of the women chiseled above the sacred altar chamber were forever etched in her mind: Agronā, Gwyn, Ceri, Rhiannon, Arial, Efa, Dona. And now her name could be added, for Tessa Wiggins drown in that ancient tomb, and a priestess walked out in her skin. Giving herself completely over to the divine madness, Tessa received the Druid mantle and, with it, the sacred responsibility of being the people's connection with The Mother.

Tessa recalled the moment she and Cian emerged from the flooded tomb. Her eyes had difficulty adjusting to the light. Holmes, Beara, Moran, and the others were faint and shadowy amid a net of silvery filaments—she could not separate the people from the landscape around them. Now, she saw the truth of all things. Her body didn't need to die for her spirit to be reborn, but only the old idea of who she once was. And so, the waters in Bodewryd offered both baptism as well as absolution. The insights, feelings, courage, and love that brought her to the altar of The Mother had *always* there, even in those dark and lonely moments in her past when she felt so empty. Like all human beings, Tessa carried within her the secrets of life, death, healing, and balance, waiting to be awakened.

A horn blast shook everyone from his and her musings and startled Clark, whose head was on Tessa's shoulder. The headlights from Ceridwen's limousine glared in Cian's rear-view mirror. "Yes, yes," he muttered, putting the auto back into gear.

"I'm fine, Tess," Clark muttered. "No need to hurry. My wrist is first-rate."

"We will see, Clark. Mr. Holmes and Dr. Watson have injuries to mend as well."

Dusk settled on the village as the autos pulled onto the town's High Street. It seemed as though their journey had come to an end, but endings occur only in storybooks. In life, something always comes after.

When they arrived at The Stag, Holmes made arrangements to have the bodies in Bodewryd retrieved. Watson resurrected his latent skills, tending to Clark's bullet wound and the gash on his own head. Neither was serious.

As the local constabulary consisted of one man, Holmes called Inspector Joshua Walls at Scotland Yard. The Inspector said he would not be able to get there until morning and asked that everyone remain at Cemaes until he arrived. Holmes was eager to go to Hellingford to search for his manuscript, but he agreed to wait.

It took no small amount of hot water to cleanse bodies and clothing. Food was next. When the entourage went downstairs to the pub, it seemed as though half the town's population of three hundred was jammed into the inn. Fortunately, Griff, the innkeeper, had saved a table for them. The menu at The Stag consisted of pork pies, fish and chips, spiced beef sandwiches, and several other dishes where cutlery was not required.

Holmes made inquiries regarding Brady, but no one had seen him, and no bodies had washed up on the beach. "I believe the tide got a hold of that fellow," Holmes said to the innkeeper—which was not untrue. Cian had told Holmes he was certain the fellow was dead.

There were many ears about, so after dinner, Holmes assembled everyone in his room. He shared his news that Inspector Walls was on his way. He urged everyone to stay within the facts during their interviews the next morning—with one exception. They all agreed not to reveal Tessa's actions at the cromlech—that secret would remain with all of them forever. And long after this day, each of them, in their own way, would recreate this story in their heads until it finally fitted with their current stitched-together reality. When magic is afoot, bamboozling themselves is the way human beings maintain their tenuous grip on sanity.

The Stag was a small inn, so rooms had to be shared. Tessa and Beara were the first to retire. The others desired a nightcap—or maybe two. No sooner had Tessa climbed into bed than a disturbance outside called her to the window. Townsfolk had poured out of the inn and gathered around a lorry in the street. "It's the bodies," Tessa told Beara. Moran and Beatrice Corder had been found and brought to town. Beara peered down and offered a generous epitaph: "Two of a kind. They struggled to find their way amid the darkness of greed and revenge."

*****

The stormy veil lifted overnight, and by degrees, the sun's glow restored color to the earth, gentling all and sundry spirits. Tessa awoke early with Pamela Fritzwaller on her mind. She had made a promise to the woman and intended to honor it. She understood that it wasn't Hellingford that imprisoned Fritzwaller so much as sorrow. Holmes said he would take her to the asylum with him later that day.

Eager to depart for home, everyone was pleased when Inspector Walls arrived mid-morning. The young man had quickly climbed the bureaucratic ladder to the top of number four Whitehall Place, and Holmes had come to respect him. When he arrived, Walls sent his associate, Constable Rafferty, to the oldest church in Wales to examine the bodies. Llanbadrig Church was founded by St. Patrick and became the hub around which the small seaside community revolved—serving not only as a place of worship but as a meeting hall, polling station, and mortuary.

Walls conducted interviews over breakfast—beginning with Clark Button and ending with Holmes. "Quite a tale, Mr. Holmes," he said, closing his notebook. "Rafferty confirms that Moran's timely death was by a lightning strike." He eyed Holmes closely. "Any further thoughts on the matter?"

"I cannot explain it."

"Or will not," Walls rejoined. "And what of your manuscript?"

"I may find it at Hellingford. The Crossley I mentioned may provide a lead as well. It's parked behind the inn."

"I would like to look it over."

Curious eyes followed Holmes and Walls as they went outside. Approaching the Crossley, Holmes stopped and stiffened to attention.

"What is it?" Walls asked.

"The number plate."

"LY-1089?"

"I thought it was familiar. It's the magician's number." Walls looked perplexed. "Inspector, do you recall a chap named Dai Vernon—the professor?"

"The magician fellow?"

"Exactly. I have always been fascinated by magic, and Dai Vernon did the trick where he asks a person in the audience to pick three random numbers and be prepared to do a little subtraction and addition. He was able to predict the answer even *before* the three numbers were revealed to him."

"Did the trick work?"

"Every time, because the answer is always 1089. It's a mathematical anomaly."

"Your point?"

Holmes turned to the Inspector. "Who would select a plate number like this?"

"A magician?"

"Or a mathematician."

This new insight prompted a change in plans.

Holmes hurried back to the inn to find Watson in their room. "The old hounds are on the scent again," was all he needed to say.

As Watson said his goodbyes, Holmes took Tessa aside to explain that he would not be able to go to Hellingford just yet. "I no longer believe that my manuscript is there. I do not know for certain, but something tells me it awaits me in London."

"So, you are listening to your instinct," Tessa said.

He cocked his head and grinned. "I don't know as I would use those words, but yes."

"I have a strong feeling too, Mr. Holmes—that you are courting danger."

Holmes chuckled.

Tessa took the druid's glass from around her neck and handed it to him. "Keep this with you," she said, placing it in the palm of his hand.

"Magical amulets? I live in the real world, Tessa."

"I lived in that world, but I have been fortunate enough to experience things that man's reason cannot defend."

"So, you think this hunk of stone will protect me?"

Tessa smiled and folded his fingers around it, gripping his fist tightly in both of her hands. "Think of it as a way for me to be with you."

Nodding, he put it in his pocket. "Go on to Ceridwen. If you still wish me to go with you to Hellingford, I will do so in a day's time. However, I think you can manage without me."

Tessa took in the measure of her friend. "Like Ganna, you have a higher estimation of me than I have of myself."

"I do not agree with people who rank modesty among the virtues, Tessa. To underestimate oneself is as much a departure from the truth as it is to embellish one's abilities. I do not flatter or exaggerate when I tell you that you are more than able to manage without me."

THIRTY-EIGHT

IT WOULD BE DISINGENUOUS to say that things had returned to normal, for if there would be but one lesson that nature teaches, it would be that nothing remains the same. Today appears like yesterday only if one is not paying attention. And there are times when the earth beneath us explodes and recreates itself in an instant. So it was for Tessa. Within the tomb of an ancient tribal lord, her choice to live gave her life's consummate gift—something to live for.

Cian drove Tessa, Beara, Stone, and Clark to Ceridwen. Their journey was silent and peaceful, one of those rare times when everyone was too exhausted to make plans. When they arrived at the manor, Gwendoline and Margaret Davis were overjoyed, insisting they all enter through the front door. "Mud be damned," Margaret said.

Tessa put off questions from the sisters and went to her room. As she stood before her mirror, she recalled looking at herself at The Stag, covered in dried mud that flaked off and fell in patches at her feet. *Like a snake that sheds its skin as it grows*, Tessa thought. Indeed, she felt a sense of newness not experienced since she was a child when every day offered new places, faces, creatures, sounds, and words every day. After thirty years, newness is rationed out— but not so with nature. The Mother is not sentimental. She does not hang on to old things but continually creates new life. That is what Tessa felt inside her now. She could never be the woman she was. This thought, in the same moment, was both frightening and exhilarating.

The next morning, Margaret and Gwendoline Davis hosted a hardy Welsh breakfast in the hope of learning more about what had transpired at Hellingford and beyond. But those at the table offered only sparse information—the barest facts. They had emerged from a storm and would never be the same. Resting in momentary peace and contentment, they did not yet appreciate that this is the purpose of a storm. Only Tessa knew that another tempest loomed in London for Holmes.

After breakfast, Professor Stone hurried off to the library to chronicle recent events. As he departed, he asked Tessa to stop in and share whatever she could about what happened inside the cromlech. His was an honorable effort, for the Professor held the deepest commitment to history. But even as he made his notes, he knew that his account would never find its way into a book or lecture.

Tessa knocked. Without looking up, Stone asked her to come in and close the door. When she settled in a chair next to the desk, the Professor opened a drawer and removed the gold torc. "I took this from the Hellingford woman as we left." He held it out for her. "It doesn't belong in a museum."

Tessa smiled. "But your whole life has been about museums."

He nodded. "This is true, but something singular happened at that burial site."

"Magic?"

He chuckled. "It might surprise you to know that I believe in magic—although not in the way most people do. You see, what we call magic is simply something waiting for science to understand."

Tessa took the torc. "I accept this as your offering, and I will see that it ends up where it belongs." She rubbed the torc with her fingers. "In my experience, Professor, magic is not waiting for new science, but rather for our senses and awareness to grow sharper. Magic is everywhere if you care to notice it."

He nodded. "Can you tell me what happened inside that tomb?"

"Some things can only be experienced," she answered.

"As with all the best things in life."

Eager to show Beara the torc, Tessa took leave of the Professor.

Clark had not attended breakfast but instead stayed in his room. From his back window, he watched Tessa and Beara. They were bundled up against the chilly morning mist, merrily chatting away in the garden. He envied the bond between the two of them and between Tessa and the herb lady Nell Rees. As he looked on, a sense of loss crept into his heart, for he knew he was losing Tessa. He told himself that this should come as no surprise. He realized his rough manner made for an awkward courtship. He would console himself with the memory of their two loving nights.

About to turn away, he noticed Cian join the two women in the garden. The big man doffed his cap respectfully, holding it at his belt as he approached. Tessa went to him and touched his unshaven cheek and said something. He took her hand in his and kissed her fingertips. She was thanking him because he was the one who had dashed into the cromlech to save her. Clark recalled how he hesitated at the cave entrance, and he vowed to remember that moment if another fateful opportunity should present itself in another time and place.

Finally, Elis joined the garden party—bringing word that the Davis sisters had asked Tessa to join them in their upstairs sitting room. She was obliged to go because they were elders in her tribe.

When Tessa arrived at the upstairs salon, she found the double French doors closed. Hearing quiet conversation and the clink of teacups, she knocked, entered, and wordlessly took a seat opposite Margaret. They made inquiries as to her health before getting to the heart of the matter.

Margaret set her cup down and lowered her head. "My sister and I owe you an apology." Tessa did not acknowledge the comment, but her expression did not discount it. Gwendoline continued her train of thought: "When Ganna shared her plan, we did not know—"

"That she would take my body," Tessa said. "Ganna fled for those who bled, giving on and living on the lives of the *Cymry* sisters. Does that sound familiar?" The ladies glanced at one another. "You must have known what happened to the others. Even when I was losing myself and doubting my sanity, you said nothing!"

Gwendoline held her hands up as if to shield herself from Tessa's words. "The others who sheltered Ganna's spirit did so willingly, as an offering."

Tessa shook her head. "After Ganna's spirit drove them mad, they gladly threw themselves into a river. I nearly did myself."

Margaret looked into Tessa's eyes. "But you are here—alive, and we are grateful. Gwendoline and I want to make amends, but first . . ." Tessa knew what they wanted and waited for them to ask. "Ganna, is she with you?"

"No." She went on to tell them of the raging waters in the field near Bodewryd, the altar, and offerings in the cromlech. She said nothing about the cubbyhole where Ganna hid from the Romans two-thousand years ago. Her own secret battle with regret and shame taught her to honor others who grapple with inner demons bent on unmaking them. Silence is the only real defense. Those fortunate enough to move beyond their ordeal are not cheered or congratulated by friends and family because their fight would rarely be known or understood.

When Tessa finished her account, she realized her anger had abated. She knelt before the sisters and took their hands. "When I stood at the altar in that grotto, I received tidings from The Mother: 'Be not troubled. I will abide.' This message came to me, I thought from The Mother, but now I wonder if it was from Ganna."

"Both," Margaret replied. "For Ganna is with The Mother." Tears glistened in Margaret and Gwendoline's eyes. "I want to believe the message was for all of us."

"Especially the women who sacrificed themselves," Tessa said. "They did not go the easy way. Dangling at the edge of the whirlpool in that tomb, I experienced what they must have felt, the clash of fear, love, panic, and joy.

THE MAGNIFICENT MADNESS OF TESSA WIGGINS

Margaret offered a slight bow. "We're sorry for not taking you fully into our confidence. We wish to make amends.

"Amends are not needed," Tessa said. "All my life, I longed for a home I could never quite find. Not long ago, I served porridge in a Salvation Army dining room. Later I found my way to running a home for young women like Eva. Now, I serve not only our tribe but all people. Can you imagine what a wonderful gift this is? By embracing the illusion that I would lose everything, including my life, I gained everything and found a home, but it is not the manor house."

Gwendoline's mouth gaped in surprise. "Where will you go?"

Tessa smiled. "Not far. I wish to ask a boon."

Eva was waiting at the bottom of the stairs when Tessa came down from the sitting room. The two women embraced and remained wrapped in one another's arms for some time before Eva spoke: "I wanted to come with Clark and the others."

"It is good you did not. What is it you want to tell me, Eva?"

"I'm moving to the city. Professor Stone offered me a room until I can find a position."

Tessa laughed. "How lucky he and Dr. Watson will be to have a lovely young woman in their lives. I will miss you."

"But you will always be with me, Tessa. I owe my life to you."

Tessa took Eva firmly by the shoulders. "No. You are a world of possibilities in the form of a woman, and you will find your unique expression. Your only obligation is to yourself—to manifest your singular purpose."

"I have no idea what that purpose might be."

Tessa smiled. "What best way to begin a journey.

"And you?" Eva said. "What will you do now?"

"I only know what I will do tomorrow and probably that I want to serve young women like yourself."

Eva nodded and took Tessa's hand as they walked toward the kitchen. When Tessa and Eva entered, they found Beara and Cian enjoying a cup of tea. Tessa stifled a laugh as she noticed Cian nervously cradling a fancy china cup in the palm of his hand, his thick fingers unable to fit through the dainty handle. The two were chatting in Welsh—a musical language with gliding sounds and rhythmic inflection. When they turned, Tessa pointed a playful finger, "Someday, I'll understand *everything* you are saying, and there will be no more talking behind my back."

"Nay, nay missy. Beara and me, we was talking about the old cottage in the—" Cian glanced at Eva. "Does she know?"

"More or less, but Eva's off to London. I've talked with the sisters, and they have given us the use of the gamekeeper's cottage." Cheers of delight arose from Beara and Cian, then suddenly hushed. Following their eyes, Tessa turned to see Clark standing in the doorway. "What's all this about the old place?"

Tessa motioned to an empty chair next to her. Clark remained at the door. "There are several homeless people in this room," Tessa said, "Beara, Cian, and now me. The Davis's have agreed to let us make a home in the old gamekeeper's cottage."

"I see," he said.

"Would you like a cup?" Beara asked Clark.

He shook his head. "I have work to do."

"But your wrist is injured, and it's about to rain," Tessa said.

He laughed. "I'm just crazy enough not to care." As he turned to leave, there was a knock at the back door. Before Tessa could rise, Clark went and opened it to find Nell Rees. The old woman stepped back on her heels and looked up awkwardly. "Come in, Nell," Clark said, "There's a cup waiting for you and some interesting gossip as well."

THIRTY-NINE

RAINDROPS DRUMMED on the gallery windows as Tessa made her way to the garden. The brown flowerbeds were caked in mud, and the bare branches of the azaleas were twisted into a tangle. Clark was tending the mahonia, hoping that it might survive the recent storm and honor its promise to bloom in a couple of months. The mud stuck to his trowel as he tried to bank the soil around the base of the plant. The rain was light, but he was already soaked to the skin. Within his patient tending, she saw the sweetness of the man. She recalled the yellow bird that Beara buried in Hellingford's garden and the old woman's words as she cupped the dead swift: "She waited too long."

She opened the door and went to Clark. He heard her footfalls but didn't turn. "What is it, Tess?"

"It will take but a moment. I want to thank you for coming for me."

"I didn't. It was—"

"You. You came for me. " She paused and looked down. "Clark, do you remember what you said about me the night we first made love— about being a raging river? Ironic now, given what's happened. You were right. And a river can't stop flowing even if it wants to. Do you understand?"

Clark pushed himself to his feet. His hands and knees were caked with mud. "I'm not afraid of wild waters, Tess."

She laughed. "But you may tire of swimming upstream."

"Maybe you're right. But the current is not important if it takes us in the same direction."

"I don't see as we are going the same way, Clark."

"Where are you going?"

"I want to live my life in the ways of a different time, a forgotten time. I intend to walk in the olde way with Beara, Cian, and Nell as we serve The Mother."

"It's clear you've made that choice."

Tessa came closer, and in a wistful whisper, said: "It isn't a choice. In my heart, I know it's something I must do. I don't expect you to understand."

"Why? I have a heart too. I don't always listen to it, but my heart is shouting at me now. Do you want to know what my heart is saying?"

Tessa lowered her head. "I think I know."

They startled as Elis approached, shuffling toward them with an umbrella in one hand and a silver tray in the other. "Beg pardon, mam, a telegram. It was marked urgent," he said, proffering the tray.

Tessa opened and read it, then turned to Clark. "It's from Dr. Watson. Holmes is going after his manuscript and heading into trouble, as I knew he would. Will you put on your chauffeurs' hat and drive me to London?"

* * * * *

Arriving at 53 Conduit Street, Holmes asked the cabbie to let them off around the corner. "Loan me your revolver, Watson. I may have the element of surprise, but there is still danger."

"Why not wait for the Inspector?"

"You know better, my friend. It's a matter of honor."

"Dash it, Holmes, talk sense to a fool, and he calls you foolish. I never thought you a vengeful man, but here you go. You know the saying: Before embarking on revenge, dig two graves."

"Confucius, I believe," Holmes remarked as he opened the barrel of the Webley and spun the cylinder to confirm it was loaded. "You know my ways—I will not be dissuaded."

"Neither will I. I'm going in with you."

"No, you must wait here for the Inspector," Holmes said.

"Just one more question, Holmes: What words would you like on your tombstone?"

"Hmmm, 'last mystery solved,' I suppose."

Watson chuckled. "I might have known you would have thought about that. If you get killed, I shall be extremely cross with you."

"Fair enough. If that happens, count to ten and box me up."

When number fifty-three was in sight, Watson opened his notebook and put his finger on a page. "If the vehicle licensing agency is correct, Mr. Farhad Turani lives here."

"I shall be surprised if that is true," Holmes replied, putting a hand on Watson's shoulder. "This is as far as you go, my friend. This is a corner I must turn alone." Watson nodded as he took the hand of his dearest friend.

Holmes mounted the stairs and knocked. An unattractive woman with coarse, skeletal features answered the door. She wore a blue nurse's uniform, a white apron, and a surgical mask.

"Sherlock Holmes to see Mr. Turani."

Offering no words or resistance, the nurse turned to show the way.

When they came to a large oak door, his escort knocked once, waited a few moments, and swung it aside. As Holmes took the pistol from his pocket, he felt another poking in his back. "I'll take that," a gruff voice ordered.

"Foolish me, I should have seen beyond the dress," Holmes remarked.

"Just like a bloke," he chuckled. Taking the pistol, he patted Holmes's pockets and pulled out the druid amulet before prodding the detective through the door.

The curtains in the room were closed, and there was no lighting. A flickering fire cast the room in a scarlet glow and danced russet shadows across the walls. Holmes made out the edges of a person sitting at the far end of the chamber. "Dr. Hermann Mayer . . . or should I say, Professor James Moriarty?"

A low, raspy laugh emanated from the gloomy figure as he rolled his wheeled-chair into the amber light. He had a villainous face with a low beetling brow. A shawl was draped over his shoulders and gathered in his lap where his boney hand folded around a pistol. "I had every confidence you would find your way, Holmes."

The phony nurse handed Moriarty Holmes's pistol and talisman and left the room. The old man put the detective's pistol in his pocket and dangled the amulet in the firelight before dropping it in his lap. "If you've come for your manuscript, it's on the mantle."

"So, you too survived the falls at Reichenbach."

"Just barely, as you can see. Lost the use of my legs. It was a long, painful recovery, and when I was finally able to return to London, I discovered that you and your minions at Scotland Yard had decimated my enterprise. Everyone was snatched up—all but the Colonel."

"Was it you who saw the potential in Hellingford and Mayer's orgone machine, or Moran?"

"The Colonel is tenacious and loyal, but he's fundamentally a crude fellow. I wove the web at Hellingford strand by strand, and you fell neatly into it."

"Your conceit mystifies me, Moriarty, as I can see little excuse for it. I knew, almost from the start, that it was all done for my benefit."

"For your death, you mean."

"Yes. And for a time, I thought Moran was behind it all because I couldn't imagine that your ungodly presence was still plaguing this world."

"Insults, the last refuge of the hopeless."

Holmes came a step nearer.

"That is near enough, sir."

"What do you fear, Moriarty? You have the pistols."

The old man picked up the druid's glass. "And you have this superstitious nonsense." He rocked back in his chair, raised the pistol, and put Holmes in his sights. "It's not so much your death I have been craving. I realize now that I simply needed to know that I *can* kill you. And finally, here we are. I have the gun, and you have this." Moriarty dangled the necklace from his fingers. "This bit of mumbo jumbo."

"It's from Tessa Wiggins."

"What has happened to that great brain of yours? Is it superstition or sentimentality that has you carry this rock in your pocket?" He shrugged. "Whatever it is," he tossed it into the fire. "it is no more."

Suddenly the room exploded in light. A blinding yellow flash burst from the fireplace, and suffocating sulfuric fog spewed into the room.

A volley of gunshots rang out, and Holmes fell to the floor.

FORTY

THE WAITING ROOM AT ST. BART'S HOSPITAL was cool, but Tessa wasn't pacing to keep warm. "Don't worry, he'll pull through," Clark said. He wanted to offer more hope, but he had seen chest wounds during the war and knew they were usually fatal.

On the way to the city, Clark had asked her about what happened inside the tomb at Bodewryd. She did not answer, and he was content to let it rest. But Tessa knew others would ask, and she wondered what she could say or would say. Most would not believe her, and those who might wouldn't understand. Tessa was many women: the brazen thief, the humble flower vendor, saintly Salvationist, and the common housekeeper. All of these women harbored a certain dishonesty about them because none were who Tessa was in her heart. But how do you tell someone you are a druid priestess?

Dr. Watson came out of Holmes's room and walked up the hallway. He smiled when he saw Tessa. "You're here! I do not know how he knew, but Holmes asked me to find you."

Tessa quietly opened the door to Holmes's room. A spike of light cut through the shadows and fell on his face. A halo of grey hair frayed on his pillow, framing Holmes's pale complexion. "Come in," he said. As she walked to his bedside, she noticed opened letters piled on a table next to his bed. A notebook and pencil lay in his lap, and his manuscript was precariously balanced at the foot of the bed.

"You've come a long way," Holmes said.

"Of course, I've come."

Holmes nodded. He tapped the notebook in his lap. "I was writing to you, looking for the right words."

Tessa reached into her pocket and produced a penny. He laughed as she held it out and dropped it into his waiting palm. "I am sorry for sending you to that horrible place."

"You didn't send me. I wanted to go." She motioned toward the stack of letters on the table. "You have many well-wishers."

"No. Old mail—letters sent to Watson requesting my help. People don't believe I have retired."

"Do you?"

"Yes. My manuscript was an attempt to turn the last page on that long chapter of my life."

"An *attempt*? You are planning to publish it, are you not?"

"I'm not certain. I had fallen under Watson's storybook spell, thinking that mysteries begin on one page and end on another. Our recent escapade has shown me that life goes on after my cases end . . . and not always well." He reached out and placed his hand on the stack of letters. "And then, I'm left to wonder about all the people I refused."

"What are you saying?"

"You mentioned Lady Fritzwaller in your first report from Hellingford. I didn't recall at the time but later remembered that her maid had written to me on her behalf. I chose not to offer my services. Now I am left to wonder if, with my assistance, Pamela Fritzwaller might not have ended up in an asylum. And then there is Jack Ferguson."

"The man who betrayed me."

"He didn't. He thought he was betraying me. Thirty years ago, I resolved a strange little mystery where Jack was the culprit. Rather than prison, I suggested to Jack's father that he be sent to sea."

"But you are not responsible for Jack or Lady Fritzwaller."

"Possibly not, but the fact remains that Watson's fictions and my manuscript do not tell the entire story."

"But the manuscript is your legacy."

"The capture of Moriarty is my most fitting legacy."

A cheery spirit suddenly overtook him. Holmes straightened up and turned a keen eye on Tessa. "And what of you? What does the future hold?"

Tessa grinned. "I am leaving the manor house and taking up residence in Ceridwen's gamekeeper's cottage with Beara and Cian."

"And Clark?"

"He thinks that he wants to be with me."

"But?"

"We're just so different."

Holmes chuckled. "Rather like you and me."

"No, I'm *too* different . . . mad some would say . . . have said."

"Yes, but yours is a magnificent madness, Tessa. Plato would be quick to remind us that it was when they were mad, that the priestesses at Delphi did so much good for the Greek people. Madness is a gift when it's tempered with virtue."

Tessa's grinned. "Delphi is long gone. Where does a priestess look for employment now?"

Holmes took a fistful of letters and cast them on the bed between them. "Take your pick. Here are half a dozen people here who need help. Read their letters."

"I'm not Sherlock Holmes."

"No, but you are astute and tenacious, and you have your own gifts." Holmes's eyes flashed upward in thought. "Women have an abundance of passion and feelings; I had always thought that emotion clouds reason. But now . . ." Holmes opened the notebook in his lap and poked a finger on one of the pages. "In this note I was crafting; I was telling you that the amulet you gave to me . . . it saved my life."

"And that surprises you?"

He nodded. "I won't speculate but will simply make the point that you have gifts of the heart—instincts and intuitions—something akin to the kind of wisdom that comes too late in life for most of us.

Moreover, like me, you prefer moral justice over the legal." He reached out for Tessa's hand. "You would make a splendid consulting detective—albeit a different species altogether."

She clutched his hand and gazed at the letters on the bed. "I would need your help."

"And I would give it." Then he pointed to the manuscript at the foot of the bed.

Tessa retrieved the tome and began to place it in his lap.

"No, it's for you. Keep it at hand. When the day comes that you no longer need it, burn it."

"But your legacy?"

Sherlock squeezed her hand. "Tessa, *you* are my legacy."

Clark rose from his chair as Tessa entered the waiting area. "He's doing well," she said with a nod. "I think we can leave him in Watson's good company."

Doctor Watson offered to walk them to their auto, but they declined and left with a handshake and look that spoke volumes.

Clark opened the door of the Daimler for Tessa. She took the chauffeurs' cap from the passenger seat and handed it to him before getting in. He starred for some time at the hat before he placed it on his head with an air of acceptance or resignation. Coming around, Clark climbed in and reached for the starter button. Tessa's hand suddenly shot out to halt him.

"Do you understand," she began, "Can you see how things are? How they can't work for us now?"

"It seems more apparent to you than me," he answered without turning.

"Clark, really? Something happened to me in Bodewryd. I don't fully comprehend it, but I know that I will no longer have an ordinary life. I'm chosen to serve The Mother. It's extraordinary, wonderful, and scary."

"You *can* be a scary woman, I'll give you that, but it's not because you rein down lightning on people. It's because you can't see what's in your own heart. You've spent your whole life rescuing people." He chuckled. "Hell, you were a Salvation Army slum sister out to save the world. Now it's Beara, Cian, Nell and Lady Fritzwaller. In a way, I'm jealous, but I'm also I'm happy for you."

"What are you saying, Clark?"

"I'm saying that I see your heart; what makes it beat. You think everything has changed, but one thing has not, you're a woman. And in all your new, wonderful, scary extraordinariness, you may need someone ordinary." He turned to her and put a hand on his chest. "They don't come any more ordinary than me. You want to serve The Mother, but maybe a part of you wants to be a mother and make a home." He shook his head and turned away. "I'm sorry . . . I don't know what I'm saying."

Tessa took in the measure of the man sitting beside her. "How did you get so bright?

"Hangin' about with the likes of you. It rubbed off, I suppose." He took her hand and placed it on his chest. "If you need to rescue somebody, rescue me. I love you."

A tear streamed down Tessa's cheek. "You don't need rescuing, my sweet boyo, but you just may need a good woman, and I may need a good man to hold onto when things get too extraordinary." Tessa leaned in, kissed him softly, and yanked down on the visor of his cap. "Take me home, Mr. Button."

From The Journal of Tessa Wiggins

November 3, 1920 —

I wondered if a detective is an anathema to a priestess, but Mr. Holmes said I would make "a splendid consulting detective—albeit a different species altogether."

The world is full of crime that is not evil people doing evil deeds. The line between good and evil is drawn within each human heart and shifts with awareness, circumstances, and compassion. Countless crimes go unnoticed, minimized, or disregarded: assault on the human heart, abuse of privilege, the robbing of self-respect, emotional as well as physical rape, and desecration of the earth.

Thirty years ago, I became a recruit in the street army of Sherlock Holmes—one of his "irregulars." Now, I'm becoming the 'irregular detective'—trading intellect for instinct, coolness for compassion, and a sharp eye for intuition.

Holmes has Watson, and I have Beara and Cian who walk in the olde way. As a handmaiden of The Mother, I recognize that Nature has no favorites, nor anything resembling a childlike conception of good and evil. Nonetheless, at the heart of Nature are powerfully persistent forces that seek balance and offer healing. I wed myself to those energies.

Wretched Gods and Gargoyles
A Tessa Wiggins Mystery

By

Kim Krisco

I

STONE GARGOYLES SQUATTED along the lengthy roofline of Hartfield Manor, their hollow eyes watching Beara, Cian, Clark, and me, as we passed through black iron gates. Our driver, Clark, could not turn his eyes away. "Do folks believe those carved stones keep evil away?"

"Belief makes things real," Beara answered, without looking from her knitting. "Is that not right, priestess?"

"Please don't address me in that manner," I said.

Our quartet was odd enough, but the notion of a Druid priestess in 1920 Britain would be too much for people to understand or accept. "If we wish Lord Henry to heed our counsel and bring his wife home from Hellingford Asylum, we must keep the olde ways between us. Mr. Holmes lent us his name, and the Davis sisters loaned us their auto. We must do nothing to tarnish their reputations."

Everything had been calculated to get me through the door—the posh clothes we borrowed, the rouge on my cheeks and lips, and gleaming Crossley auto we rode in. Clark had donned his chauffeur's uniform to complete the picture.

Drawing closer to the entrance, we fell under the spell of Hartfield's gothic splendor with its finials, lancet windows, and vaulted rooflines. Resting in Warwickshire, Hartfield endeavored to hold back the encroaching iniquities of London. As we passed under the bronze splendor of the Beechnuts lining the drive, it appeared that Lord Fritzwaller had succeeded. Amber light filtered through the quaking leaves, attempting to whisk away marauding shadows.

We were expected, so I was not surprised to see a man waiting atop the broad steps to the front door as we pulled to a stop. As I reached for the door, Clark stayed my hand. "Let me get the door, madam," I chuckled. The waiting butler's eyes became saucers as we all climbed from the Crosley. Mounting the stairs, he offered a token bow. "Lord Henry is expecting you, Miss Wiggins," he said, glancing warily at Beara and Cian. "Your man can get a cup of tea 'round back."

"He is content to wait," I replied, extending my hand. "Pleased to meet you . . ."

"Beeker, mam," he said. This gesture caught him by surprise, and he gingerly took my hand. His pulse was fast. He could not know that, only a month ago, I was a housekeeper on an estate much like Hartfield.

Beeker's uneasy eyes darted to my companions, riveting on Cian, who was a solid mass of man. We were a strange sight, to be sure, and might have momentarily been mistaken for nomadic performers from a circus we passed along the way. Cian was well over six feet and weighed eighteen stone. He had olive skin, shaggy black hair, and steel blue eyes that popped from his swarthy complexion. His ancestors were *Tuatha-de-Danann*—true servants of The Mother. In stark contrast was diminutive Beara with snowy hair and dazzling hazel eyes that bounced between the ever-present knitting in her hands and whomever or whatever stood before her. Beara was a *dryw*—a seer, bard, and herbalist. She had a disarming smile that she turned on Beeker when I introduced her. I stood between the two.

As for me, I would simply say that I am of average height, slight build, with hair of black and eyes of green. But let me add the words of my mentor and friend Sherlock Holmes, who I once overheard describe me to an associate. He said: "She is more than not bad looking, and her pleasing appearance masks a strength lacking in most women." While I believe those words say more about him than me, I pass them on because Mr. Holmes is unhampered by standards of comparison when it comes to women, and because I would like to believe they are true, false modesty not being among my vices. I am a descendant of Queen Boudicca, and the newly anointed Druid priestess of the Iceni tribe, tutored by my ancient predecessor, Ganna.

Lord Henry Fritzwaller came to his feet as Beeker showed us into the parlor. The grey-haired man was casually dressed in a brown tweed Norfolk coat and grey flannel trousers. A bushy salt-and-pepper mustache did not hide a kind mouth. As we approached, his body lengthened and stretched as if he were making himself taller. He measured us calmly through squinting eyes as we took seats around a low table set before the hearth.

He waited until all our eyes were upon him before he spoke: "Please excuse my surprise, Miss Wiggins, but Mr. Holmes's letter did not mention your companions. No matter, you are all welcome." Mr. Holmes's letter had loaned me credibility and served as an entrée to an unaccustomed social class.

Fritzwaller turned to the butler who was waiting at the door. "You may go, Beeker." His casual dismissal embodied all that was shameful about rank and status in our world. Ganna taught that, while we have roles, none come with rank.

When the door was closed, he turned a keen eye on me. "Mr. Holmes was vague in the extreme." He picked up a letter from the table, and glancing at it, continued: "It said only that you were coming on an urgent and delicate matter that deserves my attention."

"Thank you for receiving us, Lord Fritzwaller. I come on behalf of your wife—Lady Pamela."

Lord Henry's brow tightened. "My wife? May I ask how it is you have come to know Pamela?"

"We met in Hellingford."

The color ebbed from his face. "Hellingford . . . then what . . . are you a matron or nurse?"

Beara lowered her head to hide a grin.

"If you had visited her more often, you might know that I was a neighboring patient on her ward."

His jaw clenched. "You are a plucky woman, Miss Wiggins. I hope you are not one of those people who sit in the sun and preaches to others in the shadows?"

"I do not preach. Your wife is suffering from neglect and not from mental illness. She holds an abiding sorrow for the loss of her child."

"A child that died eleven years ago!" he exclaimed. His body was rigid. "The child died at birth eleven years ago," he repeated, pushing himself up from his chair. He walked to the fireplace, grabbed a poker, and stirred the embers on the grate. "It's not the loss of the child that has warped her mind, but superstition." His tone was smug. "Did she tell you that she believes that the spirit of her dead child haunts her?"

"She clings to this belief because she has not fully come to grips with her loss."

He became gimlet-eyed, immobile—his thoughts turning inward. "It *was* hideous. A ghastly experience for which there are no words."

"Of course, a difficult birth, but—"

"My heir . . . my son. It was a boy." Then, as if a warm breeze blew over him, Lord Henry's shoulders relaxed, and an empty smile came to his face. He was in control again.

I turned to Beara, who was looking at me—telling me to hold back. I became aware that I had been carrying Pamela's Fritzwaller's resentment and anger, and it had given me a false sense of righteousness. "Lord Henry, I apologize if my words are hurtful. I care deeply for your wife. I know neither of you will have peace until you are willing to grieve the loss of your child, both individually and together. I resided at Hellingford and can tell you that she will not get well there. Dr. Mayer is gone. Your wife receives no treatments. She spends her days alone in a dreary room. She will get better care here." I rose and went to him at the hearth. "I beg of you, bring your wife home."

I waited as he was stared into the flames. In a soft voice, he said: "I did not know these things." Then, as if unfamiliar compassion unsettled him, he turned and narrowed his eyes. "But who will take care of her? Who will care for Pamela when she is raving like a madwoman at his grave . . . when she calls out at night to his ghost . . . when my wife refuses to sleep or eat?"

"We will!" Beara exclaimed, her words slicing through his indignation like a saber through silk.

We turned toward Beara's genial face.

I echoed the commitment: "If you will allow us, Beara and I will care for her."

"I . . . I must have time to consider this," he said. "I had hoped that once removed from the influence of Doyle and other fanatical spiritualists; my wife would return to her senses. But . . ."

"If you can consider spiritualism as grieving, it may stir compassion rather than ridicule. Lady Pamela is not alone in her belief that it is possible to commune with the departed. Though it has been nearly two years since the Great War guns fell silent, people still grieve for the millions who lost their lives. To this day, many hearts in Britain remain in the grip of grief. Your wife's heart is one or many."

Fritzwaller nodded. "You are a canny woman, Miss Wiggins. There is truth in what you say, but I feel it would be prudent to consult our physician." He made a slight bow. "You are all welcome to stay the night. Beeker will arrange rooms for you."

Beara's and Cian's eyes followed Lord Henry as he departed. When the door closed, I turned to them. "What do you sense?"

Beara shrugged. "He is lying. There is more here than a dead child."

Cian nodded. "He is afraid."

"I sense that much was left unsaid . . . secrets," Beara added.

I took their words to heart because Beara and Cain walk in the olde way where instinct is valued above reason. It is called *greddf* and is rooted in a time when survival depended on the subtle knowledge that abides within our animal nature. "But he cannot hide secrets from himself," I said. "The man is suffering."

"It's good we're staying," Beara added.

"Yes. He's listening to his heart. His mind will soon follow. I'll ask Clark to bring Pamela here."

II

Lady Pamela Fritzwaller arrived. True to our word, Beara and I took her into our care. Her opulent bedroom suite was on the second floor and opened onto a roof terrace that overlooked the front steps and driveway that curved out toward the front gate. Her bed was massive. Like great tree trunks, four carved posts supported a velvet canopy the color of maple leaves in autumn. As Lady Pamela stood in the open door, a long-absent smile blossomed upon her face. In her early forties, she still possessed great beauty, but it had been hardened and coarsened. Her hair was a full rich brown, and her eyes were hazel with glints of amber. Taking her hand, I felt her conflicting sense of joy and trepidation. Pulling away, she entered her old bedroom cautiously, walked to the bed, and ran a hand over the satin *duvet*. Then she turned, closed her eyes, and lowered herself onto the bed. A sigh escaped her lips as the plush mattress enfolded her. Lady Pamela was home.

Rising from the bed, she walked to windowed doors, pushed aside the curtains, and pressed both hands against the glass. As she stared beyond the terrace, the lady repeatedly mumbled something under her breath, pressing her body against the door. It made me worry that Beara and I might have put too much faith in our ability to heal this woman.

Lord Henry appeared at the door. A momentary look of concern flashed across his face when he saw his wife at the terrace doors; then, he quickly put on a smile. "There's my lovely lady," he said, walking to her side.

Observing Lady Pamela and her husband over the next several days, I was heartened to see that they shared a genuine affection. Every day they strolled in the garden. When Pamela paused to look at a rose or dahlia, her husband would take her hand and hold it as if it were a fledgling bird. Other times they wandered in silence, amid the flotsam and jetsam of words waiting to be said.

A small bed was moved into Lady Fritzwaller's *boudoir* for Beara. My room adjoined. It had been empty, but Beeker and the gardener put a bed and wardrobe in place. A fanciful mural on one wall told me that it had been intended as a nursery for the child Lady Pamela had lost. Cian, who shuns creature comforts, made a place for himself in the loft above the carriage house near the room of the estate's gardener, Moffet.

While Beara and I shared breakfast and dinner with the Fritzwallers, Cian ate with the servants. Occasionally, Lord Henry would ask the cook, Jeddie Bell, to come to the table. "My, my Jeddie, you've done it again," he would tell her, and her already beet-red cheeks would turn crimson. Jeddie would nod, offer a perfunctory curtsy, and leave. Such innocuous events would unleash a rush of dark emotion within me. I was embarrassed for Jeddie and felt sadness for a world that condones the human spirit's subjugation, however small the act. I envied Cian's guileless nature. When I endeavor to explain the notion of class, his face contorts, and he scratches his chin. For Cian, all people are equal, and a person's only obligation is to be helpful, which he was to a fault. Indeed, it was not long before Cian's ever-present helping hand put him in good stead with the small, overworked staff at Hartfield. Doing so, he was able to learn that there had been recent reductions among the manor's servants, and the gardener Moffet feared more would come. "He cain't keep proper help, but cen toddle off to Africa," Moffet groused one afternoon as he and Cian struggled to remove an old tree stump.

It soon became apparent that Lady Pamela's obsession with spiritualism had not diminished during her six months at Hellingford. Beara reported she frequently saw Pamela standing trance-like at the doors to the terrace. "She calls out to the spirit of her child: 'I'm here . . . your mother is here," Beara reported. "It breaks your heart. I shall make a bedtime brew for her, lemon balm and lavender."

I should have partaken of Beara's tea myself, for I also found it difficult to sleep amid a recurring dream that I initially attributed to the mural in my room—a fantastic zoo of mythical creatures scampering among pink, white, and blue clouds.

The beginning of my dream is peaceful: Unicorns, centaurs, and the winged-horse Pegasus prance amid a verdant meadow on the edge of a lush forest. My spirit soars as I see these bewitching creatures dance and play in the sunlight. But then a great shadow falls over the meadow, and all the creatures freeze in place. Looking skyward, we see a great bird-like beast hovering above. Covered in coal-black feathers, its wings are tipped in scarlet and orange flames. Panic grips us as the creature becomes consumed in flames and tumbles from the sky. We scatter to make way and, when the beast hits the meadow, it is ashen—the only sign of life is its sad green eyes fluttering for a moment before they close. I join the unicorn and centaur as they cautiously approach. Then, as the smoke clears, there is a movement among the embers. Bending lower, I see something moving among the hot ashes. Suddenly a hand lunges at me, and I startle awake.

Dreams are rooted in our souls. When our mind sleeps, our spirit finds its voice. My nighttime fantasy of death and rebirth was telling me about Lady Pamela, and I hoped Beara might help me reveal its whole meaning.

Beara's eyes glazed over when I shared my dream. "I had a similar vision. I was sitting by a cradle when I heard whimpering, and I drew closer to comfort the babe. But as I did, an odd creature leaped at me."

"What does it mean?" I asked.

"Our creatures could be evil or fear,' she said. "This household is in the grip of fear. Cian said as much the day we arrived. You can sense it."

"Yes, but there is more . . . the hand . . . I keep seeing the hand reaching for me. Maybe the spirit Lady Pamela imagines is real. Make a strong tea for Pamela tonight, and the two of us will keep watch in her room."

So Beara and I shared the bed in Pamela Fritzwaller's room that evening. We took turns keeping watch. Sometime after midnight, I heard noises outside—a rustling sound in the bushes. I opened the French doors and heard Lord Henry's hounds yowling. It was several minutes before the dogs ceased their caterwauling, and I returned to bed.

When I awoke, I was not greeted by the muted footfalls and quiet chatter of the servants that typically announce a new day in Hartfield. Rather, I heard Lord Henry bellowing downstairs. I dashed from the room to look over the railing into the hall below, where I saw Beeker pausing and wiping his brow. Deciding a strong cup of tea was in order, I donned a robe and went to the kitchen, to find Beeker at the table holding his head in his hands.

"What's happened?" I asked.

"A theft . . . a burglary."

"What was taken?"

"A gold idol . . . jewels."

As Mr. Holmes taught me, I let silence spin its web. The butler continued: "A hideous golden idol that Lord Henry and his nephew brought back from Africa and Lady Pamela's family jewels."

"Any idea who—?"

"No. Lord Henry is furious." The beleaguered man was shaking. "I locked the windows in the study last night. I'm certain I did. I secure the manor every evening promptly at eleven—*every* window and door."

"Does he blame you for the theft?"

9

"He did not say so."

"The authorities will soon have things sorted," I remarked.

"He won't involve them. I am to keep this matter to myself."
Beeker shook his head. "The idol is one thing . . . what of Lady
Pamela's family jewels?"

I understood his concern. This loss could deepen the Lady's
despondency. I decided to gather more facts and seek Mr. Holmes's
advice.

Dear Mr. Holmes,

> *Your letter of introduction allowed me to accomplish
my mission. I am pleased to report that Lady Pamela is
home. Beara, Cian, and I are staying on to care for her.
However, this letter is more than an expression of
gratitude. I need your help.*

> *There was a burglary at the Fritzwaller manor last
evening. A gold idol from Lord Henry's African collection
was stolen, along with most of Lady Fritzwaller's family
jewels. I am not a judge of such things, but the theft must
amount to tens of thousands of pounds. Lord Fritzwaller
brought the idol back from a recent safari. Just under a
foot in height, it is an effigy of a bat with an arrow in its
jaws. It may have value beyond the precious metal.*

> *Lady Pamela confided in me that the family is
struggling financially. She had hoped that the figurine,
along with some of her family jewels, might be sold to
solve their pecuniary troubles. I do not know if the idol or
jewels were insured, but I imagine that any insurance
company would insist that the police be called in to
investigate—and herein lies the mystery.*

> *Lord Fritzwaller has refused to call the constabulary
despite the insistence of his wife. She begged me to
summon the police. At the same time, Lord Henry told me*

if I did so, Beara, Cian, and I would be sent away. I hope that you will lend your singular mind and help me bring restitution and peace to Hartfield Manor.

I have made inquiries of the staff. Beth, the young parlor maid, had nothing but superstitious gossip to share. Cian sleeps in the gardener's quarters and, like me, was awakened sometime after midnight by Lord Henry's hounds on the evening of the theft. The gardener Moffet did not investigate because he thought marauding foxes, or hungry rabbits, were the cause.

Beeker, the butler who discovered the theft, assured me that, the evening of the burglary, he secured all the windows and doors in the house before he retired. The next morning he found the window to Lord Henry's second-floor study unbolted and open. Further investigation revealed the loss of the jewels that had been locked in Henry's desk.

I examined the window in the study and found no scratches or marks on the exterior, and the latch was in good order. Not so the desk drawer that held the jewels— someone had tampered with it to break the lock.

I cannot say how the thief made his way into the second-floor study. However, I have a suspicion given that the burglar would have to be agile enough to climb the vine-covered stone walls to the upstairs study. I realize that I may be the victim of a classic prejudice, but I believe the burglary at Hartfield Manor may be related to the presence of a gypsy circus nearby. This traveling show comes in the summer and stays for several months. There are likely agile performers among the troupe who might easily scale the walls of the manor. Also, Cian learned that there had been other thefts in the area recently, although these were minor compared to a gold idol and family jewels.

I will continue to investigate. Please send your thoughts and advice to my care via the post office in Warwick.

With affection,

Tessa

As anticipated, the theft affected Lady Pamela deeply. The loss of her family jewels resurfaced a belief that she was cursed. This fear was precipitated by the loss of her child and jewels and the fact that she had miscarried prior to the stillbirth. Beara, the wise one, said: "There's no need to believe in curses; life is enough." And went on to warn: "If the lady is not heedful, her thoughts will create a curse." This was not idle prattle. As a seer, the ebb and flow of past and future time flows through Beara. At times, when I watch her nimble fingers working the yarn, I imagine her as one of the Fates spinning human destiny—Clotho, the sister who spins the thread of the lives of all mortals. Now it seemed that Pamela's fate was resting in our hands.

I unsuccessfully tried to lift Pamela's spirits with games, books, and other diversions, but when Beth told me Lady Fritzwaller enjoys the circus, I went to her suggesting that we investigate the gypsies. For the first time in days, the Lady smiled. The idea that she might restore the jewels and save Hartfield inspired her, and she insisted we attend the circus that very evening.

There were many amusements: animal acts, aerial performances, sideshows, and games of chance that you expect within such an enterprise. We strolled the midway among colorful flags, banners, and posters touting the Flying Zendoras, Gentry Brother's Ponies, and curiosities like the Living Doll, the Cannibal Chief, and the Two-Headed Lamb. As I reviewed our options, Lady Pamela confided in me that having her fortune told by Queen Cinka was what she most wished to do, so we sought out the fortuneteller's tent.

Circling the midway, we walked among the gypsy wagons at the edge of the pasture. Pamela, Beara, and I received strange looks, some menacing, from the Romani, so I was not surprised when Queen Cinka herself confronted us. She was dressed in a colorful red skirt encircled with a rainbow of silk scarves tucked under a wide black belt. Her face was deeply furrowed, and coarse black hairs sprouted from her upper lip and chin. Her broad smile did not hide her curiosity.

"You appear to be lost," she said in a teasing manner.

When I explained that we were simply curious, she pointed a finger, closed her eyes, and put the other finger on her temple. "No, I see now. You are looking for something . . . yes, someone. Am I right, Lady Fritzwaller?"

Pamela startled when the gypsy said that. Cinka motioned for us to follow, and we went to her tent at the far end of the midway. She pulled back the flap and waited. In the center of the space sat a small round table with two chairs. A silver bowl filled with what looked like water rested in the center of the tabletop. The only light came from candles blazing atop a large candelabrum in the corner of the tent. When Lady Pamela passed through, Cinka told me to wait outside and dropped the flap.

I pressed my ear to the tent, but the noise from the barkers and crowd obscured the exchange inside. I do not know what transpired between Lady Pamela and Cinka; however, when she emerged thirty minutes later, Lady Fritzwaller was in a daze. I thought she might be mesmerized. She did not want to stay for the show, and so we went home.

Upon returning to Hartfield Manor, Pamela said she wished to go to her room. I retired to my quarters and left her in Beara's hands.

As I began my evening ablutions, a knock came on my door. It was a red-faced Lord Fritzwaller. "What on God's green earth processed you to take Lady Fritzwaller to the gypsy circus?" he asked, struggling to control his anger. I explained that I thought a diversion would help his wife's mood.

13

"What did you do . . . who did you see?" he demanded.

When I mentioned Queen Cinka, a fierce look came over him. He stood wordless for a moment, and then as quickly, composed himself and bade me goodnight.

The next morning, as is my custom, I brought tea and toast to Lady Fritzwaller's room at eight. She must have slept well because her smile had returned, and she was affable. I remarked that I had worried about what occurred in Cinka's tent. The lady motioned for me to come closer, and lowering her voice, said: "Cinka knew about my baby boy."

"Is that so surprising?" I asked her. "It may not be common knowledge, but it's likely that other people in the parish know of your misfortune."

She scowled. "I'm not a child. I know that there are unscrupulous people who profess to ply the mystical arts, but Queen Cinka knew things that could not be explained. She knew of his visits here at Hartfield."

I know that it is possible to connect with the spirit world, but not in the way Cinka conjures. However, Lady Pamela was so jolly I could not crush a fragile hope budding within her.

"Tessa, I'd like you and Beara to go to the gypsy camp . . . to Queen Cinka." She took her purse from a dressing table, retrieved a shilling, and handed it to me. "Give her this and tell her I wish her to visit me here and that there is a sovereign in it for her. She must come the day after tomorrow when Lord Henry and his nephew Gregory Slater will be hunting. They will be gone for the day, so Cinka can discreetly come and go."

She went on to explain that Gregory often visits—too often for her likes. "He has a cottage not far, but he spends more time at Hartfield than at his own meager lodgings," Pamela told me. She described Gregory as a sycophant who ingratiates himself in the hope of inheriting his uncle's fortune. His hope is not unreasonable, as the Fritzwallers have no children and are not likely to have any given the lady's age.

Lord Fritzwaller's nephew Gregory Slater arrived the next evening as anticipated. A welcoming dinner was held, and we were all asked to attend. As Lady Pamela's dislike for Gregory's tableside conversation was known, Parson Jacobs was invited to ensure that the dinner remained cordial. Spiritualism and big game hunting being prickly topics, the talk instead touched upon such things as the riots in Belfast and the seating of the first woman juror in British courts.

As the burglary was something akin to a family secret, there was no mention of it. Yet there was innuendo in Mr. Slater's reference to the circus nearby. "You best keep an eye on your valuables," he warned. I wondered if he had somehow learned about the theft.

"Have you attended the circus, Mr. Slater?" I asked.

"I have. What else is there to do in Warwick? The amusements are rather jolly however; I cannot say that I enjoy having gypsy neighbors."

With the topic of the circus on the table, Parson Jacobs expressed his righteous indignation. "The idea of making money on the backs of poor unfortunate human beings afflicted with physical ailments is wholeheartedly repugnant. The authorities must do something about this dreadful spectacle." The reverend was referring to the freak show at the circus. Lord Henry agreed and went on to share his opinion that it was time for the circus to find a new home. Dinner ended early when Henry announced that he and his nephew planned to rise before dawn for a hunt.

As the parson left, I heard Henry invite Gregory to have a drink and cigar in the library. I accompanied Lady Pamela to her room and then went to see if I could ascertain the nature of the *tête-à-tête* in the library. I caught Beeker as he was entering with a tray bearing whisky and glasses. "Is it possible to get a glass of milk for my bedtime?" I asked the butler.

"One moment, madam," he replied as he went in. He left the door ajar while he served, and I could see Lord Henry and Gregory settle themselves comfortably by the fire before Lord Henry spoke:

15

"Gregory, it behooves me to tell you that the idol we brought back last year has been stolen."

"Stolen! Horrid news. That was nearly two hundred ounces of gold. Why that's . . . that's over twenty-five hundred pounds!"

"The price of gold is relevant," Lord Henry answered.

"Not to me," his nephew remarked. "Have you forgotten who found the idol?"

"You were the first to lay eyes upon it, but we agreed it rightfully belonged at Hartfield because I bore the cost of the safari."

At this point, Beeker emerged from the room, and he asked me to follow him to the pantry.

Lord Fritzwaller and his nephew Gregory were on the hunt before the sun rose. I went to the kitchen knowing that I would find Beeker. If anyone knew more about the gold idol, it would be him.

"Togo," the butler told me," when I asked precisely where the idol was found. "Lord Henry got the figure in Togo, West Africa. Master Gregory and his uncle fled into a cave near the Aboney plateau to escape a storm. They stumbled upon the idol sitting upon a stone altar—a fitting location for the effigy of a bat."

My interview with Beeker had barely begun when the cook and her helper arrived to prepare breakfast. I explained that I would forgo the morning meal in lieu of a healthy walk. Jeddie, the cook, blew a lock of red hair from her sweaty forehead and warned me: "The creature may be lurking about, so stay to the road and out of the shadows." She went on to tell me that a local man reported seeing a strange beast prowling about last evening. Jeddie added, in a whisper, that she thought the creature may not be of this world and offered a string of garlic for my pocket. As I took my leave, sans garlic, she also suggested a sweater as cool winds were blowing in. I thanked her for her concern, bundled up, and went to find Beara.

Beara and I left quietly and walked to the gypsy camp with the hope of escorting Queen Cinka to the Hartfield. Clouds were gathering, and the wind was fierce, making our long walk disagreeable.

It was early, and the circus camp was quiet. Beara's eyes roamed the grounds warily. "The people without a country," she remarked as we made our way. "The Romani are old, but not as ancient as our people," she continued. "They value personal freedom above all things."

"We all do, do we not," I commented.

"But we have a country . . . a home, government, schools. The more we possess, the less free we become."

Beara never failed to surprise me with her insights. I wonder if I will be as wise when I am her age. Such thoughts ceased when we found ourselves at Cinka's tent. I called out.

"Come in, Miss Wiggins," a sly voice answered. "And bring your friend."

Obviously, the camp had eyes on us, probably from the moment we arrived. The gypsy bore an arrogant smile when she greeted us. "What do you want?" Cinka demanded to know.

Our request was a simple one, but the gypsy was reticent to come with us until we offered assurances that Lord Henry would not be at home. "So, you walked here in this wind?" she asked. I explained that we needed to be discreet. She agreed to come and quickly gathered up several items and put them in a shoulder bag.

A gypsy trap transported us to the estate within minutes. Wishing to remain unobtrusive, I halted the driver before we passed through the front gate and suggested that we go in on foot. The wrought-iron entry was crowned with the family crest, and beyond it was Hartfield Manor. Cinka seemed enthralled by the manor's gothic splendor and its rooftop gargoyles standing watch.

I could not help but notice that the gypsy's eyes roamed freely as we made our way to Lady Pamela's room. I was pleasantly surprised to find four chairs set around a card table in the center of the bedroom. Cinka noticed also and raised her brows.

"I want Miss Wiggins and Beara to partake," Pamela asserted.

Cinka shrugged and began emptying her bag onto the table. Lady Pamela interrupted Cinka's preparations to explain that she wanted a séance, adding that it needed to be held here because the spirit visits this upper room.

"Is it a benevolent spirit?" the gypsy asked. Pamela said that it was benign but troubled.

Cinka turned and asked if Beara or I had seen or sensed the specter. "The spirit world is real, "Beara answered. This response seemed to satisfy Cinka. She went to the French doors, latched them against the wind, and released the ties on the curtains to lower the light. When she returned, the gypsy lit a single candle in the center of the table and bid us sit and join hands.

The fortuneteller explained that she usually summoned a helpful spirit to act as a medium, but since the spirit had visited this place, it would be best if Lady Pamela herself would summon it. "I have called to it many, many times," the Lady answered, "but it is wary."

"Very well, " Cinka said. "We will summon this spirit with our collective wills." With that, she instructed us to close our eyes and hold fast to each other's hands. "Reach out . . . beyond. Open your heart and mind. Invite the spirit to come." I felt Lady Pamela's hand trembling in mine as the gypsy continued her invocation: "Do not be afraid, little one. You are welcome. Come to us . . . come my darling."

I furtively kept one eye on Cinka, who remained motionless with her eyes shut. Lady Pamela was likewise, but there was a small tear on her cheek. We sat silently for a long time. The only sound was the howling wind rattling the door.

It was ironic to hear myself calling to ghosts, for I struggle to rid myself of them. Maeve, my mother, Benjie, and brother Rory—they are more than memories to me, for the residue of who they were and what they believed is burrowed deep inside me, lying dormant and waiting for doubts and low moments to rise and rattle their chains. Their haunting comes as I imagine they are judging me, and I often wonder if they are helping me, taunting me, or simply begging me to remember them?

Suddenly, the French doors blew open, and the white curtains fluttered into the room. The candle went out, and we all squinted into the glaring daylight pouring through the doorway. Cinka asked me to bolt the door and close the curtains. I did so. She struck a match to relight the candle and gasped. "I thought so. Look. He was here."

I turned to find the gypsy pointing to markings on the tabletop—a crude drawing in what looked like red crayon. "What is it?" Lady Pamela asked, bending closer to study the image. She cried out—her hands covering her trembling lips. A rough approximation of the Fritzwaller family crest was scrawled on the tabletop.

"The spirit is telling us that it is a member of the Fritzwaller family who has gone beyond the veil," Cinka declared.

"It's him," Pamela sobbed, collapsing in her chair.

The séance was over.

Preparing to leave, Cinka retrieved a bundle of dried plants tied with string and handed it to Lady Pamela, explaining that it is henbane used to attract spirits. "He will come again," Cinka promised. "Keep this with you."

Cinka was paid, and I escorted her downstairs. We went to the front door to avoid prying eyes in the servant's hall. However, foul weather had caused Lord Henry to return early from the hunt, and he waylaid us in the front hallway. His fierce eyes locked upon the gypsy, but his voice remained composed. "So, you darken my door again, woman."

He asked me to leave, saying that he would show the gypsy out. As I turned toward the stairs, Cinka and Lord Henry walked into the library and closed the door. They exchanged heated words in forced whispers. I realized that I must let Lady Pamela know that our secret was out. When I got to her bedroom, Beara had the sobbing woman in her arms. "I never saw his face. I thought he cried but . . ." she mumbled, as tears streamed down her cheeks. "I must go to his grave."

I caught Beara's eye and shook my head. "No, you must rest," I told her and went on to explain that her husband had returned from the hunt and discovered Cinka. "It is best if you wait. Dinner will soon be served."

Beara took Pamela to her bed and then followed me into the hall. "Priestess, I did not sense the presence of a spirit."

"It was a trick. Cinka is deceiving the lady, and yet . . ."

"Go to Cian," Beara said. "He is a good judge of such things."

I took Beara's advice, and knowing Cian spent most of his day in the gardens, found him trimming the bushes around the Fritzwaller family cemetery. When I told him about the séance, he entered the cemetery and stood silently before an alabaster headstone with a cherubic angel perched atop. The inscription on the stone read: 'Baby Fritzwaller, July 21, 1909.' As I approached Cian, he spoke: "I sense nothing here."

"What does that mean?"

"The child may have died in the womb and never crossed over or . . ."

"What?"

"He's not buried here."

I asked him to walk me back to the house. "Cian, what have you heard about a marauding creature hereabouts?"

"The whole village is babbling 'bout it. There is somethin' there for sure, but it is likely a beast. When I find where the creature has tread, I will tell you what it is." I thanked him and went to dress for dinner.

Lord Henry remained closeted in the library until dinner was served. He was still in his hunting garb when he came to the table. Gregory had changed and was his usual verbose self, carrying most of the conversation during the meal. "Uncle and I talked with the beaters and learned that there had been many thefts hereabouts. The head man, Sean Mahoney, claimed that he saw the thief as he went home late from the pub two nights ago—a smallish man that hobbled. That was near the Jeffords's place just down the road."

Gregory's ramblings disturbed us all, but Lord Henry became incensed. He threw his napkin on his plate and stalked out of the dining room. I was dismayed at Gregory's impudence as he continued gushing on about the marauder. "We should hunt him down," he declared. "No doubt it's one of the gypsy scum. Hunt him like the beast he is, I say." That pronouncement drove the rest of us from the table.

Later that evening, I went down to the pantry for a glass of milk. Judging from the light peeking from under other bedroom doors along the way, I was not the only one suffering from sleeplessness. A lonely floor lamp burned in the downstairs hallway casting deformed shadows on the stairway and walls as I descended. My body impulsively froze upon hearing shuffling sounds. The noises came again—a faint scraping sound beyond the front door. On cat-feet, I moved down the stairs and put my ear to the door. Something was there—alive and breathing. But before I could unbolt the door, it was gone. Returning to my room, I waited until a crimson glow tinted my curtains before donning a robe and slippers to go downstairs. Throwing the latch on the front door, I swung it wide. There at my feet sat a parcel the size of a loaf of bread. It was wrapped in torn canvas. I prodded it with my toe before pulling the covering off an ornately carved wooden box.

"It's my jewels!" Lady Pamela exclaimed the moment she laid eyes upon the case in my hands. The jewels were all there—nearly. One item was missing, a broach with the family crest on it. If there had been any doubt before, it was now clear that the burglary at Hartfield was more than a common theft.

Dear Mr. Holmes,

I am grateful for your prompt reply to my previous letter. I will diligently pursue the avenues of inquiry you

21

suggested and convey what I discover. I can answer one of your questions immediately: Several staff members were discharged during the last year. I will endeavor to learn the whereabouts of those dismissed as I broaden my inquiries into the surrounding community. Also, I will get more details from Lady Pamela about the spirit's visitations—times, places, and manifestations. Finally, in anticipation of your advice, Beara and I have agreed that we will remain with Lady Pamela whenever she is with Cinka. I have already made that point with her.

I have additional facts to report that; I think you will agree, transform a common burglary into an interesting case. Last evening, Lady Pamela's jewels were secretly returned—all but one item, a family broach. Also, it may be that what Pamela perceives is the spirit of her dead child is a nocturnal creature, human or otherwise, stalking about. There have been several local reports of such. Cian will tell us more when he finds its tracks. Lord Henry's nephew, Gregory Slater, believes it is one or more of the gypsies and has declared that he intends to hunt them down. All my intuition tells me that such an action will lead to disaster.

Yours humbly,

Tessa

I did not tell Mr. Holmes about the séance for two reasons: First, I know it was a fraud. When Cinka closed the French doors and curtains, she left the door unlatched and waited for the wind to blow it open. When it did, the distraction of curtains and the glaring daylight allowed her to surreptitiously scrawl the heraldic emblem she had seen over the front gate onto the tabletop. I realized this when I resealed the doors. The latch is heavy and could not have been undone by the rattling of the wind. Secondly, the mention of a séance might create a judgment in Mr. Holmes that Lady Pamela is unhinged or lacks credibility. He likes to say that he is 'all head' and I am 'all heart,' but this distinction trivializes the difference between us. Mr. Holmes believes the human heart is too easily fooled. While this can be true, my experience is that a heart can only be deceived for a time. Eventually, hearts come to know the truth. On the other hand, our mind can be fooled forever, and often is, because most of what we think we know comes from others rather than our own experience. To make this point, my suspicion that Gregory Slater's rashness would lead to a disaster was not a thought but intuition, and it was accurate.

III

Two shotgun blasts woke the manor. Pandemonium broke out bringing the entire household to the roof outside Lady Pamela's bedroom. Gregory Slater was poised on the edge of the roof—the barrel of his shotgun glinting in the moonlight. He explained that he had decided to stand watch on the roof to see in all directions. He must have dozed off because he reported being suddenly startled by scrapping and rustling sounds in the front entry direction. "A claw reached around one of the gargoyles. Something was attempting to pull itself onto the roof. When a hideous head emerged, I fired," he said. "It's like no creature I have ever seen. It had small arms with . . . I suppose you could call them hands . . . crooked hands."

All the while Gregory was recounting his gruesome tale, Lady Pamela sobbed uncontrollably. She was convinced that the specter was the spirit for her dead child, and Gregory had frightened it away. Lord Henry took the shotgun from Gregory's hands and peered over the edge of the roof. As he did, he noticed that Gregory's shot had hit the gargoyle, scattering chunks of stone across the parapet and rooftop. Beara and I took Lady Pamela to her back to her room, but none of us could sleep.

The next morning, when I brought Lady Pamela her tea and toast, I noticed Lord Henry outside his wife's room. Moffat and Cian were with him examining the gargoyle. I went out to learn more.

The gardener ran his hand over the foot of the chipped statue. "Rather! Your nephew got a piece of him," Moffet noted, pointing to a blotch of blood at the base of the figure. Next to it was a bloody fingerprint. Lord Henry examined the print, remarking that it looked human to him. "Spirit indeed," he scoffed. "Gregory's story is the hysterical ravings of a sleep-deprived man." The rest of the community did not share Lord Henry's rational assessment.

When word about the shooting got out, the town was abuzz with stories about a night-crawling creature that scales walls like an ape. This report gave me pause, and I wondered if monkeys or chimpanzees have fingerprints. Regent's Park Zoo was miles from here, but it might be possible for an ape to travel unseen over long distances at night. However, I knew of a more likely prospect nearby and determined another visit to the circus was in order.

Hartfield Manor was an emotional tinderbox, and I knew that if I am to go to the gypsy camp again, I must slip away on the sly.

Lady Pamela confined herself to her room. Meals were brought to her, although she had little appetite. Lord Henry visited her several times in the course of the day but was unable to cajole her into a garden walk. After one visit, he joined me in the hallway, where he shared a confidence: "Hellingford is not the first hospital in which Lady Fritzwaller has been treated," he told me. "After the miscarriage, she was sent to St. Mary Bethlehem in Southwark, where she resided for two months before returning home. This is how it begins. She can be well for months at a time; then she suddenly claims to be visited by the spirit of the dead child, and melancholia sets in. A fair-weather spirit I call it because it comes in the warmer months. This night creature is resurrecting her delusions."

"Surely not," I remarked, "The blood on the gargoyle shows that it is not a spirit but a flesh and blood creature."

He grimaced. "I told her as much, but she believes that the blood is a sign." He waved his hands overhead in a derisive manner. "Woo-o-o . . .the spirit is telling her that he is of her blood. No, she is more convinced than ever that his spirit seeks her."

I began to believe her husband's fears might be justified, for when I returned to her bedroom, I found Lady Pamela lying in a fetal position in bed. I assumed she was asleep and motioned to Beara that she could leave. But when I went to cover her, I found her eyes open but oblivious to my presence. She was clutching the dried henbane Cinka had given her. Hearing voices on the terrace, I went to hush them. Moffat and Cian were removing the damaged gargoyle from its resting place with chisels and crowbars. Once they loosened it, Cian lifted the heavy statue and set it on the roof. Together, the two men tied it with rope and lowered it to the ground. I waylaid the gardener as he went to leave and was told that Lord Henry insisted that the statue be restored and replaced as soon as possible. "The master wishes to put a stop to superstitious rumors about a gargoyle come to life."

When I returned to Lady Pamela's room, I was pleased to see that she had drifted off to sleep. I decided to seek out Gregory Slater to see if I could learn more about the idol, but he was nowhere to be found. Beeker told me that, in the aftermath of the shooting, Gregory cut his visit short and retreated to the city. In my conversation with the butler, I wondered openly if the gold idol was insured. Beeker surmised that it was not because Lord Henry and his nephew were making inquiries regarding the artifact's historical and intrinsic value. "I assume they were doing so to insure the horrid object," he remarked.

I looked in again on Lady Pamela and, finding her still asleep, told Beara to care for her while I ran an errand. In light of recent events, I needed to get to the circus as soon as possible. Along the way, I would send a reply to Mr. Holmes's last letter along with an updated report.

Dear Mr. Holmes,

You will not be surprised to learn that some of our concerns and suppositions have borne out in the last two days.

It is fortuitous that you know Professor Augustus Stone, and he was able to share a more detailed assessment of the gold idol. It was fascinating to learn that the idol was something akin to a god of the underworld and was typically put at the entry to important African tombs. Also, the confirmation that chimpanzees and apes have fingerprints opened a new avenue of inquiry I plan to pursue.

I continue to follow your advice to put more attention on Cinka. I recently learned that the visits from the spirit coincide with the arrival of the circus in Warwick. Also, the conversation that took place between Cinka and Lord Henry after the séance shows that Cinka and Lord Henry have had dealings in the past. He likely sought to keep Cinka away from his wife, fearing she will become more entangled in spiritualism. However, I will know more after I visit the queen of the gypsies.

Thank you for your concern for my safety and that of Beara. As you know, Cian is protective and is keeping watch over the rooms where Lady Pamela, Beara, and I are staying.

With affection,
Tessa

As I left the estate, I noticed Cian and Moffet loading the stone gargoyle onto a wagon for transport. Lord Henry was overseeing the process. "Moffet, cover it with canvas before you depart. We don't wish to add to the hysteria of the villagers," he ordered. "And make certain you are back by nightfall with the statue. I want you to stand guard tonight." When Lord Henry added that he would be providing a shotgun, the gardener's brow tightened, and my body tensed as well. My intuition again told me calamity was imminent.

As I entered the circus, I wondered how Cinka would receive me. But with or without her help, I would learn if the circus possessed a chimpanzee or ape, and the midway seemed a good place to start.

A wide aisle formed by two rows of colorful banners produced a spellbinding promenade to the main tent. Each flamboyant banner beckoned with tantalizing diversions, temptations really meant to appeal to our darker nature. Games of chance that invited greed, scantily dressed women giving rise to lust, and freaks and curiosities that appealed to the macabre. One flagging poster touted 'The Human Doll,' another 'The Human Skeleton.' But one poster, in particular, caught my eye: 'The Cannibal Chief.' I wondered if this African potentate might be from Togo and made my way toward the freak show tent. Suddenly, I was aware that I was being watched. The members of Cinka's clan regarded me with wary looks and hushed remarks.

A man in a rhinestone-studded suit shouted in the distance from entry to the freaks and curiosities tent. The barker was elevated on a podium and brandished a long golden cane. His bilious banter was designed to vanquish any last inhibitions a curious customer might have as they approached: "Beyond your wildest dreams . . ." he cried, then bending lower added: ". . . and more horrifying than your worst nightmare. Come cast your eyes upon the strangest creatures in God's creation."

I knew I would not be allowed to gain entry unless money changed hands, and I had none. I approached the tent flap in the hope of slipping inside unnoticed but, as I glided by the podium, the barker slapped his cane on the placard beside me. "Ten pence, milady," he said. The intuition that brought me to the tent suddenly shifted. I knew that there was nothing inside for me. However, as I turned to leave, a poster pinned to the front of the pavilion caught my attention. Sprawled across the top were the words: "The Missing Link." Below was a colorful illustration of a gentleman in formal dress holding hands with a childlike creature covered in brown hair. The brute had a human head but the body of an ape. I approached the barker. "The missing link, sir. What is—"

He cut me off with a chuckle. "The missing link is missing tonight, but not the human—" Suddenly, his eyes flashed to one side and his mouth closed. Following his gaze, I saw Cinka standing with her hands on her hips. "This is not a place you should be, Miss Wiggins. My people don't like strangers, and I cannot guarantee your safety if you snoop about."

"Someone was wounded at the manor the night before last. Was it one of your people?"

Cinka laughed. "You are a bold lady," she said. "I like you." She turned and motioned for me to follow, and I hurried to catch up with her.

"Did you hear about the shooting at Hartfield?" I asked as we moved away from the midway.

"Yes . . . a great mystery." It was a casual comment, but there was something odd in the way Cinka said it.

"It is not the mystery that concerns me but Lady Pamela's health. It is on her behalf that I come. You know how she grieves for her lost child, yet you—"

"How could I know? Only a mother who has lost a child can understand."

"Why do you hold out the false hope that she can be reunited with her lost son?"

Cinka eyes hardened for a moment before her hallmark smile reappeared. "You have a good heart, Miss Wiggins, which makes it difficult for you to recognize deceit."

"Not in you, I assure you."

"I am not speaking about me," Cinka snarled. "Deceit may be the wrong word . . . let us say *secrets*."

"Secrets that the Fritzwallers keep?"

"Ha! I take back what I said about you. I am not sure if he keeps the secret or if the secret keeps him." She coyly put her hand over her mouth. "Oh my, did I say *him*?"

"Tell me!"

"Some secrets we dare not let out," she mumbled as she turned away. Then she pivoted back toward me, pointing her finger. "If you pursue this, Lady Fritzwaller's greatest hope will come to pass . . . and also her greatest fear."

As the gypsy walked away, I asked one more question: "Does the circus have a monkey or ape?"

"Horses, dogs . . . an old bear, and a magnificent two-headed lamb," she said, with a chuckle.

Feelings of dread overwhelmed me as I hurried back to Hartfield.

IV

Mirroring Lady Pamela's deepening depression, a somber gloom shrouded Hartfield Manor the next day. The Lady lay motionless in bed—unresponsive. Heeding Mr. Holmes's warning, Beara or I stayed with her at all times while Cian kept watch along the perimeter of the property.

Lord Henry continued in his daily visits. When he came, I left the chamber, so I did not know what transpired during their talks, but his ministrations did not alter his wife's blue mood. On one occasion, I stopped him as he left her room: "What are you going to do about Lady Pamela's condition?"

"Do? I'm not a doctor."

"A doctor cannot heal a broken heart. Your wife needs the simple truth."

His desolate eyes pierced my pretense. "The truth is never simple, Miss Wiggins," he remarked. As he turned to leave, he mumbled: "Tomorrow . . . maybe tomorrow."

It wasn't sure if he was speaking to himself or me.

Later that afternoon, Lord Henry escorted a doctor into his wife's room. She passively complied with the examination. "It is not a sickness of the body," the physician later confirmed in the hallway. There was no talk of sending Lady Pamela to Hellingford or St. Mary Bethlehem, but we all knew that possibility loomed large as she had not eaten for two days.

Lady Pamela's despair gripped the entire household. Beeker, Beth, Moffat, and Jeddie went about their daily chores without their usual chatter and frivolity. The rooftop statue had been repaired, and I watched from the windowed doors in Lady Pamela's bedroom as the gargoyle was hoisted onto the roof and set in position. Lord Henry inspected the repair and told Moffat to cement it in place the next day.

I received a belated response to a telegram I had sent to Regent's Park Zoo. They evidently took my inquiry as an affront, for their brief reply read: "A ridiculous assertion. No animal has escaped in our 92-year history."

That evening, Lord Henry again posted Moffat on watch. Cian offered to stay with him, and the gardener gratefully accepted. At sundown, the two men took up their post on the roof as Gregory had done. Visibility would be good in the light of a full moon.

As I closed the curtains on the doors of Pamela's room, I saw a shotgun leaning against the chimney. It sent a shiver through my body. I asked Beara if I could again share her bed so I might be close by.

Lying awake, I heard Moffet's measured footsteps on the terrace roof like a dreary metronome. Then, just as I was dozing off, I heard the gardener's hoarse voice in a whisper. "Sh-h-h! Ya hear that, Cian?"

I rose from my bed and went to the terrace doors where I saw Moffat and Cian crouching low. Then I heard it too—scratching and rustling punctuated with grunts and sharp breaths. Someone or something was struggling to climb the wall above the front stairs as it had done before.

We waited—then it came. A hand on the edge of the roof. Next, the top of a head emerged with its wide white eyes flashing in the moonlight—long hair twisting in the breeze. Moffat and Cian remained still, hunkering lower still. The gardener reached out for the shotgun. Then the other hand came up, wrapping itself around the gargoyle. Moffat shouted: "Here now! Who's there?"

The climber startled and tried to pull itself onto the roof, but the gargoyle gave way and tumbled down with the unfortunate soul. There was a bloodcurdling cry followed by a horrible whomp as the statue shattered on the steps below.

I burst through the doors toward the edge of the roof, where Moffat and Cian were already peering down. Amid the shadows below, we made out the form of a small creature writhing, struggling to right itself, and clutching at the stone statue in its final death throes.

The crash awakened the household, and I could hear the clatter of Beeker's and Beth's feet in the hall below. I told Beara to keep Lady Pamela in her room and found my way to the entrance.

Beeker held a kerosene lamp high as we gathered around the sad tableau. It was human—a badly misshapen boy. His head was round and seemed too large his torso and limbs. Blood oozed from his knobby ears, and his outsized lips gave his mouth an inexplicable smile. It seems horrible to say it, but he was the embodiment of a human gargoyle.

In all the commotion, I did not notice Lady Pamela standing behind me with Beara anxiously tugging her arm. Before I could stop her, the Lady pushed by and knelt at the side of the boy child. Noticing something shiny, she reached into his shirt and pulled out a necklace—the broach with the Fritzwaller family crest. It was covered in blood. She began to cry.

Lord Henry stood motionless. He did not speak for a long while. Then he said: "It's him."

Tomorrow came too soon for Lord Henry.

Jeddie threw a tablecloth over the body, and Beeker called the police. Lord Fritzwaller asked Moffat and Cian to wait until the authorities arrived, and then he slowly walked away. Beara and I took Lady Pamela back to her room. She was strangely calm.

Despite the police and other local authorities' best efforts, no one was able to identify the body. The poor lad had no identification or anything in his pockets that might tell who he was. Lord Henry arranged with the authorities to have the boy buried in the family cemetery. He told them it was the least he could do since he was partially to blame for the boy's death, the stone gargoyle having not been cemented into place. But Lady Pamela knew the truth. The unfortunate boy who died on the steps of Hartfield Manor was her son.

The Lady was inconsolable. She kept to her room, refusing to see Beara or me. Likewise, Lord Henry cloistered himself in his study.

The next day, when the golden idol appeared on the doorstep in a wooden box, the final piece of this mystery was to be revealed.

"You know what must be done, priestess," Beara told me.

I knocked on the door of Lord Henry's study. His footsteps padded closer, but he did not answer. I put my right hand on the door. " Shame only has power when it is unspoken. You must tell your wife about the boy."

He swung the open, walked to his desk, and slumped in a chair—his eyes downcast. I noticed the gold idol on his desk as I entered and took a chair nearby. I waited until he spoke. "I told myself I did it to save Pamela from grief and guilt, but it was for me."

He went on to tell me how, when the misshapen babe was born, he swept it away before his wife could see it. "It was a revolting little thing . . . covered in blood. It looked like something from the depths of hell." Tears streamed from his eyes. "But I couldn't kill it."

"Because he was your son," I said.

"My son," he repeated. "I wrapped him in a blanket and left him at the gypsy camp."

Evidently, from the swaddling blanket, or some other clue, Cinka learned that the child came from the Fritzwallers. She confronted Lord Henry, demanding that he provide support for his son. Each year she demanded more. "I didn't have the money the gypsy demanded," Lord Henry told me. "So I arranged to let one of her people take the idol. Whoever was sent got greedy and took the jewels as well."

"But the jewels and idol were returned," I noted.

"Yes, I suppose that even among thieves, there is some honor."

"Except for the broach," I reminded him. "I believe Cinka gave the broach to the boy as a way for him to claim his heritage." I put my hand on his. "Now *you* must claim him." Lord Henry was shaking and weeping. "Your son made many desperate attempts to find his family. Now you must honor him and bring him home."

"What do you mean?" he asked.

"You made a grave for your son eleven years ago, now you and your wife must lay him in it."

He did not answer.

"Lord Henry, if you put your son in his grave, he will have died but once, if you do not, he will die again every night from now on."

Later, Beara explained that the Romani have a strict code called the Romano Zakono. "At the heart of their code is the Romanipen— the set of rules for Romani life. One of the most important tenets of the Romano Zakono is that you are bound to help unfortunate people that cross your path—beggars, the homeless, the hungry, and the ill and dying. "So, by Cinka's way of thinking and living, she and her clan had no choice but to take in the poor deformed child when he was left at her camp," Beara said.

"And Cinka, or someone in her camp, cared for him and helped him make a living. If I had been more observant, I might have found the banner proclaiming 'the missing link' sooner."

Mr. Holmes later told me that the poor boy was likely born with a form of phocomelia, having foreshortened limbs and a small torso that made his head appear large.

V

It was agreed we would bury the Fritzwaller boy in the Celtic tradition. As a ritual caster, I washed and wrapped the broken body in the *eslene*—the death shirt, and Cian and I laid it in the manor house's parlor. Beara set candles around the body to hold back the darkness and to light the way below the waters.

Celtic law recognizes the rights of the corpse, and so Pamela's broach with the family crest was placed on the boy's chest. When all was ready, I called Lady and Lord Fritzwaller to the parlor, asking them to stand at either end of the body and to gaze upon their son and each other.

"Be with your own thoughts," I said. "But among your reflections, consider the love that brought this poor boy into the world, for it is that love that he came to claim."

Beara, Cian, and I waited in the hallway, gathering silence and holding it up as a shroud for Lady Pamela and her husband. Finally, Lord Fritzwaller opened the door and motioned for us to pass through.

As we took our places around the corpse, Lord Fritzwaller stood with his arms around his wife—her red, tear-stained face pressed against his chest. "We are grateful for all you have done for him and us. You've given us the hope that we might be able to put this tragedy behind us. "If only . . ." His lips trembled. "If only—"

Lord Henry's feeble words of regret took on new meaning as he went to his son's body, tenderly caressed his cheek, and laid a hand on his chest. His wife came to his side and laid her hand over his, and they gazed upon him for some time before Henry turned to me: "Has his grave been prepared?"

"Cian will do that," I told him.

Cian replied in a coarse whisper: "It is not right that he is buried without a name." We all turned to the huge man, his eyes glistening in the candlelight. "His name is Mack . . . Mack Fritzwaller."

Beara smiled. "Yes, Mack. It means *son*."

At that moment, I came to understand why Mr. Holmes struggled to stay apart and aloof. A good detective becomes tangled in people's lives, loves, and secrets. Without wanting it, you become their friend or their worst enemy, and they forever become a part of your life. As I gazed down upon young Mack's peaceful face, tears slipped over my lips, and I tasted the salty tang of life in all its bittersweet glory.

ABOUT THE AUTHOR

KIM KRISCO is the author of three previous novels: *Sherlock Holmes — The Golden Years, Irregular Lives: The Untold Story of Sherlock Holmes and the Baker Street Irregulars*, and *The Celtic Phoenix*. He continues in the footsteps of the master storyteller, Sir Arthur Conan Doyle, but more recently featuring a formidable female protagonist in *The Magnificent Madness of Tessa Wiggins*.

Meticulously researched, Krisco's stories read as mini historical novels. His attention to detail, which includes on-location research, adds a welcome richness to the tales. His fascination with ancient Celtic culture brings a mythic dimension as well.

Prior to writing full-time, Kim served as a consultant, trainer, and coach for business and non-profit organizations and their leaders. You can find out more about Kim and his books at: www. MysteryBookAuthor.com.

He and his wife, Sararose Ferguson, live high in the Rocky Mountains in tiny homes that they built themselves on the North Fork of the Purgatory River. Kim likes to say that "living on the Purgatory River is not always heaven, but it's a writer's paradise."

CPSIA information can be obtained
at www.ICGtesting.com
Printed in the USA
LVHW112034010422
715000LV00022B/153/J

9 781787 058590